LEGACY

THE SHROUD OF DARKNESS

LEGACY

THE SHROUD OF DARKNESS

BOLGER BOOKS

Cover Design: Vila Design
Developmental Editing: Jonathan Oliver
Copy Editing and Proofreading: Enchanted Ink Publishing
Book Design and Typesetting: Enchanted Ink Publishing

The text type was set in Minion Pro

ISBN: 978-1-0694771-3-2 (E-book)
ISBN: 978-1-0694771-2-5 (Paperback)
ISBN: 978-1-0694771-4-9 (Audiobook)

WWW.BRADLEYELLIOTT.CA

For the Hellfish

LEGACY

THE SHROUD OF DARKNESS

BRADLEY ELLIOTT

BOOK 3 OF THE LEGACY SERIES

PROLOGUE

THE RAID

Sierra Winters looked up, an expression of disbelief written across her face. "Bullshit," she said firmly, glaring across the table at her opponent.

Denver Pollock flashed a taunting smirk in response. "It'll cost you sixty more to find out," he goaded, his white teeth a sharp contrast to his thick dark beard.

Winters watched him closely, her instincts telling her something wasn't right as she eyed the cards on the table, quickly calculating the odds.

Her head told her to fold. To cut her losses while she could.

But her gut told her something else.

She took a quick breath, subtle enough that no one would notice. Then, abandoning all logic, she pushed sixty credits' worth of chips towards the center. "I call," she said defiantly.

The dealer reached forward, flipping the last card on the table, revealing a white holographic comet hovering above the card.

Pollock's smile widened as he leaned in, flipping his cards with the casual, all too cocky grace of an experienced gambler, revealing two holographic red stars.

Groans and hushed comments from the gathered crowd filled the room as all eyes turned to Winters, who sat unmoving as she eyed the comet hovering in place.

"Yeah, I thought so." Pollock chuckled, turning to face the amassed crowd with a smirk. He reached for the pot, his hands greedily scooping it into a larger pile, when Winters's cards rained down on top, Pollock looking at them in disbelief.

"Full Nova," Winters said casually, her hand reaching out and pulling the pile of chips back towards her. "Better luck next time," she said, flashing Pollock a cocky smile every bit the mirror image of his own.

Pollock's hands slid back to his lap as he met her eyes. "Damn, I really thought I had you, Commander. Can't believe you won that on the river," he said, shaking his head. "I'll give you this, you've got nerves of daramite."

Winters tilted her head and smiled. "I never liked probability," she said. "Sometimes you've just gotta say to hell with it, and take a chance."

An alarm rang out, drowning out the sound of Pollock's response as the officers in the rec froze, listening intently. A message blared out across the ship a moment later. "Action stations, action stations! This is not a drill!"

The crew quickly filed out of the rec room, the pot on the table forgotten as they dispersed, making their way to their stations.

Winters reached the briefing room where her squad of twenty-four marines stood waiting in formation. She quickly looked them over, taking her place at the front while her AI pulled up the situation status update. "As you were," she said, skimming the brief from a pad on the podium while her squad took their seats. "All right, here's what we've got. The *'Lex* has been rerouted to the Milakra System in response to a distress call from the colony there. Their transmission only partially made it through, but it indicated a Canid raid in progress. We're inbound now, ETA thirty mikes. I want you all prepped and ready to deploy in twenty. Intel's sketchy, but scans pulled from the sensor array in the system indicate a sizable enemy force, so we're going in hot. Questions?"

The room was silent. "All right then. Saddle up, marines!" she called, dismissing her squad as she pulled up the full unabridged report and sensor data. "Damn," she whispered, looking down at the colony's stats. Just over thirty thousand souls lived on Milakra, nearly half of them children, as was common on colonies in the first few centuries after colonization, when growing populations were needed and people tended to have a lot of offspring.

The *Alexia* had been stationed on the edge of GCH space, where the Confederation bordered the Canid Empire, for the past three months, having seen heavy combat in the early days of the war with the Imperium. After nearly two years of active frontline duty, the ship had spent the past four months in space dock for a retrofit and to repair the extensive battle damage it had suffered in the last engagement, where it went toe to toe with two of the Imperium's advanced battleships.

Once the ship was finally ready, GCH Command had redeployed her to the frontier for a shakedown cruise.

Winters had transferred on board two days before the ship left the shipyards in Delconia from the Temporal Response team, where she'd been stationed for the past ten years, eager to get off the sidelines and into the fight. Temporal Response, while a critical role, was generally quiet, with sometimes years between incidents and far from the war. Her new role was one she'd been all too eager to accept, tasked with leading the *Alexia*'s armored tactical assault unit.

Things had been quiet for the first two months while the *Alexia* went through the usual shakedown drills, and the captain put the ship through its paces. All of that changed just over a week ago, however, when the Insectoids launched a devastating surprise attack in the Kuteria System.

Since then, the Canids had grown bolder, with many of the GCH ships from the frontier having been redeployed to shore up the core systems and other strategic locations along the Holt Line.

This was the third emergency response the *Alexia* had been called to since that time.

Command hoped that pulling the mighty dreadnought from its shakedown cruise and having it fly the flag while patrolling the outer colonies would quell the Canids' boldness, reminding them who the alpha predators in the sector were.

But with the Fleet spread thin along the frontier, so far, the response had been the opposite.

Winters had lost six marines three days earlier in close-quarters combat with the much larger Canids. They'd responded to a distress call from a GCH cargo ship that was attacked, and the fighting in the corridors to repel the boarders had been bloody and intense.

The burden of their losses weighed heavily on her as she joined her troops in suiting up, knowing her team would be put in harm's way once more.

The Canids, she'd quickly learned, were not to be underestimated.

At nearly four meters in height and built like tanks, they were formidable opponents, and their speed and strength made them a threat to even the fastest and toughest GCH armor if it got too close. This time, however, she hoped to turn the tables, eager for some payback and to try out their new ground-based assault armor.

Command had sent the *Alexia* a squadron of twenty-five new suits of armor called Sprinters, designed specifically to take on the Canids. Winters had been training her squad on them for the past few weeks in the IRC, getting them up to speed on the new design, and was eager to see how the armor performed in the field.

A moment later, she felt the telltale motion of the ship exiting hyperspace as she stood ready with her team in the deployment bay, standing by should the order come to descend to the planet. She held her breath while her AI patched in a feed from the bridge, the sensors showing a large fleet of Canid raiders in orbit around the colony.

No battleships at least, she thought to herself, knowing the Canids possessed very few of them, preferring fleets of smaller, more versatile raiding craft. Unlike the other major empires in the galaxy, they held only a small territory consisting of eighteen star systems and were otherwise nomadic, surviving by hunting and raiding rather than cultivating resources at an industrial level.

The core Canid Empire, based on what little was known about them, was overpopulated, forcing those packs not of noble blood to be pushed out and requiring them to hunt in an increasingly crowded region of space. These new packs often looked for targets of opportunity, striking with speed and taking what they wanted before retreating back into the black.

Several of these outcast packs had become powerful in recent years, challenging the dominance of some nobles, adding more pressure to an already unstable region, and it was one of these that they'd faced on the cargo ship just days before.

Winters pulled up a sensor feed, zooming in on the markings of one of the raiders, recognizing the insignia of one of the newer packs. She'd read half a dozen reports in the previous months, indicating that it had absorbed several of its rivals, increasing its stature in the empire and becoming more brazen with each passing year.

The feed showed a tactical analysis, which counted more than six hundred raiders in total, with three hundred and ten in orbit and close to three hundred and twenty-five more down on the surface.

The raiders around the planet quickly formed up in a defensive posture, challenging the mighty GCH dreadnought to try to break through. Even with its advanced weapons and formidable firepower, that many ships still posed a significant threat, and their size made them harder to target, forcing the *Alexia* to hold back while reinforcements arrived.

Winters watched as a few Canid ships foolish enough to enter the *Alexia's* weapons' range were quickly dispatched, leaving a stalemate as the opposing forces stood their ground, each daring the other to blink.

She turned to face her squad, pulling up a holo-map of the colony and the surrounding area on a large display. "Ops is reporting a large force of Canids on the ground. The *Valiant* and *Yamato* just entered the system and are en route to form up with the *'Lex*. Two other ships, the *Dakota* and *Eliquias*, are inbound as well. Once they arrive, we'll attack in force. With that much firepower, it shouldn't take long to break the Canid blockade. As soon as there's a window, we'll deploy. Squads of Sentinels from the *Dakota* and *Eliquias* will follow, and the *Valiant* also has fifty Widow Makers on board, but it will take them longer to deploy.

"Our mission is simple. We're to head for the main gates, right in the thick of it, while squads from the other ships respond to the smaller settlements outside the main colony. Our assignment is to secure the main gates while a group of fighters provides cover overhead. Three squads of Widow Makers from the *Valiant* will join us, so we'll have to hold the line till they arrive. Once they're with us and the fighters engage from above, we should have more than enough firepower to drive the wolves back."

She waved her hand, zooming the map in on the main gates. "Based on the latest scans, they haven't been able to breach the colony's defenses yet, but there's a horde pressing hard at the main gates and several more attacking along its flanks.

"We'll go in with speed and hit the wolves hard. Our goals are to keep them on the outside of the walls and focus our attack on breaking their lines. Once our backup arrives, we push them back. If any make it in, then we'll split into smaller squads, once the main gates are secure, and clear them out street by street if we have to. Remember, the Sprinters are untested, so we work in squads, watching one another's backs. They've been impressive in the sims thus far, but don't get cocky. The enemy down there will adapt in ways we can't predict and won't be taken off guard for long. We need to hit them fast and hard, but be ready to retreat if you're cornered, understood?"

"Yes, Commander," the room replied in unison.

Winters nodded. "We drop as soon as there's an open window, but we may still be harried by raiders as we deploy. Several squads of fighters will provide cover, but be prepared for a rough and rapid drop. The *Hyperion* is also inbound. Their current ETA is nine minutes. It's carrying two legions of class 3 mechs. Their orders are to drop to the north, here, and to the south, here. Each group will then sweep along the colony's perimeter, driving the enemy back. Questions?"

The room remained silent, the marines all knowing their assignments. "All right then, armor up! Be ready to drop in the next few minutes. Form up on me once we hit the ground. Dismissed!"

The marines moved quickly, climbing into their Sprinters and powering them up, a hum filling the bay as the reactors came online. The dropships began pulling the armor into deployment bays, the noses of each hanging out, ready to release them as soon as they reached the ground. Winters climbed into her armor last, giving the deck chief a thumbs-up, while continuing to monitor the intel stream from the bridge.

Moments later, the rumble of the battle beginning emanated throughout the ship, the mighty dreadnought shaking as it took heavy fire. She watched on the sensors as the *Alexia* gave back every shot it took and then some in return, while the four other warships flanking it dished out a heavy barrage of fire and hundreds of GCH fighters launched into the fray.

Several minutes passed, the battle still raging outside, when an alert appeared on her HUD and she opened a channel to her squad. "The Fleet's broken their lines! Prepare for drop in five, four, three, two, one!"

The dropship suddenly fell from the bay at the bottom of the *Alexia*, pulled downward by the planet's gravity as they dove towards the blue-green sphere, accelerating rapidly. She looked from side to side, getting a shaky thumbs up from the marines in their Sprinters next to her, the dropship rocking as waves of fire streaked past the protective bubble of the shields, and they broke through the atmosphere.

Winters looked up as the five GCH warships appeared through the cockpit window while they fell. Her HUD pulled up more details, and she could see that the Fleet had destroyed at least eighty raiders while the rest were breaking formation and attempting to escape. Winters smiled as she looked at the sensor data, the readout showing that the *Alexia* was jamming the enemy's comms, leaving the Canid ground forces with no idea what was happening above, or what was coming for them.

She braced herself as they continued to dive through the atmosphere, watching on her holo-feed as the other dropships, each carrying a payload of five Sprinters, flew in formation. Three Canid raiders appeared on sensors a moment later, lining up for a strafing run.

The dropships had decent shields but limited offensive capabilities, and she knew they wouldn't last long if the raiders closed and got a solid lock on them.

She grasped her controls, waiting helplessly, unable to do anything while the dropship shook, taking fire as the raiders closed on them. Winters watched them swing around for another pass, steadying herself for the impending assault, while the pilots took evasive action, attempting to outrun their pursuers.

The ship shook hard once more, and she looked at the display in her HUD, the dropship's shields down to fifteen percent as the raiders shot past, banking hard into a turn, then coming around once more.

Just as they approached for another strafing run, three

wings of GCH fighters came out of the cloud cover from above, hitting the raiders hard and destroying several ships outright, while forcing the rest to break off their attack.

Winters breathed a sigh of relief as they approached the surface of the planet and the dropships pulled up, stopping just meters from the ground while the Sprinters deployed.

"Squad, on me," she commanded, her armor dropping from the bay and landing with a thud. "The colony is six klicks to the east, through the forest. Fall into Delta formation. Let's show these mangy dogs what a real raid looks like! Move out!"

The dropships pulled away, deploying drones as the ship rocketed out of the engagement zone, and Sprinters leapt into action, the fast, lithe constructs moving with incredible speed. Unlike other GCH armor, which took humanoid forms, the Sprinters resembled huge cats seven meters long and three high, with sleek, powerful bodies. Four rapidly moving legs, along with multiple weapons packages designed for high-speed engagements, deployed as they prepared to engage the enemy. A long metallic tail flowed from the back of the armor, tipped with a razor-sharp blade, swinging from side to side and providing a counterbalance as the armor weaved through the trees. The Sprinters leapt over obstacles with graceful ease as they closed the distance, the light but durable alloy allowing them to move swiftly and effortlessly.

"We're coming up on them shortly," Winters said, watching in her HUD as the overhead view from the drones the dropships had launched provided detailed data.

She zoomed the feed in, the Canid ground forces outside the colony walls becoming visible ahead of them: a horde of huge wolflike creatures, standing on two legs, wielding powered axes, maces, and energy weapons. Huge plasma cannon batteries bombarded the colony's shields, lighting them up with each hit.

"Sensors indicate just over two thousand Canid warriors in total at the gates. The colony's shields and forcefield barriers are still holding, but the main gates have several gaps in the grid and are taking heavy fire. The forcefields are the only thing keeping the Canids out, and they won't last much longer," she called out.

"Alpha squad on me. The rest of you, follow your squad leaders. I'm going to go straight in on the left flank and see if we can disrupt their ranks, then get to the gates and hold. Beta squad, follow my path and hit those batteries once we've cleared the way. Delta and Echo, take the right flank and do the same. Gamma, hold back, then cut through the horde wherever their ranks open up and take out as many as you can in the chaos. We'll meet up at the gates and hold the line there. Data uplink reports that the two mech legions have landed farther down along the colony walls and are about to deploy, so we shouldn't have to hold the gates for long. Fleet's almost done mopping up, and the *Valiant*'s dropships are en route with the heavy armor for backup. For now, it's our turn. Ready, break!"

The marines fell into their assigned squads, charging towards the Canid mass. The Sprinters in Alpha and Delta hit the thinner rear of the horde on the flanks, tearing through them with deadly grace. Razor-sharp blades deployed from the sides of the armor, cutting down enemy soldiers as they weaved in a zigzag pattern through the mass of muscle, claws, and fur. The Sprinters' tails flicked back and forth, wounding and decapitating several warriors still in range while plasma cannons on their heads fired forward, clearing a path.

Winters charged for the nearest battery, taking it out with her forward cannons, then turned for another one while magnesium flares launched from either side of the armor, igniting any Canids unlucky enough to be in range and forcing the horde to scatter to avoid their burning comrades.

Beta squad followed the trail of destruction, as did Echo on the opposite flank, hitting the exposed batteries as the soldiers operating them scattered from the sudden rear assault.

Mortar shells and micro-missiles rained down from the streaking Sprinters as they sowed chaos all through the enemy lines, quickly closing the gap to the main gates and leaving a path of devastation in their wake.

Winters stopped just short of the gates, outside the forcefield holding back the horde. She turned her armor to face the mass of snarling predators, taking up a defensive position, her small squad quickly forming up on her. "Full power to weapons and shields. We hold the line here!" she commanded, firing into the stunned sea of enemies. "Gamma squad, looks like there's an opening on the right flank. Cut through there and see if you can thin the pack. We'll keep them focused on us."

"Copy that," Hoffman, the leader of Gamma, replied, heading for the enemy lines while the rest of the squads formed up with Alpha in front of the main gates.

The team dug in, their plasma cannons and flamethrowers keeping the deadly predators at bay while launching mortar rounds and flares into the pack. The Canids returned fire but struggled to counterattack, thrown off by the swift and unexpected rush through their lines and the heavy resistance they now faced.

Gamma joined the rest of the squads a moment later, having completed their run.

"Link shields!" Winters called over the comm, the Sprinters syncing their shields, forming a continuous barrier, each reinforcing the others. "We just have to hold for a few more minutes," she said, checking her overwatch display in her HUD, where she could see the inbound dropships from the *Valiant* closing to the east.

A squadron of fighters flew overhead a moment later, dropping heavy ordnance on the horde, massive plumes of dirt erupting all across the battlefield.

Time seemed to freeze for a moment, and it looked like the Canids were about to break, when, suddenly, a huge warrior leapt forward from the pack, tackling a Sprinter in one swift motion. The creature, in a feat of adrenaline-fueled strength, picked up the armor and smashed it into the Sprinter next to it, slamming them both into the ground. Screams filled the comms as the gigantic wolf tossed the armor back into the horde, the crippled Sprinter disappearing into the sea of fur, where it was torn apart in seconds.

The warrior spun around, swinging its massive powered axe towards the head of the other fallen armor, slicing the pilot, Davies, in half.

"Scatter!" Winters called, her line suddenly broken, her team cornered as more Canids came rushing at them in force. "Use your speed to get away. Don't let them get ahold of you!"

Her squad sprang into motion, but the Canids responded, surrounding them and slowing the Sprinters while taking heavy losses in the process. Winters moved quickly along the colony wall, firing into the oncoming sea of claws and teeth, attempting to clear a path.

As she rounded the edge of the pack, she stopped, opening fire to try to clear space for the rest of her team to retreat, when an enormous axe hit her armor, knocking it sideways and to the ground and narrowly missing the cockpit. She attempted to get the catlike armor back on its feet, firing wildly, letting loose with everything she had as the icons representing her squads in her HUD slowly turned red, the rushing Canids overwhelming them.

"Get out of there!" she yelled. "Fall back!"

But it was too late.

Winters watched in horror as the last of her team went offline, Holman's vital signs the last to fall flat as his armor was torn to shreds.

Winters fought to hold back her tears, teetering between rage and despair, when suddenly her Sprinter was hit hard, something taking out the front legs and toppling it to the ground. "Freya, eject!" she called, her AI quickly activating the emergency evacuation procedure.

Winters launched from her cockpit seconds before a huge mace crushed it like an empty beer can, the thrust shooting her high above. She landed on a nearby branch half a dozen meters from the ground, crouching and taking aim with her sidearm, firing in desperation at everything that moved. The nanosuit she was wearing activated its personal shields and formed a helmet, Freya integrating the targeting sensors with the sidearm to increase her accuracy.

"We're too exposed and cannot hold this position," her AI warned.

"I know, I know!" Winters replied, checking the tactical screen in her HUD, watching as a few dozen Canids approached from below. "Where the hell is our backup?" she asked, the fighters passing by on another strafing run seconds later, raining hell down upon the horde.

She used the momentary distraction, leaping from the tree branch and engaging her suit's flight mode, heading for the relative safety of the colony walls.

Just as she approached a gap in the forcefield, a powerful energy blast slammed into her. The impact knocked her from the sky, the shields barely holding. Freya fired the thrusters at the last second, keeping her from hitting the ground at terminal velocity. Still, she landed hard, just outside the main gates, her sidearm lost as she skidded to a stop along the muddy ground.

Winters shook off the impact, getting to her feet just as a group of Canids approached, claws and teeth ready to tear her to pieces.

Suddenly, a deafening sound erupted from above.

She turned to see the dropships from the *Valiant* hovering overhead as huge suits of armor, each six meters tall, thundered down, hitting the ground beside her, the impact knocking her from her feet.

She looked up at the closest of the group, a large spindly red spider painted on the black armor, watching as it went to work.

The Widow Makers let loose with their heavy weapons, a thundering chorus echoing off the colony wall as massive bolts of plasma tore through the enemy lines, halting the Canid advance.

The heavy armor quickly pressed the attack, pushing their advantage, not giving the enemy any time to adapt. A single Canid warrior slipped through the chaos, lunging towards the defenseless Winters when, suddenly, one of the Widow Makers turned, striking it with a lightning-fast metal fist, sending its broken body crashing into the wall of the colony just meters from where Winters sat.

She looked up as the armor turned to face her. "Get over the gates, Commander. We've got it from here," a woman's voice said over the comm. The Widow Maker turned back to the battle, raining down a barrage of micro-missiles while pounding the enemy with relentless plasma fire.

Winters scrambled towards the wall, slipping through the gap in the forcefield, then activating her thrusters and ascending the wall. She landed on the far side, bodies and burn marks scattered all around the main square.

She scanned the scene, quickly locating a rifle and moving up to the wall to cover the hole in the defensive shields.

As she looked out, she could see that the Canids were now in full retreat, the Widow Makers picking them off as they fled, flanked now by the mech legion approaching from the south, catching them in the cross fire. She turned back, noticing several colonists on the wall for the first time, many of them bloodstained but still in the fight. "Freya, scan for survivors."

"I'm detecting thirty-one survivors in the immediate area, several of whom are in need of urgent medical attention," Freya replied.

"Hail the *Alexia* and report our status. Request immediate medical support to our location," she said, moving towards the closest group. "It's all right. They're retreating!" she called, lowering her helmet and turning to face the colonists, the looks on their faces ashen.

Several of the colonists held one another and wept, the mumbled words, "They're gone, they're gone," barely audible through their sobs.

"Freya, what's wrong?"

"There," her AI said, zooming in on a man farther back in the courtyard near a large central building, the structure heavily damaged and the main doors shattered.

Winters jumped down, her thrusters activating just before she hit the ground. She darted forward, stopping just before she reached the man as he bent down on one knee over the body of a child.

"What happened?" she asked tenderly, placing a hand on the man's shoulder. He looked up, his face a mask holding back the torrent of grief inside, ready to shatter as he reached back down, closing the girl's eyes.

As his hand moved back, Winters noticed the collar around the child's neck. "No," she whispered, taking a stunned step back.

"They were..." the man sobbed, dried blood covering half of his face as he struggled to get the words out. "They were taking the children," he said, his voice cracking as he attempted to control his emotions and fight back the tears. "I tried, but I couldn't save them."

"You did everything you could," she said, patting the man's shoulder, then moving off, considering for a moment. Most Canid raids were smash-and-grab jobs, typically going after food, supplies, and weapons...but never children.

"Are there any recorded cases of anything like this happening before?"

"Negative," Freya replied. "There are some documented cases of Rii'ven taking hostages to trade, but they have never targeted children before."

"This new faction... I've read the reports. They're known to be ruthless, but this...this is something else entirely," she said, moving away from the civilians and finding a quiet area, then opening a channel. "*Alexia*, come in. This is Commander Winters. I need to speak with the admiral now."

"Commander, stand by for *Alexia* actual," a comms officer replied.

"Winters, this is *Alexia* actual. What's your sit rep?" Admiral Carter asked.

"Admiral." Winters took a breath, centering herself. "My squad was lost, sir. I'm the only survivor. We broke their lines, but they adapted too quickly. The Widows hit them hard, though, and are mopping up with the mechs. The Canids on the ground are in full retreat."

"I'm sorry for your losses, Commander," the admiral said, knowing all too well what it was like to lose someone under his command. "We've destroyed over two hundred of their raiders and dealt them a heavy blow. The rest are scattering and bugging out of the system. We're holding a perimeter and letting them go, focusing our efforts on sending down teams to assist the colony."

"Admiral, we have to go after them, now!"

"Why? What happened, Commander?"

"They took prisoners, sir. The attack on the main gates. It was mostly a diversion. They must have broken in at another location." She swallowed hard, barely able to choke the words out. "They took the children, sir!"

Silence filled the comm for a moment. "Acknowledged, Commander," Admiral Carter said, his voice firm. "We'll send scouts after them immediately. We will find them. There are several other squads that I need to check in with before we can pull out. Hold your position and do what you can to assist on the ground. Help is on the way. We'll do what we can here to help the wounded, then we'll mobilize and go after those bastards. I promise you that!"

"Understood, sir. Winters out," she said, looking back across the square at the child once more.

They'll pay for this, she told herself. *Even if I have to kill every last one myself.*

CHAPTER 1
AFTERMATH

Jackson stood in the heart of GCH Intelligence, staring up at the map of the core systems suspended in midair, taken aback by the sheer number of ships, stations, and GCH installations in the thirteen systems that comprised the core. A few meters away, half a dozen officers gathered around another terminal, staring at the display floating in the air above it. One of the officers manipulated the controls to focus in on a specific section, bringing up the most recent scans, along with dozens of other data points as they zoomed in on the Kuteria System, red symbols appearing where GCH facilities had once stood.

Jackson watched as the statistics appeared beside the map – the number of lives lost, ships destroyed, and so on – having become numb to the sheer immensity of the numbers as he tried to picture the people behind them, unable to contemplate the loss of life at such a scale.

"Looks like the hyperspace defense grid is active again, at least," he said quietly.

"Indeed. The Fleet has deployed several specialized ships to reinforce sections where the grid satellites were destroyed, and replacement units are still being deployed in the affected areas," Bits said. "The system should be secured within the next eighteen to twenty-four hours."

"That's good, at least. I know there was a lot of fear about another attack with the grid offline and the system in chaos. We'd have been sitting ducks if another wave of Imperium ships arrived while we were commencing full rescue operations."

"Unfortunately, reports indicate that the Imperium used the opportunity instead to attack several other military targets along the Holt Line once Command rerouted ships to counterattack the incursion in the Kuteria System."

"Yeah, the admiral mentioned that," he said, walking slowly along the pathway that ran around the perimeter of the room, moving past clusters of pods and other stations, hundreds of them, that filled the massive space, nearly the size of a football stadium. A dozen other displays hovered around the room, with teams gathered around them, focusing intently, each dedicated to a specific sector and task, some visible, while others just appeared as a flicker of light from the right angle, the data encrypted to the officers' individual HUDs.

Jackson took in the levels above, where floors of analysts worked, going through data, coordinating with the army of androids beneath the facility, running scenarios, processing scans, and analyzing vast amounts of data.

The entire complex reminded him of a giant ant colony with thousands of workers going about their tasks, each part of a larger whole.

He stopped for a moment, noticing a familiar star system layout on one of the displays, watching as the image zoomed in on the Kishara System for a moment, his heart sinking in his chest. He took a breath to center himself, pushing his emotions aside, noticing the icons that represented a task force of fifty GHC warships near Kishara Prime, feeling somewhat relieved that the Fleet was maintaining a strong presence in the system.

Admiral Valentyen found him a few minutes later. Jackson turned as he approached. "How was your meeting with the Admiralty, sir?"

The admiral took a breath, clearly frustrated. "They're in full defensive mode. Not that I blame them, but they aren't authorizing any ops at the moment. The entire Confederation is still in full lockdown, and it might be days before they allow even limited interstellar travel to resume."

"Makes sense. It's certainly not every day that a core system, let alone one of the three founding systems, gets attacked."

"No, it is not. In fact, the three systems that formed the Alliance haven't faced a direct attack in over six thousand years!"

"Wow, I didn't realize it had been that long. I can understand then why they're so shaken."

"That's an understatement. But, again, I can't blame them. This attack was unprecedented," the admiral said, looking around, then tipping his head to his right. "Let's get out of here and take a walk."

Minutes later, they were outside, the cool morning air invigorating as the sun crept over the mountains in the distance.

The admiral led the way through GCH Command, over several bridges and streams towards the green space that made up the Fields of Remembrance. As they walked, the admiral turned, leading Jackson down a path that he'd never been on before, through a wooded area and into a clearing filled with beautiful gardens and exotic plants. Beams of sunlight broke through the canopy, illuminating the dew on the grass. The blades bent slightly from their weight while songbirds filled the morning sky with music.

"Where are we going, sir?"

"Just over this next rise," the admiral said, leading him down a cobblestone path, through a thick copse of trees, before opening up once more, a huge monument coming into view.

As they approached, Jackson took in the sight, suddenly realizing what it was: a monument dedicated to the *Viceroy*, her valiant crew, and her legendary captain, Greyson Quentarus.

Jackson stared in awe at the beauty of it. Depicted in a massive full-color hologram stood the planet, Brestin III, with the *Viceroy* in orbit and the tiny *Phoenix* rising from the planet's surface, highlighted with a small red octagon that zoomed in on the ship to assist viewers in finding it against the vastness of the planet.

He watched as the holographic presentation played, the image zooming out to highlight a larger area of space around the planet. Seconds later, the Imperium fleet jumped in, the *Viceroy* turning to meet them. A small streak shot out from an Insectoid ship, the weapon detonating in open space and a ripple appearing across the map.

Jackson swallowed, watching as the wave expanded rapidly in all directions, remembering the moment when they realized what it was.

A subspace disruption weapon.

The wave finally dissipated, and the Imperium fleet moved forward, Jackson recalling the stoic look on Captain Quentarus's face, knowing that the *Viceroy's* fate was sealed and that there was no chance of escape.

His heart ached as he watched the *Viceroy* turn its deadly broadside towards the enemy, valiantly defending the *Phoenix* and putting itself between them and the Imperium fleet, covering their escape.

The battle began, the Imperium fleet believing they had the *Viceroy* at their mercy and launching a devastating volley of torpedoes, only to see them all picked off by the state-of-the-art dreadnought's powerful defenses. He watched as the battle played out, the mass drivers striking out and ripping through the Imperium fleet, the attackers, he imagined, suddenly aware of the folly of their hubris.

The image zoomed in for a few seconds, showing waves of Imperium fighters streaking forward, attempting to get past the *Viceroy* and engage the *Phoenix*. He watched as the dreadnought picked off dozens of the tiny fighters, along with several waves of torpedoes that were inbound for the stealth ship, never truly realizing how close they had been to being overrun or crippled as they raced to escape the range of the hyperspatial disruption field.

As he watched the rest of the battle unfold, it became clear that what he was seeing was a composite of the sensory and visual logs from both the *Phoenix* and the cloaked GCH sensor arrays in the system, giving several perspectives to the engagement.

Jackson tensed as the *Phoenix* pulled away, the Imperium fleet closing in on the badly damaged dreadnaught, going for the kill, only for the *Viceroy* to suddenly roll, exposing its other, mostly undamaged broadside.

Hubris, he thought, shaking his head as he looked at the Insectoid fleet, their formation sloppy, knowing that Captain Quentarus had played them, luring them in and catching them overconfident and unprepared once more.

He smiled as he recognized the Arachnid queen's ship in the center of the now heavily thinned out Insectoid fleet, watching as beams from the mass drivers lanced out, splitting the ship in two, an explosion engulfing it seconds later.

Jackson held his breath as the Imperium fleet closed, desperately bombarding the *Viceroy* with heavy fire from both sides while their numbers continued to dwindle.

The mighty dreadnaught exploded seconds later, taking half a dozen more Insectoid ships with it, the *Phoenix* jumping away just afterwards.

As the image faded, a display appeared, detailing the statistics of the battle – how many Insectoid ships the *Viceroy* had destroyed or disabled, how many crew members were lost, and so on. The image changed, showing a tactical display and assessment detailing, in layman's terms, how astonishing a feat it was that a single ship took on an entire enemy fleet, a credit to its captain and crew.

Little information or details appeared about the *Phoenix* itself. It was simply listed as a scientific vessel on a critical mission that escaped the Insectoid strike.

The playback concluded with a crew manifest from the *Viceroy*, scrolling for nearly a minute and forty seconds. Jackson watched as images of the captain and several of the senior bridge officers appeared at the end.

He stared at the display for a long moment in silence as a final image of the *Viceroy* appeared, the massive, elegant dreadnought floating in space, the words, *May the bravery and sacrifice of her crew never be forgotten,* being displayed above it before the holo-projection disappeared.

As it faded, Jackson saw the monument below it, an ornate display made out of stone, with an image of the ship above Brestin III etched into it.

The admiral placed a hand on Jackson's shoulder. "I thought that you might want to see this. Kelara was here for its dedication, along with her mother. It was very moving, and a fitting tribute, I think."

Jackson nodded. "Thank you, sir. I'm glad you brought me here. It's nice to know that their sacrifice will be remembered."

"Agreed. It's unfortunate, however, that not everyone can know the whole story, but I'm happy that they'll live on as heroes of the Confederation." The admiral paused for a moment, staring at the monument one last time, then turned to Jackson. "Why don't we head back? There's a lot more that we need to discuss."

Jackson fell in beside him, and the two walked back to the Command complex in silence, each taking a few moments to themselves to reflect on the sacrifices of Captain Quentarus and his heroic crew.

CHAPTER 2
REVELATIONS

The admiral led Jackson back through the myriad hallways and restricted areas that comprised the GCH Command complex. Finally, they reached a lift, which took them down thirty levels below ground to an area where Jackson had never been before.

The admiral exited first, Jackson following closely in his wake, uncertain where they were going. They turned down a huge corridor, easily five meters wide and ten meters high, before approaching a checkpoint where three heavily armed guards stood before a high-security doorway, flanked on either side by two towering Gate Keepers.

After a thorough scan to confirm their identities and verification of their AIs' access codes, they were allowed entry to the room beyond.

As they entered, Jackson stopped in his tracks, amazed at the scene before him. The room was similar in some ways to the GCH Intelligence hub, but about half the size. It stood four stories high, with a massive holo-display in the center depicting a real-time view of the galaxy spread out over an enormous space as it hovered in midair. Jackson stared as the locations of forty of the sixty-five GCH fleets, ten of them newly commissioned during the war and comprised of ships pulled from mothballs, appeared spread across the Confederation, many of them broken into smaller battle groups and task forces.

The borders of every sovereign empire crisscrossed the map, clearly highlighted in color-coded lines and labeled. Small breaks in the GCH border were visible at several points along the Holt Line, likely indicating breaches, he inferred, something the admiral confirmed a moment later as he began explaining.

"This is the GCH Central Command Center. Whereas GCH Intelligence has thousands of people working there, as you saw, fewer than four hundred and fifty officers in the entire Confederation have access to CentCom. From here, we coordinate Fleet movements and monitor the entirety of the GCH space. You'll notice there are areas where the map is clearer in focus, indicating that we have satellites, probes, or monitoring equipment present, providing real-time sensor data via compressed subspace links, while other areas where the resolution is lacking are long-range scans and updated less frequently as data comes in and is analyzed."

Jackson nodded, recalling from his basic training sessions that the GCH had deployed millions of stations, probes, and satellites throughout their space to monitor it, but he'd never realized how sophisticated the network was until now.

The admiral explained that each ship's transponder and sensor data were automatically uploaded through the network to this room, allowing Command to react quickly to most situations. He also explained, however, that there were thousands of dead zones in the map due to spatial anomalies, gravitational forces such as black holes, and other phenomena, which prevented many areas from being properly monitored or data from streaming in real time.

Jackson studied the map as they walked in a slow circle around it and Bits interfaced with the system, one of the new perks of his rank as a captain with special operations clearance, allowing him to see various details in his ocular implants, such as Outlier colonies, Vicara class planets, and quarantined systems. Small blue dots represented GCH stations, medical outposts, mining operations, refineries, and research outposts, along with other icons and dots representing ships, stations, and other facilities from the various different empires around the Confederation.

Suddenly, the map zoomed out, causing him to stop and take a step back as he realized that they'd only been looking at a small portion of the galaxy.

Jackson's jaw dropped, the updated image completely flooring him. "Oh my God! How is it possible to even *attempt* to keep track of all of this?" he asked, his mind reeling, overwhelmed by the sheer volume of information and the number of moving pieces. "I thought that the GCH Intelligence view was staggering, but this…this is a whole other level."

"It is. GCH Intelligence focuses on the micro, for the most part. Planning ops, doing tactical analysis, running scenarios, and so on. CentCom focuses on the big picture, taking in everything we have available to us. And to answer your question, *how do we keep track of this*, the truth is, we don't. We can't. But we do the best that we can," the admiral admitted. "There is a room… Well, *room* doesn't really do it justice. There's a massive warehouse, I guess is the best description, three stories down, that's nearly five kilometers long and four kilometers wide. It houses hundreds of GCH mainframes, quantum computer core processors, databases, communications relays, and an army of tens of thousands of androids to maintain it all and to process the vast amounts of information collected every second. There are four other sites like this spread across the GCH for redundancy and to share the load of the immense task we undertake each day."

"Wow, that's...amazing. It's almost unbelievable. But still, even with all of that, there's just so much space to cover. Tens of thousands of square light-years!"

"As I said, we do the best that we can, but it's never truly enough. And we continue to grow, despite what's best for us. Now we simply try to protect as many lives as possible and ensure the safety, stability, and security of our citizens. This is only part of what I wanted to show you, however. Take a look beyond our borders and tell me what you see."

Jackson studied the map carefully, the border with the Canids visible at the left side of the map, along with several of their systems marked in purple. He focused, and Bits interfaced with the map, zooming in on a section in his HUD where he could see the Rii'ven's primary fleet in orbit around Weth'rex, the Canid home world. He looked at the other side of the map and could see the same with the Reptilian Empire and the Oceanic Union, where various fleets or stations were marked on the map as he focused on each area, his ocular implants zooming in and showing him the micro-details in the massive holographic projection. On the Insectoid side of the border, however, there were only details in a dozen or so places and for no more than a few light-years across. The rest of the Imperium was seemingly empty, with known systems marked on the map, but with no ships, stations, or any other details at all.

"The Shroud of Darkness," he whispered.

The admiral nodded. "We've had to rely on short-range reconnaissance and visual scans to confirm what's still there, which is risky, as it means jumping small scout ships in-system. The Shroud has neutralized all of our mid- and long-range sensor capabilities, and even for ships in-system, they can only risk staying so long, even when cloaked, and short-range scans are limited by the Shroud. For the most part, we've only been able to react to their fleets once they enter our space. And because of the hundreds of incursions that have happened over the course of the war, the Shroud now extends beyond their borders in many places into our space, where they've dropped more satellites to expand its range. Unfortunately, this has meant that, too often, our response times haven't been quick enough.

"We know that they have similar monitoring capabilities to ours, and that's allowed them to strike at our fleets, planets, and stations when they're at their weakest. It's also enabled them to disrupt our supply lines, striking our convoys with hit-and-run raids across the border. Despite all of that, we've been lucky that they've been somewhat unimaginative in other ways. We've learned, as I mentioned a while back, that they've been operating out of many of the same bases and fleet staging areas as they did before the Shroud went up. As such, we've been able to strike out at them more recently, basing our attacks on estimated numbers of ships and ensuring a decisive advantage in each engagement. The loss of their advanced shipyards really did help to tip the balance of military might back in our favor, for a time at least. We estimate that they only have a few hundred of them left, at most, many of which have been badly damaged in recent engagements where we've made them priority targets."

Jackson nodded, a swell of pride filling him at the sacrifices he and Frederickton had made to take out the enemy's production capabilities, and seeing the tangible differences it had made. A thought crossed his mind as he stared at the map. "You mentioned something that you were planning before I was lost on the shipyard mission. What was it you wanted to show me, sir?"

"There are some things we need to discuss first," he said, gesturing for Jackson to follow him as he led him to a small briefing room.

"Security protocol Gamma-Three," the admiral said, the doors locking behind them and the glass becoming opaque, a dull hum registering a moment later as a sonic dampener activated. "I wanted to follow up on our conversation from before I went to meet with the Fleet admirals."

Jackson swallowed, dreading what he feared might come next as the admiral continued.

"I discussed several options with them, and as I mentioned, we don't have clearance to launch any operations yet, but I wanted to let you know that I brought up the Light weapons with Fleet Admiral Lighton once we were alone after the meeting."

A chill went down Jackson's mind as he fortified himself, his fears growing that he might be forced to unleash the weapons of mass destruction. A weight bore down on his shoulders at the thought of taking so many lives, despite his hatred of the Imperium.

The admiral read his expression and sensed the subtle shift in posture, meeting Jackson's eyes as he continued. "We agreed to keep their location a secret and completely off the books, Will. So even Fleet Admiral Lighton doesn't know where they are, but she knows now that we have them as an option. After talking with the other Fleet admirals and considering the dire circumstances we're in, I felt that I couldn't keep this a secret any longer. Only Fleet Admiral Lighton was there in person, so she's the only one who knows, as I didn't want to risk any of this going over subspace. Once I explained to her why I'd kept this compartmentalized, she understood and agreed that with the Imperium's espionage capabilities, it's better for as few people as possible to know of their existence or location.

"I know that we said we'd do whatever it takes, and I still hold firm to that, but I convinced her that we have a few cards still left to play before we go that route, so she's going to keep it as a measure of last resort for now. She agreed that once we show our enemies the power we possess – while it might end the war – it will make them hellbent on possessing it as well, and they will stop at nothing to achieve that. We decided that it was better to find another way for now. But…if another attack like the one on Kuteria happens, and too many lives are in danger, and she feels we have no other choice, she'll let the other Fleet admirals know of their existence and consider using them."

Jackson nodded numbly, relieved to hear that the use of the Light weapons was off the table for now, despite a twinge of guilt nagging at him, knowing that he could likely stop the war tomorrow if he used them.

The thought, however, terrified him.

Alura had explained their destructive capabilities and how they'd decimated the realm where the Phague lived.

To unleash that kind of power.

That level of destruction, the scale of which they didn't even know.

He'd felt sick since the crew had met hours before and discussed it. Though he'd meant what he said completely – that he would ultimately do whatever it took, no matter what – he felt a wave of relief knowing that they hadn't yet come to that.

"What about the mole in Command, sir? Even with just Fleet Admiral Lighton knowing about this, isn't there still a risk?"

"That was actually what I wanted to talk to you about next, and why I felt I could finally bring this to her. I've been doing some digging into the *incident* with your AI's code being tampered with," he said, the subtle bitterness in his tone unmistakable. Jackson knew that the thought of a mole in Command had unsettled the admiral deeply. After having devoted more than two hundred years of his life to the protection of the GCH, the thought had sickened him that someone from within their ranks could have betrayed them.

"I began to work backwards," Admiral Valentyen continued, "building a list of anyone who was involved in Bits's initial design and the upgrade that Admiral Thompson administered shortly before we began our search. Vetting the initial design team took time, but I was able to clear them all, deciding it was more logical that it was the upgrade, not his original code, which was the point where the tracking software was uploaded. It stood to reason that if the original team had done this, you'd be dead already, with the assassins having years to track and ambush you before you were fully trained."

"Makes sense," Jackson replied.

"Once I'd cleared the original team, I pulled up the logs on both of the upgrades you've had. There were only four techs who worked on them, along with Admiral Thompson, who oversaw the process, so I began thoroughly investigating each of them. My initial search came up empty, and I reluctantly put the project aside for nearly a year after running out of leads. During that time, the feeling that perhaps I'd missed something or was going about this the wrong way continued to nag me. Then, after you disappeared, I decided to reopen my investigation." The admiral paused, looking away for a moment before meeting Jackson's eyes. "Your loss hit us all very hard, Will, and I felt powerless as I was forced to accept that you were gone. When I received the message confirming your death and watched the video you made for me… I felt that I needed to do something to honor your memory. So, I began digging once more."

Jackson watched the admiral's face as he spoke. While he did a good job of keeping his emotions in check, it was clear that his death had affected his former commander deeply.

The admiral continued. "I had my AI pull everything she could on the four techs, going through comm logs, credit transactions, and even highly controlled tracking data recording their movements for months leading up to the upgrade. I spent weeks poring through the data, looking for something, anything, that would provide a hint of a trail to follow. Unfortunately, I came up empty. All of these men and women were completely loyal career officers who would never betray the Confederation." The admiral paused, taking a breath. "I then, reluctantly, turned my attention to Admiral Thompson, one of my oldest and closest friends."

Jackson sat in silence with his hands folded on the table before him, unable to fathom that Admiral Thompson could betray anyone.

"It was significantly more difficult to dig into the admiral. His rank and privileges give him operational anonymity, just as mine do, meaning that he can disable all abilities to track him and go off-grid when necessary. As I began my search, I quickly found several such incidents during the time period I focused on, but none of which seemed suspicious on the surface. Then I came across a comm log dated six days before your upgrade. The admiral received an encoded communication from an unknown source. Now, this wasn't suspicious in itself, as there are confidential informants who feed us intel on a regular basis, but there was an identifier embedded into the message header, which wasn't encoded, and my AI picked up on it, recognizing it for what it was."

The admiral waved a hand, and a holo-display activated, showing the header of the message.

"A GCH personal identifier," Jackson said.

"That's correct. I looked it up in the Fleet database only to discover that it belonged to an officer who'd served under the admiral one hundred and fifty-five years ago. As I dug into his file, I learned that he'd left the Fleet a few years later and was reportedly killed in a confrontation with an unknown species in the outer regions of the Cygnus Arm."

"Whoa. That's a red flag."

"Indeed."

The message appeared in the display a moment later. It read:

> Admiral,
>
> I know it's been a long time, and I'm sorry for the deception, but it was necessary for the galaxy to believe I was dead. I need to meet with you in person immediately. I have operational intel vita. to a war you don't know is coming and that I can't risk transmitting. Meet me at the coordinates embedded in this data stream in one day. You're the only one I trust, sir.
>
> A097512814-CX

The admiral switched the view to show the coordinates, and a planetary system displayed before them. "This is a small unoccupied system inside Confederation space called RG-904. It's unremarkable, with no strategic value or critical resources. However, the stellar cartography database shows that the moon orbiting the sixth planet is habitable, though just barely. This is where I believe the admiral went."

"Have you asked him about this?"

"This is where it gets complicated. Four days after the admiral returned is when you and I met for the first time to start the search for the Ancient sites. I talked with Admiral Janus, and she confirmed that it was Admiral Thompson who decided that it was finally time to pull our team together and begin the search. He contacted me the day he returned, and we arrived on the *Waverly* a few days later to collect you and Verris from Kishara Station.

"I then checked the final build logs on the code upgrade and, after considerable digging, found a deleted log that showed a new injection of code was added the day the admiral returned. The upload logs themselves were scrubbed, as I mentioned, so I couldn't see what was added, but the version tracking can't be tampered with, which is how I figured out that a change had been made. I then pulled up the build iterations and discovered that the file sizes had increased by two point three percent. I decided to ask the admiral about your upgraded code under the guise of needing to enhance one of my operatives and remembering that he'd written a custom patch for you. When I discussed this with him, he seemed confused, not recalling ever giving you the code upgrade and claiming that it was still in development when we left."

"That's strange," Jackson commented, recalling that the admiral had been very proud of the upgrades and that they were being rolled out to special-ops personnel.

"Agreed," the admiral said. "So, I continued to dig for several weeks, and what I discovered next was...*unsettling*, to say the least. Admiral Thompson dropped off the grid two days after we left for the Hideaway. The only record I found was a comm log from his AI, alerting GCH medical staff that the admiral had collapsed in his office. It took some arm-twisting, but I have a friend at the Ministry of Health who pulled the records. They indicated that an unknown pathogen was discovered in the admiral's system, which they believed had caused a minor stroke, along with limited short-term memory loss. The damage from the stroke was easily repaired, and he was only hospitalized for a few days before they cleared him for active duty. Understandably, he'd decided to keep this quiet, as it was a personal matter, so only a few people were aware that this had ever occurred."

"He did mention something about a headache when he did the code upgrade," Jackson said, recalling that the admiral had lamented not being able to join them.

"That makes sense. I then took this to Fleet Admiral Lighton, who reluctantly agreed to bring Admiral Thompson in under the guise of a routine medical checkup. While he was getting checked out, the doctors pulled his full AI logs, which I was then able to access. There were several anomalies in the logs, which eventually led me to a protected memory archive, deep within his AI's storage subsystems. As you know, your AI is able to keep a record of every moment of your life, storing this visual and sensory data for a few months, then purging all the insignificant records, while keeping anything of personal or military value. The file was heavily encrypted, and the logs showed that it had been, in fact, deleted. But it was somehow still there. I queried his AI as to the existence of this file, but it had no knowledge of it."

"Just like Bits was unaware of the code in his system," Jackson said.

"That's what I thought as well, so I put the androids to work on cracking the encryption. A few hours later, I received the unencrypted memory file." The admiral waved his hand, and a holo-image appeared, beginning playback.

The image showed a control panel beneath a wide window that Jackson recognized immediately as that of a shuttle. Data points appeared at the edges of the playback field, typical of that in a personal heads up display.

He watched as the shuttle completed a slow circle of a wide-open space, the landscape rocky and barren. A ship sat waiting on the surface, the sensor data from the recording showing it was of an unknown design. The shuttle touched down a moment later, opposite the other ship. As the shuttle powered down, the image turned towards the back of the ship. A reflection appeared for a moment on a display console, confirming that the record was indeed a buried memory from Admiral Thompson.

He watched as the admiral reached down, pulling a plasma pistol from a side compartment, then pressing it to his hip, attaching it to his uniform. He then reached for a small, circular disk and pressed it to his chest, looking down as his uniform – now clearly a nano-suit made to appear as though it were a uniform – absorbed the disk, which Jackson recognized as an advanced personal shield generator.

A moment later, he stepped out of the shuttle.

A lone figure stood waiting ahead as Admiral Thompson exited the ramp and rounded the shuttle, the face hidden in shadows beneath a heavy hood.

"Arkamus?" Admiral Thompson called tentatively, tilting his head to try to peer beneath the hood as he grew closer.

"Admiral," a rough, gravelly voice replied. "Thank you for coming. It's been a long time, sir."

"It's not every day I receive a message from one of my officers who's been dead for over a century and a half."

"I apologize for the deception, but my mission required that I operate as a ghost, completely off the grid."

"What mission is that?"

"A secret war. One I've fought for almost a hundred and fifty years."

"Why have you come to me now? What is this about a war to come?"

"You've been played, Admiral. We all have. There are forces shaping our destinies that hide in the shadows, using us as puppets."

"I don't understand. Please, let me see your face."

The cloaked figure tilted his head, then slowly pulled back his hood, revealing his scarred face. The admiral's vitals spiked as he looked at the man. "What happened to you, son?"

"It has been a long struggle. One where sacrifices needed to be made. But the secret war I've been fighting is nothing compared to the war that is to come."

"Tell me," the admiral said, stepping closer until he was just a meter away from his former officer.

"There is too much to tell, and time is short. Events have been set into motion which cannot be stopped. I need to find the second son before they do. The fate of everything hangs in the balance."

"Second son?"

Arkamus opened his hand to reveal a small data key. The admiral stepped forward, reaching out a hand to take the key when, suddenly, Arkamus dropped it and grabbed the admiral's wrist, pulling him closer. His other hand came up, injecting Admiral Thompson in the neck, the admiral's vitals in his HUD spiking.

"Why?" Admiral Thompson asked, his voice cracking.

"I'm sorry, Admiral, but it's the only way. If they find the second son, then all is lost. He will either join me, or he must die," he said, his face up close as he lowered Admiral Thompson gently to the ground.

"What hav—"

"I've injected you with an advanced nano-payload, along with a custom-tailored virus from another dimension that is undetectable. You'll wake up with no memory of this meeting. Even your AI will not be aware of it ever having taken place. The nano-payload will interface with your AI, taking control of it for what I need you to do, pushing you in the right direction. Finding *him* for me. After that, you'll then become sick for a short time, but I promise there won't be any long-term effects."

Admiral Thompson looked up at the man he once knew, his arm reaching slowly for him, then falling to his side as his vision began to fade.

"I'm sorry for breaking your trust, sir. I truly am. But time is running out, and I had to act now. You were always good to me, and for that, I'll be eternally grateful. And I hope you'll forgive me."

The admiral's eyes closed as he lost consciousness, and the recording ended.

Jackson sat in shocked silence as he tried to process everything that had just happened.

Admiral Valentyen gave him a moment, then spoke. "I believe that the admiral's AI reacted in that moment, attempting to protect the record of what happened, shunting this file to archival storage and encrypting it, then wiping all records of its existence before the foreign nanites took control of its systems."

"It's a miracle you found it, sir," Jackson said. "What did you do next?"

"Fleet Admiral Lighton and I brought Admiral Thompson in, presenting him with the evidence. He was unsurprisingly shocked and horrified at learning what had happened and had no memory of it. He recalled waking up in his shuttle, the autopilot taking him back to Archon. His AI, which we now know was compromised at the time, told him that they'd encountered a spatial anomaly and he'd simply passed out. He chalked up his foggy memory to the anomaly and moved on, keen to get back. He spent some time going through his messages and various Fleet reports on the way, still feeling off. After a few messages, he came across a report on the Ularans, which we now know was fabricated by his AI, and a reminder in his calendar to check in with Chief Johansen to see if there was any additional progress on the analysis of the Ancient tech you'd tested. He then said that he felt an urgent need to begin the search for the Ancient sites. We think that the code manipulating his AI placed subliminal messages in the report on the Ularans and that the calendar entry triggered him to act, getting him to contact me and bring you in to start the search. He also had no memory of the update to Bits's code, as I mentioned, so we think the virus was somehow affecting his memory for nearly a week before it finally died on its own, creating what appeared to be a stroke in the process."

"That's awful," Jackson said, recalling how he felt after Bits had been compromised, though this was much worse. Losing entire days. Being manipulated. Forced into actions with no memory of them. He felt as though he was going to be sick as he thought about how the admiral must have felt after getting this news.

"It is, but he took it like the seasoned officer he is and did everything he could to help," Admiral Valentyen explained. "He knew he had some memory gaps, which the doctors told him could happen from the stroke – which we now know was a side effect of the virus – but he had no idea there was more to it than that. Once he was aware of what had happened, he pulled up some old files and told us about Arkamus, a lieutenant commander who'd served under him for seven years when he was the captain of the destroyer *Theseus*. He described him as a good officer, recounting his disappointment when he left the Fleet a few years later. The only other contact the admiral had with him after that was when he received a personal message from Arkamus's AI informing him of his death."

"Where is the admiral now?" Jackson asked, concerned about what had happened to the man who had shown him nothing but kindness since the day they'd met.

"He took voluntary leave, but honestly, the feeling of betrayal, both from his former officer and in what he did to you, crushed him, and I don't know if he's coming back."

"I'm so sorry to hear that, sir. I know that the two of you have been friends for a very long time. It must have been hard on you."

"It was, but I have no regrets," the admiral said resolutely. "The truth is what's most important here, both for you and for him, and this is a mystery that needed to be solved. We now know who planted the tracking code in Bits and where it came from. We also know that there's a new player in the game, one whose motives we don't yet understand."

"What do you make of it all? Arkamus said that he wanted to find the second son, which I'm assuming means me, before the *others* did. Who do you think he meant? What do you think he wants with me?"

"It's hard to say. It's possible that he knew that the Insectoids were looking for you and that he was trying to find you before they did. In fact, I think he might be the one who saved us at Praxian Prime."

Jackson nodded. "That makes sense, actually. If he could track me, then he'd know I was there. And someone did save us that day, stopping those Insectoid ships. Can you bring up the visual of his ship again?"

The admiral waved his hand, and his AI brought up the record from Admiral Thompson's shuttle window while he circled the meeting spot.

"Bits, can you bring up the visual record of the ship from Praxian Prime?"

The images appeared next to one another, hovering in the air. "They look similar," Jackson said. "What do you think, sir?"

"Agreed. The design elements and hull construction appear to be the same. Hmm… Latara, pull up data from the

Ancient database we recovered from Vishnara. Look for ship designs or specifications," he said to his AI. A moment later, several images appeared.

"There!" Jackson said, pointing excitedly to the image of a ship. "That's it. Holy shit, he has an Ancient ship! He's like me!"

"Hmm, it does appear that way," the admiral conceded. "We never had any reason to test our officers for genetic compatibility with Ancient tech before you arrived in this time. Our scientists simply didn't think it was possible for someone to be compatible after years of failed testing." He paused, taking a breath and pulling up the image of the scarred face staring back at Admiral Thompson before he lost consciousness. "The question is, if he's the one who planted the code to track you, then how did the Cavarians get it, and why were they trying to kill you?"

"That's an excellent question, sir. We know that he took on a number of Imperium ships at Praxian Prime. It's possible that his ship was badly damaged in the process and he couldn't follow us. Perhaps he decided it was too much of a risk to let me live and sent bounty hunters after me instead. He did say that he couldn't risk my falling into the wrong hands."

"It makes sense. He told Admiral Thompson that you would either join him or die."

"So, what do we do now?" Jackson asked, taking a breath, feeling his heart pound in his chest as all of these questions, which had been left unanswered and nagged at him for years, finally came to light.

"For now, there's not a lot that we can do. We could try to send the signal again and see if we lure him into a trap, but he's likely wise to that by now, if he's even still alive. But we'll continue to work on this in the background and wait to see if anything new comes up."

Jackson nodded, knowing that the admiral was right. It had been years since the events leading up to their mission to search for Ancient tech, and there hadn't been any new information or contact with Arkamus since then. "So, what's next?"

"We can't run any ops yet, as I said, but you've gained a lot of experience infiltrating Imperium sites during the war, and I need your help in planning a complex mission. We need intel and answers about how they got the technology to create the Shroud of Darkness, and most importantly, we need to find a weakness."

"Makes sense. Where do we start?"

The admiral smiled. "We're going to break into the Imperium central database."

CHAPTER 3
SPLINTER CELL

THE FRONTIER

The *Alexia*, along with a fleet of twenty-one warships – nearly every ship the GCH had on the frontier – exited hyperspace in an unknown system twenty-eight light-years beyond the Confederation border, ready for battle.

The armada, led by the *Alexia*, included five battlecruisers, three mech transports, eleven destroyers, and one medical frigate, each falling into formation as they entered the system past the orbital plane of the farthest planet out, far enough away to ensure they would be undetected by their prey.

"Our scouts have located the Canid base of operations on the fourth planet," Admiral Carter began. "There are over three thousand raiders on the surface, spread out around a large settlement nearly twenty kilometers long and sixteen kilometers wide. We've also detected over seventy thousand Canid life signs on the surface," he added, addressing the briefing room where his senior staff were seated.

Winters, along with several other officers, stood at the back of the room while the admiral continued the briefing.

"Scans show several satellites in orbit, which we believe act as an early warning system, along with a primitive form of subspace disruptors to prevent any ships from jumping in too close. We only have two stealth scout ships available, but they don't have the armaments to take out the Canid defenses, so the plan is for a tactical strike to be carried out by Captain Medcof, along with two squads of his elite fighter wings. They'll jump to the far side of the moon in orbit around the planet and use a gravity assist to slingshot them towards the enemy positions, then power down. Once in range, they'll power up and quickly take out the Canid defenses, then signal the *Alexia*, and we'll jump in with the battle group to provide support. The *Alexia* will form up in the center with the battlecruisers, and the destroyers will flank us in gamma formation. The *Dakota* will hang back at the jump point here with the mech transports and medical frigate to provide cover until we need them.

"Our fleet will hold position in a high orbit above the colony and start targeting their ships on the ground. With that many vessels, we won't be able to get them all before some are able to take off, but any that do will be facing down the formidable firepower we have waiting for them, and we'll have the tactical advantage, allowing us to pick off more of their ships as they ascend. Once we occupy their raiders, the *Alexia* will send a signal for our ground forces to engage. Our dropships, mech transports, and fighter escorts will jump in on the far side of the planet and head for the surface. Their mission is to take down the Canid colony's defenses and search for the people who were taken from the Milakra colony.

"Based on our tactical analysis, we should be able to overwhelm their fleet, forcing them to break off or retreat. We'll then issue a demand for the colony to surrender. For this to work, however, we need those colonists secured. I don't want to give them any leverage to work with," he stressed. "This pack has become increasingly aggressive over the past few months, and it ends today. Understood?"

"Yes, sir," the room replied crisply as one.

"Very good. You have your orders. Captain Medcof, you're clear to deploy."

The room quickly emptied, Winters nodding to several other officers as they exited the room, each of them aware of what had happened back on the colony. She stayed behind and approached the admiral a moment later.

"I'm sorry for your losses, Commander. I'd understand if you wanted to sit this one out. I'm sure we can find someone else to lead this mission," he said, meeting her eyes, gauging her mental state and fitness for duty.

"Thank you, sir, but I'd like to see this through."

The admiral paused for a moment, considering. "Very well. I've assigned you a handpicked squad consisting of some of our best combat officers. You'll also have plenty of proven firepower this time with five Gate Keepers, ten Widow Makers, five Bone Crushers, and a dozen modified Strikers. Go get our people back."

"I will, sir. I promise," Winters said, the thought of payback burning in her mind.

Ten minutes later, Winters arrived on the deployment deck of the *Alexia*.

"Attention on deck!" one of the officers called out, and all thirty-one of the combat specialists snapped to attention as she entered the room.

"As you were," she said, approaching the front of the formation, tossing a holo-sphere into the air as she moved to stand before them. An image of the Canid planet appeared a moment later, hovering before her, the largest settlement marked in red. "As I'm sure you're all aware, following the Canid raid on the Milakra colony, we discovered that they took over nineteen hundred colonists prisoner and retreated here, to the fourth planet of this system."

She paused, making eye contact with each of the soldiers assembled before her. "What you may not have heard, however, is that we believe that the majority of those they took were children," she said, watching as the expressions on her team's faces shifted from disbelief to anger before they composed themselves once more. "We're in-system now, and Admiral Carter has set his battle plan into motion. A group of fighters will hit their orbital defenses in the next few hours, then the Fleet will jump in and take on their ships, while we, along with sixty other dropships and fighters, jump in on the far side of the planet, making our way to the surface.

"Long-range scans of the colony show two main entrances, one at either end of the twenty-kilometer-long settlement, along with dozens of other smaller entry points along the sides," she said, the map zooming in to show the Canid colony in detail. "The settlement is primitive, likely only built in the past year, situated in the middle of a dense forest with a river on the north side. It's made almost entirely out of wood, with some steel reinforcements on the walls, but we won't have any formidable obstacles or defenses aside from a few sentries on the walls to worry about.

"The bulk of our forces, including six legions of mechs and over two hundred armored units, will attack the gates to the west, drawing the majority of their warriors away to defend them. Once they engage, we'll break for the south side of the colony, entering here, where their defenses are weakest and there are smaller entry gates. Bioanalysis indicates several large pockets of humanoid life signs clustered in these areas," she said, the map highlighting them in green octagons located a few kilometers inside the colony. "Intel believes they're holding pens, and based on initial scans, we expect these to be only lightly guarded once the fighting starts.

"Our mission is to locate and secure the colonists, eliminating any resistance we encounter along the way. The mech dropships have the most capacity and will be on standby for evac once they offload the battle mechs at the main gates. We'll have four fighter wings providing cover while they land and load the colonists. Our orders are to hold the perimeter until they're airborne. Admiral Carter was explicit that he doesn't want any colonists left behind for the Canids to leverage when he demands their surrender, so we stay until the last transport dusts off. Any questions?"

The soldiers before her stood silently, each ready to do their duty.

"Very well. I'll assign squads and formations once we have more intel, but don't underestimate our enemy. My squad went toe to toe with them on Milakra, and this pack has some elite warriors in it. I lost twenty-four highly trained marines in a matter of seconds," she said, barely able to keep the emotion out of her voice as she tried not to think of the screams of her squad as they were slaughtered. "This is their home, and we all know how territorial the wolves can be. They won't give up without a fight. We do this by the book. Check your six and cover your squad mates. Call for backup if you need it. I don't want anyone playing hero out there, understood?"

"Yes, Commander," the room answered in unison.

"All right then. Saddle up, and safeties off once we hit the dirt. Let's teach these bastards what happens when they fuck with the GCH!"

"Hoo-rah!" the room erupted in a cheer. The soldiers cleared out a moment later, quickly heading for their armor to begin system checks and prep for the mission. Winters moved to a nearby console and was reviewing the latest scans when she sensed someone approaching. She turned to see a female officer, tall and slim, with a powerful build and three small scars across her left cheek, standing a few meters away, waiting respectfully for her to notice her presence.

"Lieutenant," Winters said. "What can I do for you?"

"Actually," the lieutenant replied, lowering her voice, "I know it's not my place to ask, Commander, but I wanted to see if you were okay."

Winters was taken aback for a moment as she studied the officer before her quizzically.

"I was in the Widow at the gates," the lieutenant offered. "I saw what happened to your squad."

Winters nodded. "It all happened so fast. I..." She paused, the screams of her team rushing back in a flood of memories. "Thanks for the save back there. You've got a hell of a right hook," she added, a weak smile appearing for a brief second.

The lieutenant flashed a quick smile back, a look of concern returning to her face.

"But I'm okay, really. And I owe you one," Winters added, sensing the officer's hesitation.

"Anytime, Commander. And...I'm sorry if I'm overstepping, but I've...I've lost a lot of people in combat as well, and

I know how hard it can be to jump right back into the fray. If you need anything, just ask."

Winters took a moment to compose herself, the act of kindness catching her off guard, her emotions wavering between putting on a brave face and breaking down into tears. "I'll be okay, Lieutenant, but thank you. I appreciate your asking."

The officer gave Winters a nod, then turned towards the rows of armor in the deployment bay. Winters watched her go, realizing she hadn't noticed a name tag on her tactical suit. "What's your name, Lieutenant?" she called after her.

The lieutenant turned, smiling. "It's Quentarus, ma'am. Lieutenant Kelara Quentarus."

Three hours and ten minutes later, Captain Medcof's fighters launched their surprise attack, wiping out the Canid orbital defenses in a matter of minutes. The Fleet jumped in shortly after, and Admiral Carter ordered all ships to open fire.

The bombardment that followed destroyed nearly twelve hundred enemy ships on the surface, and a force of just over fourteen hundred raiders made it off the ground, heading for the Fleet blockade.

As the battle raged, the dropships and fighter escorts jumped in on the far side of the planet, quickly descending to the surface. Winters's group landed to the south, a few kilometers outside of the settlement, hanging back until the Canid forces near the pens thinned out, their warriors drawn to the main gates to help repel the huge GCH landing party attempting to break through.

Winters watched from inside her Striker just over a kilometer from the enemy settlement. The tall, lean armor powered up, ready for battle. The modified version of the Striker traded the normal external weapons mounts on the arms and shoulders that the armor traditionally had for a huge rifle with a large serrated blade affixed to it and smaller integrated weapons ports in the armor itself. What the modded version sacrificed in heavy ranged weapons, it gained in speed and agility, allowing it to work more like a soldier in heavy tactical gear, while still packing an enormous punch with the meter-long assault rifle.

She watched on her HUD while the enemy forces flowed from the center of the settlement to meet the main GCH attack force, leaving their target sparsely populated. Winters waited until the last large groups of Canids were on the move, then activated her comm. "All units, we're clear to engage. Alpha squad, on me. We'll take point. Beta and Delta, take the flanks. Widows and Crushers, keep close and provide cover if needed. Keepers, bring up the rear. We'll attack the southern wall as planned. Once we're through the perimeter, the Strikers will sweep and clear, while the Bone Crushers protect from in close and clear any obstacles, and the heavy armor provides ranged support. We get to the pens and secure them at all costs. Understood?"

"Understood," a cacophony of voices replied.

"Good hunting. All units, break!" she called, launching her armor forward, accelerating rapidly. The Widow Makers and Bone Crushers followed at just over half the speed of the Strikers as they bounded forward, using their powerful thrusters to aid them, allowing them to leap great distances. The heavy Gate Keepers brought up the rear, lumbering steadily, but picking up speed and crushing everything in their path.

Within minutes, the Strikers reached the Canid perimeter, opening fire on the few sentries patrolling the walls and taking them down easily. Winters fired a rocket, opening a hole in the wall just as the Crushers and Widows caught up.

"Alpha squad, on me," she said, moving through the breach and sweeping the area. Beta and Delta squads flanked out onto either side, the deadly strike force quickly taking out any enemy targets as they appeared.

"Check those corners," Winters cautioned as the squad continued to move through the settlement, a patchwork of large log structures, many of them covered in dried mud, forming a maze of streets and alleyways with a few larger open spaces here and there. Winters held up, stopping her Striker behind a large building while her squad dealt with some light resistance. She pulled up a top-down view from one of the drones overhead, checking their position and calling out orders. "Beta squad, head east. There's a few clusters of enemy soldiers about half a klick away. Delta to push ahead to the first pen. Alpha will provide cover."

Two minutes later, they reached the first holding pen, a huge oval shape made from twisted branches wound tightly together. She ran a quick scan, confirming the number of colonists inside, as pleas for help from within cried out and small hands reached through the tangle of wood.

"Giannitsis, take your Widows and two Keepers to reinforce the perimeter along the main thoroughfare to the west. No doubt word has spread of our incursion, and more warriors will be heading back our way soon. I'll position Beta on the east side of the road once they mop up behind us."

"Copy that, Commander," Lieutenant Commander Giannitsis replied, calling out commands to his squad and quickly moving off.

"Winters to mech dropships. I'm reading two hundred and twenty-one colonists in this pen. Send a ship to my position. We'll cover you from the ground. Fighters, keep a tight cap overhead."

"On our way, Commander," one of the mech transport pilots replied.

"We're inbound now," the wing leader of Epsilon squadron added. "We'll hold a perimeter a few klicks out and monitor from here. If anything tries to come into your airspace, it won't last long."

"Copy that. Keep me apprised if there's any inbound raiders that might pose a threat to the transports launching. Let's make sure we have enough fighters on station to keep the cap up and give the transports an escort out."

"Roger that, Commander. Most of our fighters are currently engaged above, but Captain Medcof's squadron is back in the barn refueling and rearming, and they'll be ready to launch again shortly. I'll relay to him to send some more birds our way."

"Roger that. Keep me posted. Winters out."

She turned to the pen, lifting the right arm of the Striker, then flicking it down in a chopping motion. A swordlike blade shot forward from the wrist, the powered edge glowing blue. "Stand back," she called over the Striker's speakers, slicing down through the wall with two quick slashes and creating an opening several meters wide. She retracted the blade and reached forward, pulling out a tangle of wood to clear the gap.

A sea of colonists stood clustered a few meters inside the wall, most of them children under the age of twelve, crying and looking up with expressions of terror at the formidable armor.

"It's okay," Winters called, opening the back of her Striker and climbing down with her exo-suit on and a pistol attached to each hip.

She retracted the helmet of her suit as she moved around the armor and through the opening, allowing them to see her face as she stepped through the gap. Winters surveyed the group of terrified souls before her, noticing that several of the older children had collars around their necks to keep them in line. "We're here to rescue you. Follow me. We've got a ship coming in just a minute to pick you up."

The group moved slowly, several of the older children holding the hands of the younger ones to bring them along. They tentatively crossed the threshold, uncertain as to what awaited them on the other side, most of them still in a state of shock. A group of towering Gate Keepers caught up with Alpha squad and thundered nearby a moment later, splitting into two groups and setting up on either side of the opening, startling the already-skittish survivors.

"It's okay," Winters said, putting her arms out to keep the group back until the armor was in position. "They're here to protect you. Nothing bad is going to happen, I promise. We're going to take you back to your families."

A moment later, the dropship appeared overhead before landing in a nearby clearing. Two wide ramps opened to reveal a large empty bay filled with rows of benches.

"Get to the ship," Winters said to the older children, who quickly obeyed, the rest of the group filing out behind them, many of them still crying. "It's okay. Just get on the ship. We're taking you home," she said, watching the tears streak down the dirt-covered faces, her heart falling in her chest at what these poor children must have gone through.

The colonists were loaded moments later, and the ship took off shortly after the ramps closed, a blue light filling the bay to keep the children safe and locked into their seats.

"Lieutenant Jennings, good to see you," Winters said, getting back into her armor as the leader of Beta squad arrived a moment later.

"Sorry for the delay, Commander. We ran into a few friends along the way. How can we help?"

"The first pen is clear, but I can see from the orbital feeds that several groups of Canids have broken off from the main gates and are headed back this way. The next two pens are just up ahead. Take your squad and fall out two hundred meters to the east along the main thoroughfare. Delta squad is already set up on the main road to the west, and Lieutenant Commander Giannitsis has them spread out to give us some buffer room. I'll take two Strikers, the Bone Crushers, and a couple of Widow Makers with me to liberate the rest of the pens while you hold the line to the east. I'll send the rest of Alpha to reinforce you and Delta."

"We're on it, Commander. Nothin's gonna get past us," Lieutenant Jennings said before turning and moving away quickly, his squad falling in with him.

Winters opened a channel to the rest of the squads. "All units, first objective complete. We're moving on to our second target. Alpha squad, split up to reinforce Delta on the west and Beta on the east. We're expecting more incoming. Crushers, you're with me. Quentarus and Noble, you two stay behind and move to flanking positions to cover us. Keep a perimeter twenty meters out with your Widows and light up anything that gets through. Morris and Bylok, follow me – Strikers on point, Crushers right behind," Winters said, quickly relaying her orders and pulling up the next pen on her map.

The three Strikers got moving once more, the Bone Crushers right with them, headed for the next two pens. Quentarus and Noble moved farther out to either side in their Widow Makers to provide cover, while the rest of Alpha squad split and moved off with Beta squad to the east or to reinforce Delta to the west.

Winters's group arrived at the next pen a few minutes later. This one was much larger than the first and guarded by a dozen Canid warriors. The Strikers streaked forward, their shields taking several hits as they moved into firing positions, keeping their bursts short and precise to ensure that no stray fire hit the pen. While they kept the guards occupied, the Bone Crushers moved around behind them, rushing into the fray and engaging at close range a moment later.

The Strikers moved forward, taking out the rest of the defenders while the Crushers and the Canids were locked in a deadly struggle. Less than a minute later, the last Canid warrior fell. One of the Bone Crushers had suffered moderate damage, but it was still in the fight, and the two Widow Makers reported in from the flanks that the area was secure.

In the distance, Winters could hear Delta squad engaging the enemy to the west, the sounds of heavy weapons fire echoing throughout the Canid settlement.

She watched for a moment on the overhead display while Delta kept the attackers at bay. The Gate Keepers were mobile tanks, able to absorb huge amounts of damage while defending fixed positions with powerful ranged weapons.

The Widow Makers, meanwhile, poured on the offense, punishing anything that came into their range, supported by the more agile Strikers, who rounded out the defense, watching the flanks, creating a multilayered defense on each front, keeping the bulk of the enemy forces away from Winters's smaller team.

Winters pulled her attention back to the task at hand, working quickly and opening the pen. She called down for the next three mech transport ships to pick up the six hundred plus souls inside. "Cover me," she said to Commander Rioux, climbing out of her armor once more and lowering her helmet to calm the children inside the pen.

"Copy that, Commander," he said, his towering Bone Crusher watching her back as she ushered the colonists towards the opening in the fence.

The sounds of fighting grew more intense on the western front, where Lieutenant Commander Giannitsis and Delta squad held the line, Winters keenly aware that they could be overwhelmed or outflanked, even with the heavy armor, if the enemy rallied enough troops.

She focused on the survivors, hurrying the terrified children and a few adults towards a clearing, where the first mech transport ship touched down a moment later. Once the first group was loaded, she called in the second ship, then the third. The colonists filled the hold while the sounds of combat grew closer, her AI alerting her that Lieutenant Jennings was engaging another group of enemy targets on the eastern flank as well.

"Lieutenant Bylok, take Morris and four of the Crushers with you and head to the next pen. I don't know how long Delta and Beta can hold, so we need to hurry. We'll catch up in a few minutes, as soon as the last of these people are loaded up," she said, the sounds of a flight of fighters filling the air as they rocketed overhead, circling, ready to escort the last transport out.

"Winters to Epsilon wing leader," she said over the comm, looping in the leader of Delta squad.

"This is Lieutenant Oliveira," the lead pilot responded.

"We're almost done loading. Another minute or two at most. Swing around to Delta squad's position to the west of here and see if you can thin out the enemy ranks there, then circle back to escort the transport out."

"Copy that, Commander. Delta squad leader, this is Epsilon leader. Incoming ordnance headed your way. Danger close. Have your AI call the ball on targets of opportunity, and we'll do the rest."

"Roger that, Epsilon," Lieutenant Commander Giannitsis responded. "I've got coordinates on a cluster of tangos coming your way now."

Winters stood listening for a moment while she continued to wave the last of the colonists into the dropship. A moment later, the fighters engaged the Canids near Delta squad, the sound of explosions thundering through the streets, startling the children.

Finally, the last of the colonists were out of the pen, and the mech transport lifted off. Two of the fighters from Epsilon formed up on them as they rocketed into the sky, while the rest of the fighter wing continued to circle above, maintaining a perimeter.

Winters climbed back into her armor. "Noble, Rioux, Quentarus, we're good here. Let's move out and rendezvous with the rest of our team at the next pen," she said, quickly heading north to the next location.

They arrived at the next pen several minutes later to find

Lieutenant Morris standing beside the opening in his exosuit, calming the three hundred plus survivors inside while the rest of the team provided cover.

"Commander, there isn't anywhere for the transports to set down," Lieutenant Bylok called.

Winters ran a quick scan of the surrounding area, her AI identifying two large empty wooden structures. "Rioux, take your team and level those two buildings there," she said.

"Copy that," Commander Rioux replied, and the rest of the Bone Crushers fell in behind him, heading towards the buildings, quickly getting to work. Huge powerful fists smashed through the outer walls, tearing them down as though they were made of paper, while Rioux's AI scanned the internal layout, identifying the key structural pillars and load points, then targeting with micro-missiles. Minutes later, both structures were down, and the Crushers began clearing the debris, creating an open area. "That should be enough space to let the transport ships touch down and load up," he said.

"Roger that," Winters replied. "Morris, get them out of there and line them up. I've called down two ships, and they'll be here in a minute."

The dropships arrived a moment later, while two fighters came in loud and low, providing air support for Delta squad and hammering the last of the Canid advance to the west, the sounds of explosions deafening once more.

The colonists flooded through the gates, spurred on by the heavy ordnance, quickly making their way to the dropships. Five minutes later, both ships were airborne, with another squadron of fighters providing an escort.

Winters checked her HUD, locating the final pen to the northwest, this one much larger than the rest. "All squads, we're moving out. The last group of colonists appears to be in a pen three klicks north of here. Sending the coordinates now. Delta and Beta, continue to hold the main road where you are. We'll get the last pen cleared."

Winters took the lead, sweeping the area with Morris and Bylok right behind her in their Strikers, while Noble and Quentarus provided cover and the Bone Crushers brought up the rear. They reached the final pen a few minutes later.

"Rioux, deploy your team to create a perimeter. Bylok, Morris, each of you take a flank. Widows, watch for incoming while we evac," she said, running a scan, registering more than nine hundred prisoners inside, far more than they'd expected. "Shit," she cursed, careful to keep her comm off, knowing the last three transports they had on standby wouldn't be enough, each only able to cram in about two hundred and fifty people. "Winters to any ship in the area, I need another ride with capacity for at least a hundred and fifty survivors."

"Copy that, Commander. This is Captain Karaman on the dropship *Galveston*. Our heavy armor bays are empty. It won't be the most comfortable ride, but I can fit a lot of people in here."

"Are you sure, Captain? You'll be abandoning your armor back at the gates."

"We deployed mostly Gate Keepers, ma'am. They'll be fine without us for a spell, I suspect. We're standing by and ready to assist."

"Roger that, *Galveston*. Remain on standby. We only have enough room to land one ship at a time here. I'll signal you once we're ready."

"Copy that, Commander. Standing by."

Winters quickly got to work as the sounds of battle filled the air once more, a group of Canids over a hundred strong attacking from the west. The Delta squad was holding for now, but she could see several waves swinging north, around the battle line, knowing that they were going to have company before they could get the colonists loaded.

The first dropship landed, and Winters hurried the survivors on board just as another group of Canids attacked on the eastern front, where Beta squad battled to hold them back. Moments later, the first dropship was away, the second landing and taking its place right after.

Winters climbed back into her armor and called to the next group of colonists to make a break for it. She watched in her armor's rear cameras as they ran, most of them only small children with a few adults and teens guiding them, all of them terrified as the sounds of battle raged, growing ever closer.

She switched to her overhead view, a dozen more enemy targets appearing and moving rapidly, approaching from several directions.

"Incoming from the north! Keep them away from the pen and the landing area at all costs!" she called, her team moving to engage as waves of Canids kept coming. "Crushers, protect the colonists until they're on board. Don't let anything through. The rest of you, hold them back, weapons free!"

"Copy that," Commander Rioux said, deploying his team to protect the colonists.

"Quentarus, Noble, we need more firepower back here. Bylok, Morris, take the east flank; I'll cover the west. We need to hold them back for a few more minutes," she said, opening fire at a group of warriors approaching rapidly, taking them out with a heavy volley.

She darted forward, taking up a better position with lines of sight in all directions before laying down suppressing fire to keep the Canids at bay while the colonists continued to load. The group to the east was pressing hard, keeping Noble, Morris, and Bylok busy, while she and Quentarus held the west.

"Winters to any available units, I need assistance providing cover for the colonists at the south end of the pen. We're getting overwhelmed. Rendezvous on my position," she said as she fired another salvo from her rifle, taking out a group of Canids foolish enough to rush at her without cover.

She turned to sweep the area, suddenly taking heavy fire from multiple directions as more Canids took up positions, creating a cross fire and forcing her to retreat behind a structure, pushing her back towards the pen.

She turned to her left just as a Striker from Delta squad came into view, streaking towards her across the open area. Before it could reach her, a Canid axe launched from one of the nearby alleyways, cutting the Striker down, the blade smashing through its left shoulder and toppling it to the ground. Winters sprang into action, running towards the stricken armor and laying down heavy fire. A second Striker from Delta squad formed up on her a moment later, the two of them pouring on their covering fire while they took a defensive position in front of their downed team member.

With the enemy held at bay momentarily, she looked down, her AI quickly scanning the armor. "Telson, you still alive in there?" she asked as her display showed the ident tag of the fallen unit.

"That was a hell of a throw; somebody call an agent and sign that guy." Telson half laughed, half coughed, sounding as though he'd taken a hit to the head. "But yeah, I'm okay; it just took off the Striker's arm and knocked some sense into me."

"Can you get out?"

"I think so. Hang on." The back of the armor opened, and he emerged a moment later, a rifle in hand.

"Make a break for the pen and stay with the remaining colonists. We'll hold them back as long as we can," Winters called out, looking back up and sweeping the area, laying down suppressing fire once more as Telson darted for cover. She glanced up at a small window in her HUD showing that the third transport was almost full. "Telson, hold back the rest of the colonists when you get there. I need to bring the last transport," she said, turning to the other Striker from Delta standing next to her. "Yoshida, let's fall back to the pens and provide cover."

"Copy that, Commander," Lieutenant Yoshida replied, following her lead as the enemy fire increased, dogging them back to the cover of several nearby buildings.

Telson arrived at the gates to the pen, stopping the flow of colonists and taking up a defensive position inside the opening while keeping the rest of them back.

"Winters to *Galveston*, you're up."

"*Galveston* here, we're en route," the pilot responded.

"It's getting pretty hairy down here. We can't provide effective covering fire. Land as close as you can to the opening in the pen."

"Copy that."

Winters glanced to her right, watching for a moment as a Widow Maker pulled up beside her, picking off several

Canids at a distance, firing precise controlled bursts with its heavy cannons. "Glad to have you with me, Lieutenant."

"Happy to help, Commander," Quentarus replied. "There's a sizable pack coming in from the southwest though. We're going to have our hands full in a moment."

Winters checked her display, noticing the pack approaching in the distance, easily thirty strong. "Giannitsis, Jennings, can you spare anyone else? We're about to be overwhelmed."

"I can back you up," Lieutenant Commander Giannitsis responded. "My squad is holding the line, and I'm only about half a klick north. Got caught up in a running battle on one of my flanks. It'll just take me a minute to get there."

"Copy that," Winters replied.

"We're taking heavy fire, Commander," Lieutenant Jennings replied a moment later. "I can't afford to pull any of my units, or our lines will break."

"All right. Hold your positions for just a few more minutes. We've almost got the last of the colonists out of here. Once they're clear, be prepared to start falling back towards our point of entry. We'll form up in strength while we exfil."

"Copy that," several voices replied over the comms.

Winters resumed firing as a group of Canids broke from the cover of a small mound, attempting to reach a flanking position. She reacted quickly, taking down two of the four, while Yoshida picked off another and Quentarus pinned the last one in a small alcove. "Think we can hold them?" Winters asked.

"We need a more defensible position, or the next wave of inbound will overrun us," Quentarus replied, her eyes quickly sweeping the area as the *Galveston* flew in overhead. The dropship laid down a hail of fire at the approaching pack, scattering their advance, then landed near the pen. "If you take the left, Commander, using that hut, I'll go right to that small cluster of buildings. Yoshida can stay close and provide cover if anything gets through."

"Copy that, LT. Let's move," Winters said. "*Galveston*, dust off as soon as you're loaded."

Winters and Quentarus moved out, laying down covering fire while Telson guided the last of the colonists towards the ship, more and more enemy contacts appearing.

They were nearly done when a Canid leapt from atop one of the structures towards Quentarus's armor, its axe narrowly missing the body as she spun at the last second.

Quentarus dodged the next two attacks, the Candid pressing its advantage in the close quarters between buildings, the bulky armor just managing to keep ahead of the powerful swipes.

Finally, Quentarus saw an opening, stepping into the next attack and catching her attacker off guard as she barreled into it, then hit it with a close-range shot from the Widow Maker's powerful arm cannons, finishing it off.

"More inbound!" Winters called as three more enemy contacts approached, one laying down fire while the other two wielded axes and closed on them.

"This thing's too slow to engage up close! I've got an idea," Quentarus called, exiting her armor. "Helo, activate remote control. Hold the line; I'm going to go on the offensive," she said, leaping from the back of the armor onto a nearby rooftop, pulling a sword from her black tactical exo-suit.

"Lieutenant!" Winters called as Quentarus scaled the roof, then slid down the far side, disappearing from sight.

The Canids passed down an alleyway a moment later, and Quentarus jumped from the roof, taking out the leader with her sword, then engaging the other two up close. The huge predators dwarfed her, but she moved in a blur of fluid motion, her thrusters rocketing her forward, sword out, as she cut down the nearest of the two, then dodged the axe from the third, taking it out seconds later in a deadly display of speed and agility.

Quentarus emerged from the alley, rushing towards another warrior while Winters and Helo held the rest back.

The Canid warrior dropped to the ground a moment later, the fighting intensifying all around as more and more enemies arrived. Quentarus pressed the sword to her back, then leapt into the air, pulling two pistols from her hips and laying down a barrage of fire from above.

She landed a moment later, sliding in the dirt, the sword back in one hand, a pistol in the other, two enemies charging her position.

The first came at her, claws and teeth bared, too fast and close to get off a shot. She twisted, evading its assault and falling back. The Canid's claws shot forward, narrowly missing her head, when suddenly, her sword thrust upwards into its chest, punching through its back.

The warrior's arms dropped, and it fell to its knees, hitting the dirt with a thud.

Quentarus put a foot on its chest, pulling the sword while the life drained from its eyes, then turned just as the second warrior came at her, forcing her to dodge to the side in order to parry its axe. She spun into a side kick, spikes forming on her foot as it made contact with the enormous wolf's ribs, sending it back several steps, its hand clutching the wound. She lunged forward, using the opening to strike once more, the Canid falling to the ground lifelessly a second later.

Another warrior appeared, Quentarus flicking the blood from her sword, then raising a hand towards the huge predator and goading it towards her. "Come on!"

Winters stood holding the line with the Widow Maker under Helo's control, taking out multiple enemy targets and keeping half a dozen more at bay with her rifle. She checked the overhead view, noticing that the pen had emptied.

Not far away, the Bone Crushers were living up to their name, as their huge metal fists engaged the Canids that made it through, keeping them away from the stream of colonists and dropping them in their tracks.

Thirty meters away, Telson called from the base of the dropship, "We're all good here, Commander!"

"Get on board," Winters called, knowing Telson would be a liability without his armor.

"Understood," he replied, stepping into the hold and closing the ramp. "*Galveston*, we're loaded and ready for takeoff."

"Copy that; hold on back there!" Captain Karaman called, the heavy armor dropship lifting off a few seconds later, a cloud of dust and debris providing cover while the Bone Crushers, flanked by Yoshida, mopped up the nearby enemy forces that had made a last-ditch rush for the ship.

Winters cycled scanning modes, cutting through the dust cloud as she spotted another squad of approaching Canids, four of them huddled behind a tall structure, ready to attack. She was about to open fire when Quentarus appeared on the rooftop above, dropping down silently behind the predators.

As the dust cleared, Quentarus stepped out into the street, fresh blood on her blade. She moved past the nearest Bone Crusher, easily three times her size, the huge armor staring down at her as she sauntered back towards her Widow Maker.

"Nice work, Lieutenant," Winters said in awe.

"Thanks, Commander," Quentarus responded, climbing back into her armor.

"Giannitsis, what's your twenty?"

"Thirty-six meters to your west, holding the perimeter. I had a group here pinned down and couldn't risk them making a break for the colonists. They're all down now, but I'm reading a massive cluster approaching from the northwest, nearly two hundred strong!"

"All right, all units, fall back to the south. Our job here is done, and we have a large force of hostiles incoming. Head back towards the breach where we entered. Don't stop for anything. I'm calling in an emergency evac and for air cover to engage behind us, but right now there are no other ships on station at the moment, so we're on our own until we get clear."

Winters watched on her sensors as the other units began to fall back. "The rest of you, on me. Let's get the hell out of here."

"Copy that," came several calls over the comms as the heavy armor formed up and began charging back towards the entry point to the south.

"Winters to fighter wing Alpha, do you copy?"

"Alpha here," Captain Medcof said. "Looks like you've got a pissed-off horde on your tail, Commander."

"Yeah, we didn't exactly make any friends. Can you buy us some time?"

"Sure thing. We'll keep 'em pinned down while you get clear."

"Thanks. Good hunting, Captain!" Winters called, checking on the status of the other units while her Striker thundered forward.

Her team reached the hole in the colony wall several minutes later, a lone dropship waiting for them.

"Freya, what's the status of the other units?" she asked her AI.

"The Gate Keepers are still inbound. The other units from Delta and Beta arrived here ahead of us and have already been evacuated," Freya said, the roar of Captain Medcof's fighters filling the air once more as they unleashed hell on the Canid horde in pursuit of the heavy armor.

"Rioux, get your Crushers on board. Yoshida, Bylok, Morris, Noble, go with them. That should be a full load," Winters said. "Pilot?"

"Yes, ma'am," the dropship pilot replied.

"Get out of here as soon as they're on board, and call down for another ship ASAP."

"Roger that. There's another bird waiting to get the rest of you. They'll be here as soon as I'm clear."

"Acknowledged," she said, knowing it was going to be tight to get airborne before hundreds of warriors were on top of them.

She watched as the first ship took off and the second, a much larger dropship, landed in its place a moment later.

Quentarus and Giannitsis formed up on either side of Winters in their Widow Makers, leaving a path for the Gate Keepers to get to the dropship and standing by to lay down covering fire. Winters watched on her tactical display as the Gate Keepers approached, the Canid pack not far behind and gaining fast.

The powerful lumbering Gate Keepers crashed through the settlement wall a moment later, the squad taking heavy fire, several of the suits of armor smoking from repeated plasma impacts. They dashed towards the dropship, Winters and her team opening fire as the Canids darted through the breach in pursuit.

A wall of heavy fire hit the first wave, cutting them down with a relentless barrage, forcing the rest to hold back behind cover, buying the retreating squad precious seconds to get on board.

Winters and her team made a break for the ramp of the ship once the Keepers were inside, taking heavy fire as they ran. Winters turned, the two Widow Makers following her lead. They stopped and stood their ground returning fire, their shields failing and the dropship taking damage.

"Captain, we need another strafing run to buy us some time!" Winters called.

"Copy that," Captain Medcof replied. "I'm coming in now, danger close!"

The roar of fighters filled the air as four ships spread out in a staggered line and rocketed past, each unleashing a powerful barrage of plasma fire and missiles. The Canid horde erupted into chaos as warriors fought to evade the onslaught, while Winters's team turned and raced towards the dropship.

They reached the ramp seconds later, Quentarus the last up, laying down a final barrage of fire before the ramp closed behind her.

The ship rocketed forward, blue light from a stasis field filling the bay, the feet of the armor magnetizing to the deck as the ship accelerated rapidly.

"Great work out there, all of you," Winters said, proud of her squads and grateful that they had all made it out without any losses.

Half an hour later, they were back aboard the *Alexia*, stepping out into the enormous hangar bay after thanking the dropship pilots for the pickup.

"Freya, what's the latest?" Winters asked.

"Admiral Carter has demanded the unconditional surrender of the Canid forces. Several enemy ships have broken off, making a run for it, while the remaining ships have powered down their weapons and appear to be surrendering."

"That's good to hear," she said, letting out a relieved breath.

"What's good to hear?" Quentarus asked, falling in stride cheerily beside Winters.

"Looks like it's over. The rest of the wolves have either surrendered or are bugging out," Winters said. "Thanks for all your help down there. I don't know what I would have done without you. I owe you one for sure."

"All part of the job, Commander, but I'll be in the bar later, once we stand down from action stations. You can buy me a drink if you'd like, and we'll call it even."

Winters smiled, the guilt of her lost squad weighing on her momentarily as she considered celebrating their hard-fought victory. She pushed the pain aside, reminding herself that they'd saved a lot of lives today, a lot of innocent children. She'd honor her fallen squad in a day or two once the dust settled, but for now, the best she could do to remember them would be to live.

Winters pulled herself from her thoughts, meeting Quentarus's eyes. "I'll buy the first two rounds, Lieutenant, but the third is going to be shots," she said, raising her eyebrows. "Maybe a lot of them." She smiled.

"Sounds good. I'll see you there, Commander."

"Sierra," Winters replied.

"Kelara." Quentarus smiled, moving off across the bay.

Winters watched as she walked away, the same deadly grace there just beneath the surface as she moved.

Damn, she's impressive, she thought as she turned, making her way towards a lift to report in to the admiral.

Winters looked back, peering over her shoulder one last time as she caught Quentarus doing the same. A smile crossed her lips as she thought about how fate sometimes had a funny way of bringing people together.

CHAPTER 4
SUICIDE RUN

Eight days later, Jackson stood on the deck in one of the hangar bays of the massive orbital trading station called the Hub, the largest in the Delconia System, staring at the ugly beast of a ship before him.

The *Severus* was one of only a handful of ships authorized to make monthly runs between the GCH and the Mantis home world, and he watched from a distance as an inspection team finished giving it a final once-over. Jackson shouldered his duffel bag, moving around the outside towards the rear of the ship, taking it all in.

Well, it's not pretty by any means, but it'll do, he thought as he made his way towards the ramp that led to the cargo hold.

The trade route between the Mantis home world – the name of which was unpronounceable by human vocal capabilities and simply called Ulpharisha – and the GCH had existed for just over a thousand years. It was an important link between two empires that, even in times of war, was respected by both sides for the mutual benefits it provided.

The GCH had considered discontinuing the route entirely during the war. However, that would have left the Mantises, their only allies in the Imperium, to fend for themselves. As much as it was anathema to trade with an enemy, they knew they needed allies inside the Imperium, and over the past millennium, it had proven to be a valuable connection that neither empire wanted to risk losing.

For the Imperium, it allowed them to trade with the GCH for several rare organic compounds that were only found on worlds deep within Confederation territory. The Insectoids had learned to use these to extend the lifespans of their ruling classes, and they were in constant demand throughout the Imperium for the ruling elite. This trading relationship also gave the Mantises a level of power and influence in the Imperium that had elevated their species out of subjugation. In return, the GCH was able to acquire several types of biological materials that different species of Insectoids created naturally and could not be synthetically reproduced with the same quality and purity. These allowed for the production of advanced medicines and various other medical treatments.

In times of peace, many other goods flowed between the two empires. However, in times of war, only the barest of items were exempted.

The Mantises had, at one time, lived in indentured servitude to their Scorpion masters, the ruling species in that region of the Imperium.

Jackson had read up on the history during his trip there, learning how a Mantis ship on a mining expedition had become badly damaged by an unknown anomaly and drifted across the GCH border. In those days, most GCH captains would destroy an Insectoid ship without a second thought, but the vessel was beautiful and elegant, unlike any known Imperium designs. The captain of the GCH cruiser *Deventus* approached the wounded ship cautiously, with shields up and weapons locked. The weak distress call it sent out told her there was something different about them, and she decided to make contact. Much to her surprise, her boarding party discovered the Mantises – a species the GCH had never previously encountered but had heard rumors of before – and she took a risk in sending some of her engineers over to repair the ailing ship.

The reports from her first officer, who led the tactical and repair teams to the Mantis vessel, reported "gentle and communicative creatures that appeared to be genuinely grateful and posed no threat." This led to a series of covert communications over the next several years between the Mantises and the GCH, eventually leading to a secret agreement.

Days later, the GCH launched a surprise attack on the Scorpions' occupation fleet in the Mantis System, destroying them outright in a single decisive battle.

The Mantises then sent a transmission to the Imperium capital, declaring their freedom from Scorpion rule, along with their new trade agreement with the humanoids.

Many in the Imperium were enraged; however, they shared mutual hatred of the Scorpions, and the opportunity to weaken their rivals was one that the other ruling species couldn't pass up.

In the end, the Mantises were granted their freedom, using their newfound wealth and resources from the GCH to gain allies in the Imperium by bribing them and ultimately convincing them to rally to their cause while flaunting the benefits of the new trade agreement that only they could provide. Days later, their system was annexed by the Imperium Council from Scorpion control and granted sovereign status, but with several caveats.

As the centuries passed, the trade agreement proved to be extremely fruitful for both sides and became one of the few formal relations between the two empires.

Now, over a thousand years later, the Mantises had their own modest fleet of ships and a seat on the Imperium Council, where they controlled the only flow of trade and critical resources from outside, negotiating several new agreements with the Oceanic Union and two other smaller empires through their GCH connections.

In turn, the GCH had a powerful partner, allowing them to gain some insights into the inner workings of the Imperium and back channels, which proved invaluable in the centuries to come.

Though the Mantises would never outright help the humanoids, they would, from time to time, feed them information in exchange for contraband goods or other favors, particularly against the Scorpions, who still sought revenge against their former slaves.

One of the conditions from the Imperium Council of maintaining the trade route was a checkpoint through which all cargo ships were required to pass. Various species, subjugated by the Arachnids, maintained the checkpoint, using their advanced senses to root out any contraband. Each ship entering the Mantis trading station was required to submit to being boarded and thoroughly inspected before being allowed through.

As Jackson got caught up on the history of the relationship, he knew that if the GCH abandoned the route, the Mantises' clout and status would soon fail, and it wouldn't be long before they'd be consumed by their bitter rivals, the Scorpions, once more.

He paused as he reached the top of the ramp, taking in the main cargo hold of the *Severus*. The Beth'anar class cargo vessel had been assigned to this route for the past two years, and the hull bore the scars of several close calls. The tough little ship was fast and maneuverable, with decent shields and the ability to carry a modest payload. Still, the Mantis System was just over twenty-two light-years inside the Imperium border, and that made it risky work for the crews that dared to run the trade route.

The vindictive Scorpions were known to hunt GCH transports, stealing their cargo and dismembering their crews, sending them back on their way to the Mantises or the humanoids as a message. Even a thousand years later, they'd not forgotten the bitter defeat.

During peacetime, the threat of Scorpion attacks decreased, as other ruling species asserted their influence to ensure that goods made their way through. During the war, however, raiding activity had increased significantly, as the Scorpions attempted to erode the Mantises' power, forcing the GCH to run operations on a randomized schedule and use other tactics to make their ships more difficult to track.

Jackson looked at the rough, battered interior of the ship's hold, the vessel looking every one of its forty-three years of service, and then some.

"Welcome aboard. I'm Mara Lofton, the cargo officer," a short brunette woman said, extending her hand and breaking Jackson from his thoughts as he turned to face her.

"Hi Mara, I'm James Howlett, the new operations officer. It's good to be here," Jackson replied, extending his hand, the geek inside him attempting to suppress the smile at his fake name. He'd almost gone with Logan but decided that he'd never be able to focus if he did. *I am such a nerd*, he thought to himself as he let go of her hand.

"Ha!" Mara laughed. "*Good to be here,* right. That's a good one. I'm sure that you're here *willingly*, just like the rest of us, eh?" She gave him a wink along with a wicked smile. "So, what did you do? Steal something from the wrong people or run from the Confeds? Maybe get caught in a quarantined system?"

"Something like that," Jackson replied playfully. "I actually go a little ways back with Kaspar and Turner. You could say that we've gone fishing a few times together, if you know what I mean."

"I hear that," Mara said, her tone suddenly serious. "But those boys have gone straight these days, in case you didn't know," she said, crossing her arms in front of her chest. "I'm not sure what things were like when you used to run with them back in the day, but they run a tight ship around here, and we've got a good thing going, so don't fuck it up, got it?" she said bluntly, staring him down.

He smiled an easy smile, not entirely sure if she was kidding or serious.

"We've done this run over thirty times," she continued, sensing he wasn't quite getting it. "It pays well, but the 'sects ain't fucking around. Those skitters will suck the life out of you and tear you to pieces just as soon as look at you. They're as dense as a bulkhead. If you get my meaning. And if you do anything unexpected around them, they just snap and attack! And they won't just kill *you*, they're more 'n happy to do the same to the rest of us as well if you mess this up!"

The charming smile he'd put on quickly faded as he realized that she was now deadly serious, straightening up from his relaxed posture and meeting her eyes squarely. "I've got it," he said earnestly. "I'm not looking for any trouble. Just a fresh start like the rest of you."

Mara's posture relaxed slightly, though her arms remained crossed, her expression one of suspicion and doubt. "You be sure to remember that," she said. "The boys are all up on the bridge, prepping for our departure." She pointed him towards the hatch at the far end of the cargo bay. "And watch out for Desnik. He's a slimy bastard and won't hesitate to screw you over if he gets the chance. I'd keep my distance from him if I were you."

"Thanks, I appreciate the warning. It was nice to meet you, Mara," Jackson said as he walked over to the hatch and headed for the bridge.

"Mm-hmm," she responded skeptically, going back to her work.

Jackson walked the corridors of the *Severus* as he made his way to the bridge, following the map Bits projected in his ocular implants. The hallways were much larger than on any GCH ship he'd been on before, and Bits confirmed that it was a requirement of the trade agreement in order to allow for the larger Insectoids to have access to all parts of the ship during their inspections.

Jackson suddenly had flashbacks to the corridors on the Insectoid battleship in the RE-13 System as the sounds of the horde coming to rip him to shreds played back in his mind. He stopped, steadying himself against a wall for a moment, trying to push the memory from his mind as he pulled himself together, the doors to the bridge just ahead.

The doors parted, and he stepped onto the bridge a moment later, quickly spotting Turner working on an overhead access panel to his right. Another man sat to his left, his back to him while he worked at his console, Jackson inferring that this was Desnik Venborn, the logistics and trade officer. Ahead, he could see Kaspar standing by the helm, studying a holo-map.

Jackson approached Kaspar, clearing his throat. The captain turned, his expression brightening as he saw the man standing before him. "Howlett," Kaspar said, keeping up the show for Desnik's benefit as he extended his hand.

"Yes, sir. James Howlett, reporting for duty," he said, shaking Kaspar's hand.

"Good to have you aboard. It's been a long time. You remember my first officer and our ship's engineer, Evan Turner."

"Of course. It's been a while. Nice to see you again."

"Welcome aboard," Turner said distractedly.

"And this is our trade officer, Desnik Venborn," Kaspar said. Desnik looked up, giving him a nod, then returned to his work. "You'll take the ops position there," Kaspar continued, pointing to the console to his left, just ahead of Desnik's and close to the helm. "Come on, I'll show you to your quarters so you can stow your gear, then we can put you to work."

Kaspar turned, leading Jackson towards the doors at the rear of the bridge. "Hey, Ev, you get that lateral sensor array calibrated yet?" Kaspar asked Turner.

"Yeah, I'll get to it," Turner responded, not looking up from his work.

"I'd appreciate it if you could look at that *now*. I want the rook here to have full sensors before we leave. Don't want him missing something and getting us all killed."

Turner closed the panel he was working on with a bang, then walked over, his posture rigid as he met the two standing by the door. "After you, *sir*," he said coldly, the three of them exiting the bridge and then proceeding down a series of hallways to Jackson's quarters.

The door closed behind them as they entered a moment later. Kaspar locked it, turning to face Jackson, both men clearly on edge.

Turner stood with his arms crossed, his posture tense. Kaspar gave him a sharp look, shaking his head slightly, then looked back towards Jackson. "I'm sorry for the less than warm reception," he said, nodding to Turner. "But as you can imagine, we're not used to having a GCH *operative* on board our ship. Our business is risky enough as it is."

"I appreciate the lift, guys. And I'll do my best not to cause any trouble."

"You've already caused trouble," Turner retorted snidely. "What, our ship wasn't good enough for you? You just had to have them pull it from rotation and do its six-month maintenance overhaul now, kicking us off it for the past four days while your precious GCH techs went over every inch to make sure you're comfy while throwing us off our schedule?"

Jackson paused for a moment, recalling what the admiral had told him about how superstitious some cargo crews were with regards to picking certain times to make their runs, quickly realizing that Turner was amongst their lot.

"Sorry to throw off your schedule, but with all the travel lockdowns after the attack on Kuteria, I figured a few more days wouldn't make too much difference. Besides, I have a plan, and hopefully, if all goes well—"

"*Hopefully!*" Turner spat. "We're risking our lives on hope now! This is just fucking great! This is shaping up to be a fucking suicide run, Kas, just like I said!"

Kaspar was about to step in when Jackson beat him to it. "This is a risk, Turner. I'm not going to lie to you. But there are always risks. Sometimes they pay off, and sometimes things go to hell. I can't promise you anything except that I've done my research and I've got a plan. And you'll be compensated extra for this run, I promise."

"*If* we live to even get paid. If we die, then it's all for nothing," Turner griped.

"It's never for nothing," Jackson replied. "We're helping to save lives, and even if we fail, at least we'll die doing something to help others and not just ourselves. If we don't make it back, my contacts will transfer what's owed to you back to your families on Dantun. They'll be well taken care of, thanks to the two of you."

Turner looked down at the deck, feeling a twinge of guilt at the mention of the family he'd abandoned and put in harm's way all those years ago. If it hadn't been for Jackson, he knew he wouldn't be there today, let alone his partner and the love of his life, Kaspar.

"All right," he said. "I'll do everything that I can. I owe you that much…and more," Turner conceded grudgingly, unable to meet Jackson's eyes.

"You don't owe me anything, Turner. I helped you that day because it was the right thing to do. Just as this is the right thing to do now," Jackson said, giving him a nod. Turner's rigid posture softened slightly as he returned the gesture, if somewhat halfheartedly. "And like I said, I have a plan."

CHAPTER 5
LUCK AND TRUST

Jackson had traveled through Imperium space dozens of times before but had rarely felt this nervous for an upcoming op. On all of his previous forays, he'd been on the *Phoenix,* cloaked and with at least the illusion of control. Now, on the unarmed cargo ship, he found himself questioning his plan, wondering what he'd gotten himself into.

The tension on the bridge was almost tangible once the ship left the Hub; the crew barely spoke each focused on their duties.

Close to half a dozen ships made the trade run between Delconia and the Mantis home world. Of those, two had been attacked by the Scorpions in the three weeks before the attack on Kuteria had locked down all travel. One of them didn't make it back. The second ship was able to escape, its hull bearing the markings of the close brush with death and its crew shaken from the close call, forced to turn around and abandon their trading run.

The *Severus* had been docked at the Hub for the past three weeks and was next in the rotation. After the last two attacks, the ship's ops officer decided to quit rather than risk another run, leaving them shorthanded and vulnerable. The opening in the crew turned out to be the perfect opportunity for Jackson, as it was less likely to draw suspicion than if he were an extra hand throwing off their expected numbers.

Still, the crew was clearly rattled as they settled in for the journey ahead.

Six hours had passed since they left Delconia, with another two and a half hours to go before they reached the border. The route took them through several GCH checkpoints, where they were required to drop out of hyperspace and verify their flight path before carrying on — a new precaution instituted along the handful of travel routes near the core systems that were now open in the hyperspace defense grid. GCH Traffic Control was still only allowing limited travel in the aftermath of the attack on Kuteria, and this added time to their trip. Traffic Control routed the *Severus* as far from the front lines as possible, but as they approached the border, the risk of exiting a jump into an ambush became an increasing possibility.

Finally, they dropped out of hyperspace for the last time on the GCH side of the border.

"Howlett, open a channel to GCH Traffic Control," Kaspar ordered.

"Channel open," Jackson replied.

"*Severus* to GCH Traffic Control," Kaspar said, doing his best to project confidence in his voice.

"*Severus*, this is Traffic Control, awaiting code verification and flight plan confirmation," a serious voice spoke over the ship's speakers.

"Transmitting now," Kaspar replied, initiating the upload and entering his authorization code.

The crew sat in silence as a flash of light appeared on the viewscreen, a GCH destroyer jumping into view. Jackson straightened in his seat, appearing to look as nervous as a rookie should be when facing down a heavily armed patrol ship. Inside, however, the sight of the destroyer gave him a sense of comfort that'd been missing thus far, helping to steel his will for the trials ahead.

"Stand by for bio-scan. Hold your position and do not raise your shields or you will be fired upon," the operator warned, her voice stern with military authority.

"Understood, Control. Standing by," Kaspar replied as the destroyer grew closer, running a thorough scan of the ship.

Jackson looked around the bridge, taking in the faces of each of his crewmates, while his ocular implants relayed their bio-signs in his HUD. Despite having been through this procedure many times before, they were still clearly rattled by the military protocols and appeared to take the warning with a full measure of respect.

Seconds passed, the destroyer cruising by their bow, its bulk filling the main view screen as it dwarfed the cargo ship. A moment later, it moved off, and the operator spoke once more. "*Severus*, you're clear to proceed. Uploading an updated nav plan now with the latest astrometric data. Your flight path to Ulpharisha is clear as per last reports, with minimal turbulence anticipated on your route. Be aware that the enemy presence in the Lkarus System has increased in recent weeks. Keep your shields down and power levels to minimum to avoid detection."

"Thanks for the warning, Control," Kaspar replied.

"Transmitting return codes now. These are valid for the next twenty hours only," the operator stressed, "and you must jump back to these precise coordinates. If you miss your window or jump target, you will be required to hold position and *will* be boarded. You will also be required to submit to a full quarantine and inspection upon return. Failure to meet any of these requirements will be met with terminal force."

"Understood," Kaspar said.

"Good luck, *Severus*," the operator said, her tone conveying the slightest hint of emotion for the first time. "May the stars light your way."

"Thanks, Control. We'll be back before you know it. *Severus* out," Kaspar said, nodding to Jackson, who closed the channel.

Mara blew out a breath while Desnik shifted uncomfortably in his seat. Turner sat unflinching, attempting to keep a cool confidence for the rest of the crew, as did their captain, but Jackson could see that their pulses were racing.

Kaspar entered the flight plan, and the ship jumped back into hyperspace, the crew sitting in silence, each doing their jobs and following the protocols to the letter, all on edge as they crossed the border into Imperium space.

Forty minutes passed as they approached the Lkarus System. "Dropping us out of hyper in two minutes," Kaspar called.

"You ready for this, *rook*?" Desnik sneered.

Jackson smiled to himself, having run into people like Desnik many times before: those who needed to put others down to raise themselves up. He put on his game face, turning across the bridge to meet his antagonist, a look of concern written plain as day across his face. "Why do we have to drop out of hyperspace *here*?" he asked nervously, playing into his character, knowing the answer already but figuring that giving the crew a chance to gripe would settle their nerves.

"Well, the space between the GCH and the Mantis System, Ulpharisha, is extremely volatile," Kaspar began in earnest, turning from the helm to face him excitedly. "Two nearby neutron stars create a strong gravitational pull and emit highly disruptive electromagnetic radiation. A proto-nebulae also covers a large portion of the space between the border and the Mantis System, and if that's not enough, there's at least six documented spatial anomalies in the region."

"So, what the cap's trying to say is that travel's a bit of a pain in the arse on this route. Not your simple A-to-B milk run, if you get my meaning," Desnik chimed in, the condescension clear in his voice.

Kaspar continued, either not noticing or just so used to his logistics officer's attitude that it no longer fazed him. "Right, but GCH Traffic Control gives us a flight plan each trip with updated conditions from a series of cloaked satellites, which allows us to jump here safely. It's a pretty good jump distance, considering we're in enemy space. Unfortunately, the distance is too great to make it all the way to Ulpharisha, and the conditions can change rapidly, so we have to exit hyperspace at a waypoint in the Lkarus System and get an updated flight plan with the current conditions, then make a second jump for the rest of the trip."

"That's where the Scorpions wait to ambush their prey," Turner cut in, his voice vicious.

A quick scathing look from Kaspar seemed to humble him, and he turned back to his console while the captain continued. "Unfortunately, as Turner mentioned, the Scorpions continue to threaten the route's stability virtually unchecked."

"It's hard to know what to expect," Mara chimed in. "Most of the time, we jump in and our sensors are clear, but every now and then, we spot a patrol. The only thing the Scorpions *don't* try to destroy is the small waypoint station in the system, as they need it as much as we do to safely jump in."

"Okay, cut the chatter, people," Kaspar said as he turned back to the helm, attempting to focus their attention. "We're thirty seconds out. Everyone ready?"

"Engines are optimal. Shields are standing by if we need them," Turner said, having become less sullen since they'd left, immersing himself in his work while only complaining under his breath, for the most part. Jackson was somewhat impressed that he actually appeared to be quite a competent engineer.

"Cargo is secure," Mara said.

Desnik remained quiet, staring at his console, his foot tapping unconsciously, its pace increasing.

"Sensors are optimal. Defensive countermeasures standing by," Jackson reported.

Sensors were, in fact, better than they had probably ever been. Jackson had used his experience on the *Algeron,* and Bits's assistance, to modify them from their base parameters and increase their sensitivity considerably. The modifications he'd made were classified and limited to military personnel, but for the purposes of this operation, he figured that the *Severus* was acting in a paramilitary capacity and that it justified risking Turner or someone else noticing the modifications. He had also suggested to Kaspar that they reroute the defensive controls to his station. Turner usually operated these, but neither of them doubted Jackson's tactical abilities and were happy to have his expertise.

Bits interfaced with the ship's systems, but kept his presence hidden from the rest of the crew. Since none of the others had AIs, Jackson didn't want to raise any suspicions and throw them off their routine any more than his presence already did.

The *Severus* exited hyperspace in the Lkarus System, one point five million kilometers from the waypoint beacon. GCH Shipping Operations had changed the protocols after the last two attacks and now had each ship jump in at a different set of coordinates in an attempt to randomize their ingress points and reduce the risk that they would fall into a Scorpion ambush.

"Power down to silent running," Kaspar said, his voice tense. "Howlett, check for enemy contacts."

"Passive scans initiated," Jackson said, already one step ahead, knowing that civilian crews were trained to follow similar protocols to military vessels. He was responsible for monitoring the system for activity, while Kaspar manned the helm, running the navigational calculations. "I'm not detecting any ships so far, but there's a lot of interference in the system."

"It's the neutron star that's less than a light-year from here. It's a pulsar that throws off a lot of EM rads, limiting our scanning range," Turner explained. "There are better positions in the system, where our sensors are more effective, but those are the spots that the Scorps like to hunt in."

"Good to know. Well, I don't see anything so far, but I'll keep my eyes peeled."

"All right, I'm linking up with the computer on the waypoint and scanning ahead to get the latest astrometric conditions on our route," Kaspar said, his hands working the controls.

"Let's just hope it's faster than last time," Desnik muttered under his breath, just loud enough for the crew to hear.

"Knock it off, Des!" Mara shot back. "You know I hate this part. I already feel like I'm gonna puke!"

"How long does it usually take?" Jackson asked.

"Well, it depends on the conditions between here and the Mantis System. Grav spikes and heavy EM rad pockets make navigation tricky. It may take a few minutes for it to update with a jump solution," Kaspar replied, not looking up from his console.

"There was a spatial anomaly a few months ago, rook. Caused the nav computer to have a fit. It took nearly twenty minutes to plot a safe course," Desnik said. "We were lucky to get out of here with our lives."

Kaspar shot him a look that clearly told him to shut the hell up, while he turned to Jackson, flashing him a fake smile in an attempt to put him at ease. "Hopefully we're in for better luck today," he said, trying to keep his crew upbeat.

If the Scorpions attacked, they could try to hold them off with the ship's powerful shields and countermeasures for a short time, but they needed a clear window to be able to initiate a jump into hyperspace. The Scorpions were also unpredictable, trying different hunting tactics to throw the cargo ships off, sometimes driving them into an ambush.

Two minutes passed while they waited, each second feeling like an eternity.

Kaspar stared intently at the progress bar as the navigational computer processed the data from the *Severus*'s sensors and the waypoint, the calculations seemingly moving at a glacial pace.

Another minute passed, and Jackson swore that he could hear the ticking of a second hand on an old-fashioned watch while they waited, the sound grating on his nerves. He'd been in a few tight spots working search and rescue and on missions from FoxBlind, but he had always felt a relative sense of safety knowing that the Fleet was never far away or he had a level of control and options onboard the *Phoenix*.

This was completely different, however.

They were truly alone, deep inside enemy lines, and unable to even jump until the calculations were complete or they risked a catastrophic exit from hyperspace due to the unstable gravity and electromagnetic fields.

A small beep emanated from Jackson's console, breaking the near silence. Another beep followed seconds later.

"Howlett, what do you have?" Kaspar asked.

"Not sure yet. Something is moving out there. Sensors can't lock on. But whatever it is, it's just at the limits of our range," he responded.

"Shit. Nav is still computing. We can move, but if we stray too far from this position, it will add more time to the calculations," Kaspar warned.

"Turner, anything else you can power down?" Jackson asked.

"Not much, just sensors, nav, life support, and the drive are up; the rest of the systems are already powered down."

"Hang on," Jackson said, studying the readings on his console. "I think we should raise the shields and invert their polarity."

"Are you insane? That would light us up like a beacon," Turner snapped.

Jackson turned, meeting Kaspar's eyes, giving him a slight nod.

"Do it," Kaspar said decisively, trusting Jackson's skills, while Mara and Desnik gave one another a concerned look, wondering why their captain was listening to the new guy over Turner.

Turner huffed, reconfiguring the shields to an inverted polarity, then powered them up while the crew sat perfectly still, none of them daring to breathe.

Jackson put a map of the system up on the main viewscreen, each of them watching as the readings from the sensors became clearer, the computer confirming the enemy contact as several Scorpion ships, growing closer as the seconds passed.

"They're closing, Kas. We have to jump now!" Turner implored Kaspar, watching as the patrol grew ever closer.

"The computer's not done," Kaspar shot back. "We can't risk it!"

"Look!" Mara called out, watching the patrol, less than twenty thousand kilometers and closing, as they altered their course and turned away.

Breathless seconds passed while the ships moved off, finally leaving the *Severus*'s sensor range once more.

"What the hell just happened?" Desnik blurted out.

"Just because I'm the new guy doesn't mean I don't know a few tricks," Jackson replied, eager to get the crew off his back so he could focus on the tasks ahead.

"No, really?" Turner asked, his voice suddenly lacking the edge it had carried for the past day and seeming genuinely interested. "How'd you do that?"

"Well, from what I can tell, we're in one of the worst places in the system for EM interference, and sensors show several nearby pockets of radiation. So, by raising our shields and inverting the polarity, we amplified the radiation signature our core would normally kick out with the hyperdrive spun up, while reflecting any direct scans, thus making us harder to detect through the interference," Jackson explained.

"So, you make us look like a big, nasty pocket of radiation?" Turner asked.

"Exactly."

The engineer nodded his head appreciatively, turning back to his console while he stroked his chin. "Nice work, rook."

"How were you able to detect them so far out? The sensors on this bucket are shit," Desnik said suspiciously.

"Like I said, I know a few tricks," Jackson replied slyly, turning to look Desnik in the eye. "Not my first time trying to hide from the authorities," he added, raising an eyebrow and flashing a smirk, hoping to add some mystery to his character while avoiding having to explain himself.

"Works for me," Mara chimed in, clearly relieved. "Now, can we please get the hell out of here, Cap?"

Before Kaspar could answer, the nav console beeped. "Hmm. It looks like we can," he said cheerfully, a broad smile crossing his face. "Space you, Lkarus!" Kaspar called out, Turner, Mara, and even Desnik responding with enthusiastic cheers. A ritual, Jackson suspected, that they'd established over time while he joined in the revelry, finding that the release helped to relax his nerves considerably as the ship jumped out.

The next hour and twenty minutes passed uneventfully as they continued their journey through Insectoid space.

"We're approaching the Ulpharisha System," Kaspar said, the *Severus* exiting hyperspace a few second later just over two hundred thousand kilometers from the Mantis home world at a designated egress point. The captain brought up the forward visual sensors on the main viewscreen while the crew watched, waiting silently.

A few thousand kilometers from the egress point, a massive structure floated in space, ominously blocking the path of the *Severus*. It stretched out in both directions, easily five kilometers long and three kilometers high, constructed from a mix of metal and asteroids that had been woven together to create a solid barrier. A large octagonal ring sat in the center, with four enormous doors coming together that met in the middle, large enough to allow even a battleship to enter through.

"This is the Wall, as we like to call it," Kaspar said, piloting the *Severus* slowly towards it.

The Wall bristled with weapons, its massive bulk dwarfing the ships flanking it on either side. Jackson zoomed in on his console's visual display, taking in the breathtaking Mantis warships around it, their colors and designs stunning. A group of five other ships of various Insectoid classes approached them from behind, escorting them towards the Wall. Jackson recognized several of them as destroyers and cruisers, but there was at least one design that he'd never seen before.

"What is it?" Jackson asked.

"It's a gateway. You see, the Mantises have deployed a network of tens of thousands of hyperspace disruptors all around their home world, similar to the hyperspace defense grid used by the GCH, but a little more basic. Anyway, it creates a web preventing any ships from attempting to jump in close to the planet without going through the checkpoint. The web would tear apart any ship passing through it in hyperspace, and the waypoint just behind us is the only safe place to jump into or out from."

"Makes sense," Jackson said.

"All right, people, enough staring at the big scary death wall. You all know the drill," Kaspar said, his voice suddenly booming with authority. "Howlett, power down the sensors; only minimal navigational readings are allowed. Whatever you do, do *not* scan anything while we're here. Understood?"

"Understood," Jackson replied, sensing there was a " *'cause if you do, they'll blow us to atoms*" response waiting should he ask.

"Good. Just do what I say, and we'll be fine. Open a channel to the station."

"Channel open."

"Ulpharisha Gateway, this is the GCH cargo vessel *Severus* requesting permission to dock," Kaspar said clearly, his voice cordial and respectful.

A series of clicks echoed over the speakers a moment later, Bits translating them into Jackson's ear while the ship's computer took several seconds to catch up. "*Severus*, proceed to inspection station three. Any deviation from protocols will be dealt with severely," the computer said, reading the message aloud.

"*Severus* acknowledges. Proceeding as per protocols," Kaspar replied, gesturing to Jackson to close the channel.

Kaspar took a deep breath. "All right, here we go. I'm taking us in, slow and steady."

The doors in the Wall retracted, revealing a massive entryway. The *Severus* slipped through the opening, dozens of weapons mounts visible on the main viewscreen, all trained on the small cargo ship.

Once inside, a vast open space spread out before them with half a dozen docking ports and more weapons spread around the perimeter, while several small shuttles scurried about, the entire inside dimly lit and providing an ominous feel, as though stepping into the lair of a predator.

"Mara, take Howlett back and show him *exactly* what to do. Desnik, Turner, prepare for docking. Let's get this over with," Kaspar said, maneuvering the ship.

Jackson followed Mara back to the mess, a large open area just off the main cargo bay. Once they arrived, she had him help her move the table and chairs off to the side to clear the room.

"We dock in about a minute. Once we do, we'll be boarded by an Insectoid tactical team first. Just stay calm, okay? Protocol is to sit silently against the far wall and stay *completely* still. Once they sweep the ship, the roaches come on board to do the inspection, and the fucking skitters will come to babysit us."

"Got it," Jackson said, his ocular display showing Mara's vitals spiking with fear as she spoke. "How many runs have you been on?" he asked, trying to put her, and himself, at ease.

"Me? I've been on nineteen runs over the past year and a half. I sit one out every once in a while, just to keep my sanity, you know?"

"Yeah, not exactly a stress-free line of work," Jackson said, a sound echoing inside the ship as it docked with the station.

Mara moved to the empty wall and sat down, wrapping her arms around her knees. Jackson followed her lead, settling in beside her as she lowered her head, staring down at the deck.

"Just be sure to stay perfectly quiet and still. The skitters aren't much more than animals. To say that they are sentient would be an insult to all other sentient life," she said, cracking a slight smile as she looked his way.

Her smile quickly faded, however, as she continued. "Oh, and don't look directly at them. If you lock eyes with them, they can become aggressive. Try your best to breathe deeply and stay calm. If your heart rate gets too high, it can also whip them up into a frenzy. From what I've been told, skitters are extremely deadly in battle, and they're known for their bloodlust, not for their self-control. I think that's why they use Venarian mosquitoes as close air support in some of their ground actions. Their reputation precedes them, if you know what I mean," she said, giving him a knowing look.

She's fishing, he quickly realized, trying to see if he was ex-military or had any experience with the bugs before in battle. *Smart*, he thought, realizing that he'd underestimated her. He nodded, giving her the barest indication that he knew what she was talking about without giving away any more than was necessary.

Bits continued to display her bio-readings in Jackson's HUD while he watched out of the corner of his eye as she calmed herself, cracking her neck to one side then the other before running through a series of breathing exercises to slow her heart rate.

"I've heard that if someone panics, the skitters impale them with their bloodsuckers for a taste," he said nervously, careful to sound like a rookie caught up in the local scuttlebutt and more afraid than she was.

"Don't believe everything you hear." She chuckled, her tone and expression becoming deadly serious as she continued. "They don't just stick you; they suck you dry!" she added, clearly enjoying having some fun at his expense. "Once the blood starts flowing, they can get caught up in the frenzy like a pack of Galathayan wolf sharks! The good news is that you'd be dead in less than ten seconds, pretty much just a husk at that point."

Jackson played along, looking amply horrified while Mara smiled mischievously at him, patting him on the shoulder. "You'll do fine. Just remember what I said, okay?"

Jackson nodded weakly. "Got it."

"It won't be long now till they come," she said, the sounds of the rest of the crew approaching on the metal decks growing louder as they headed back to join them.

A few seconds later, Turner, Desnik, and Kaspar entered the mess, each giving them a nod, then silently sitting down along the wall next to them. Jackson wasn't particularly worried about himself, as Bits could intervene and control his heart rate if he got too nervous, but he had never been face-to-face with an Insectoid before without having a plan to deal with them. To be so small, so helpless, was difficult for him to accept.

The crew each focused on their breathing exercises, attempting to stay calm. Seconds later, the sound of the cargo bay ramp descending, followed by dozens of heavy footsteps, filled the ship, echoing throughout the corridors as the boarding party began their sweep.

Desnik, Mara, and Turner closed their eyes while Jackson and Kaspar kept them open, both careful to keep them low. He risked a quick glance up as a large armored ant-like creature, similar to the ones he'd faced on Brestin III, entered the mess, sweeping its rifle past each of the crew, quickly assessing them. He then heard several clicks that Bits informed him meant that the crew was accounted for and in position, inferring that Kaspar had likely transmitted a crew manifest as part of the inspection protocols.

The tactical team continued their sweep while a lone Ant stood guard.

Minutes passed, the crew staying perfectly still until the team completed the sweep, the sound of their metal exoskeletons moving on the decks indicating that there were at least a dozen of them. Their guard left as the sounds faded, silence filling the ship for several seconds until a dim buzzing sound registered in Jackson's ears, growing closer and louder.

A moment later, three huge mosquito-like creatures appeared in the mess, spreading out before them in a line, standing almost upright on four legs, while distant sounds of scuttling could be heard throughout the ship.

Jackson continued to lock down, catching a reflection off a metal door on the far side of the mess of the ugly, spindly creatures while they watched the crew intently, their eerie compound eyes unmoving. He thought back to his training, recalling that the Imperium deployed dozens of species of mosquitoes as air support. Venarian mosquitoes were the worst, however, and the most notoriously vicious in combat.

The guards stood less than a meter in front of them, appearing more like animals than other Insectoids he'd encountered. He recalled the Wasps from the Insectoid battleship, which had more evolved properties and features that separated them from their more primitive, animallike kin. Still, standing at nearly three meters tall, with a wingspan of close to seven meters and a sucker thicker than his wrist, he knew that the creatures before him were feared for good reason.

Seconds passed while he tried to stay still, focusing on his breathing as Mara had suggested, when the smell hit him.

The putrid scent filled his nostrils, reminding him of devastatingly bad BO mixed with rotten chicken, as he tried to breathe slow, shallow breaths through his mouth. The odor, however, was overpowering, quickly filling the room with its stench, entrenching itself deep within his sinuses as his eyes began to water. He coughed slightly, doing his best to suppress it while attempting to breathe as little as possible.

The mosquito in front of him twitched slightly at the sound, forcing him to buckle down and bear it, closing his eyes and fighting to hold back the tears. He focused on the sounds throughout the ship, rather than the smells filling his senses. In the distance, he could hear the roaches crawling all over, checking everyting. How many, he couldn't be sure, but it sounded as though there were hundreds of them.

He tried to focus on something else, but the smell overwhelmed him once more, and his skin crawled at the thought of the creatures surrounding him, scuttling about.

Finally, after what seemed like an eternity, he could hear the roaches file out of the ship. The mosquitoes buzzed at one another, then turned slowly, lumbering their way out of the mess. Jackson dared to open his eyes, watching as the disgusting creatures moved away, their wings twitching with each step.

A few seconds later, he heard the cargo bay ramp begin to close, shutting with a thud.

The crew turned to look at Jackson, tears still trickling from his eyes as he attempted to clear the smell from his nostrils, the scent still hanging heavily in the air. Jackson looked up and met their eyes just as they broke into a fit of uncontrollable laughter, Turner and Desnik nearly rolling on the deck while they cradled their sides in pain.

Desnik looked up at Jackson. "So, rookie," he said with a chuckle. "What did you think…of the smell?" he stuttered out between fits of laughter, the rest of the crew roaring uncontrollably, Mara and Kaspar each with tears streaming down their reddening faces as they fought to rein themselves in.

Jackson shook off the stench, watching while the crew attempted to compose themselves, noticing for the first time that they were all wearing small transparent nose plugs that appeared to filter the air. They were subtle, so much so that he hadn't seen them when they walked into the room or noticed Mara putting hers on.

After a moment, he couldn't help but get caught up in it himself, even if it was at his own expense. "Yeah, you assholes, you got me!" he admitted, feeling good to laugh, despite it being at his own expense, and knowing that the crew needed it as much as he did.

After a few moments, they all managed to compose themselves.

"All right," Kaspar said. "Enough messing around. Howlett passed his initiation. Now let's get back to work," he added, the crew quickly making their way back to the bridge.

The *Severus* backed out of the inspection bay, heading towards the gateway at the far side of the structure, the doors opening as they approached. Once clear of the Wall, Kaspar set a course for the massive station in orbit of the Mantis home world.

Jackson sat at his station, watching on the main viewscreen as the planet, a rich, tropical paradise full of vibrant colors, came into focus. The crew was silent, still clearly on edge but appearing to relax somewhat now that they were past the hard parts.

The station grew closer, the design clean and bright, a stark contrast to the ugly utilitarian ships that made up the bulk of the Imperium fleet. Gleaming metal shone in the sunlight, and a huge glass dome revealed a massive tropical habitat covering the upper levels, easily a few kilometers wide and a hundred meters high. The rest of the station spread downward into a circular shape with huge cargo bays and berths extending out for larger warships. The overall design resembled a GCH station, but with clear aesthetic differences and more windows to allow natural light inside.

Jackson took a slow, deep breath, preparing himself for what lay ahead. He'd made it this far in his journey, but his real mission was just beginning.

CHAPTER 6
OUT-OF-BODY EXPERIENCE

"Well, looks like my job's done," Jackson announced with a touch of arrogance. "I'll be in my quarters taking a nap if anyone needs me," he added as he stood up and stretched while yawning loudly.

"What? Why the hell does he get to sleep?" Desnik asked, his voice bitter.

"Because *he* did his job already and got us here in one piece. Now go do yours so we can get the hell out of here," Kaspar scolded.

Desnik gave Mara an imploring look, trying to get her to back him up. She rolled her eyes and stared back down at her console, firmly ignoring him. Finally, Desnik got to his feet, glaring at Jackson while he smirked back, then turned to leave.

"Oh, and Des?" Desnik looked back, the stern expression on Kaspar's face stopping him in his tracks. "No trying to negotiate or swindle our gracious hosts this time, or I *will* leave you here. Got it?"

Desnik looked across the bridge, Turner staring him down a few feet from Kaspar, his body language equally hostile as he glared, his arms folded across his chest. "Sure, no problem, boss," he said in his best slippery-car-salesman voice. "Come on, Mara, let's get this over with."

Mara and Desnik exited the bridge, leaving Turner and Kaspar alone with Jackson. The three of them waited until the door closed before they turned to face one another.

"So, what do we do now?" Turner asked, still clearly unhappy about the risks they were taking.

"Absolutely nothing. You two do exactly what you always do. As I explained, I'll be in my quarters the whole time. There's nothing to worry about," Jackson reassured them.

Turner shot Kaspar a look, clearly still hoping that, somehow, they could back out of this, but knowing that his partner felt indebted towards Jackson for saving his life and would do anything for him.

"Just let us know if you need anything. We'll be checking the ship's systems and keeping an eye on the cargo transfer if you need us," Kaspar said.

"I'll be fine, but thanks," he replied. "Just give me as much time as possible before we leave," he added, turning and exiting the bridge, eager to get started.

The doors closed, and Turner shot Kaspar a scowl. "I don't know how you talked me into this."

"It's the right thing to do," Kaspar replied. "And we *owe* him."

"We don't owe him anything! He was just doing his job when he saved us."

Kaspar tilted his head, giving him a look. "You all thought I was dead; you've told me so yourself," he pressed, pausing, his tone softening as he continued. "Ev, we *owe* him. He took a huge risk saving me. Not a lot of people would have done that. Then he kept us out of prison, giving us a second chance. I know you don't like it, but he's assured us that he's going to do his best not to put us in any more danger than we're already in, and I believe him."

Turner's scowl faded, knowing that Kaspar was right and that they were already well past the point of no return. "Okay," he said softly. "I just don't want to lose you again," he added, moving and embracing his partner in a hug. "I can't," he whispered, his voice shaking.

"I know," Kaspar replied kindly. "And I appreciate that you think I've got my blinders on when it comes to him, but it'll be okay. We just have to put our faith in him and focus on making sure that everything else goes smoothly on our end. We'll be back home in no time, and we'll take that vacation you've been bugging me about."

Turner nodded, a smile crossing his lips for what felt like the first time in years. "Okay," he said finally. "Let's go keep an eye on our other miscreants, then. I still don't trust Desnik as far as I can throw him."

Kaspar smiled. "At the very least, we can bust his ass to make ourselves feel better."

Jackson reached his quarters a few moments later, locking the door, then moving to his bed and lying down on his back with his hands folded across his stomach, fingers interwoven. He took a deep breath, attempting to calm his mind, knowing that the task ahead required his complete concentration and focus.

After taking a few moments to center himself, he whispered, "All right, buddy, let's begin."

A sensation of falling hit him almost instantly as Bits activated the Cognitive Remote Projection implant, newly installed in the base of his skull. The technology was similar to the cognitive headsets miners used to project their consciousness into mechs or mining drones, allowing them to perform dangerous and complex tasks to extract resources from asteroids or other environments too hostile to risk humanoid lives. The military also used the same technology, enabling a humanoid operator to take remote control of specialized battle mechs for specific ops. This allowed a highly trained, highly skilled soldier to take on missions where the hazard level was extreme or the likelihood of returning from the mission was highly improbable. In these cases, a soldier's consciousness could be transferred into a mech that was specifically adapted for advanced physical combat, allowing the soldier to take their personal experience, skills, expertise, and judgment into extremely volatile situations without risking the lives of the highly valuable assets.

During his covert-ops training, Jackson had learned a little about these types of mechs and operations, but his specialty almost always demanded a physical presence.

All of that changes today, he thought, *if I can pull this off.*

Days before, during the planning phase of the operation, the admiral reached out to a former colleague of his, Professor Kensington, who ran the Advanced Remote Operations (ARO) department at the University of Technical Sciences on Pentara III, one of the best technical schools in the entire Confederation. After reactivating her classified operational clearance, he brought her in to consult on the op they were planning. As he described the basic challenges, she offered up something new that might do the job.

The next morning, a team of specialists arrived from the ARO at a small orbital station around the seventh planet in the Archon System, a GCH tactical staging site. After brief introductions, they jumped right in, reviewing the mission parameters and explaining their plan. The team then demonstrated the technology they proposed and how it could work.

Jackson pulled the admiral aside during a break from the session, moving into a small conference room away from the ARO team. "I want to be the one to go, sir," he said, imploring the admiral.

"We need to keep you safe, Will. If all else fails, you're the only one who can use the Light weapons. We simply can't risk you going."

"I know, sir, but we don't have a lot of time, and you said it yourself: There are very few operatives with as much experience infiltrating Imperium sites as I have. I know where the Shroud tech likely came from and what to look for. I can do this, sir."

Admiral Valentyen thought for a moment. "All right," he said reluctantly. "But we'll need to take some precautions."

Half an hour later, the team prepped Jackson for the minor surgical procedure, installing an advanced Cognitive Remote Projection implant into his brain stem. Once installed, they then talked him through the basics, instructing him on how things worked in the virtual world, then running him through a series of simulations for a grueling eight hours to get him used to the new environment.

The next morning, the team started early, helping Jackson to refine his control in the virtual world and, once satisfied, introducing the Remote Construct, or RC for short.

"The RC is an advanced and highly classified nano-tech package made from nanites constructed using a combination of alloys and synthetic compounds, making them light and flexible but also incredibly durable and adaptable. The nanites can morph into almost any shape or form that the user can imagine," Professor Kensington explained excitedly. "It also has a large data storage capacity and advanced sensors, which process data in real time into the virtual world, making it a nearly perfect representation of the real world surrounding it."

The team set Jackson up, starting him off with his first challenge: morphing the construct into a ball. It took him several tries, but after about fifteen minutes, he had the basics down. Next, they asked him to make the ball move. He sat for several minutes, focusing intently, the task proving to be surprisingly difficult. Finally, after close to an hour with the team's patient coaxing and training, he learned several techniques for locomotion.

First, he learned to alter the weight and density of different parts of the ball, such as the top, slightly off center, using the force of gravity to tip it over by pulling on the heavier side. Next, he learned how he could make the nanites partially fluid across the bottom, having them push it in the direction that he wanted, and then combining the changes in density at the top to increase its speed and maneuver it around objects.

After several hours of practicing, he was beginning to get the hang of it and had the ball moving with excellent agility and control around the room, weaving and dodging at his command. He even experimented, making the ball into a passable BB-8 from Star Wars, but found the construct's head too difficult to maintain on top indefinitely while it moved.

Once the team was satisfied that he had the basics down, they moved on to more advanced forms, building up his repertoire and mental capabilities for several hours.

Professor Kensington stopped the team for lunch after the intense morning session to let him recover. Over lunch,

Jackson got to know the team better. There were two nano-technicians, a junior tech named Maraleh and a senior tech named Whitson. Maraleh was the young prodigy of the group, joining the project shortly after she graduated. She appeared to have a father-daughter relationship with the older Whitson, who was clearly very proud of his apprentice and the advances she'd made to the program.

Next there was the bio-science lead, Dr. Devesh. The doctor was quiet and very serious in most of his interactions, focusing on his work intently while monitoring Jackson's brain waves and sensory inputs into the CRP implant, then tweaking the interface to optimize the connection while fine-tuning the hardware to Jackson's neural patterns. Jackson liked him but found his bedside manner to be slightly cold. Still, he could see why Dr. Devesh was on the team; he was clearly very good at what he did, and, after several hours of tweaking, Jackson conceded that the neural connection between his mind and the RC had grown considerably stronger.

Finally, there was Professor Kensington, the leader of the team and the visionary behind the project. She'd developed the integration between the virtual world and the cognitive transfer into a dynamic construct, something which had never been done before. She and her team also rebuilt the interface system from the ground up, coming up with the Cognitive Remote Projection implant, which was considerably more efficient and intuitive and provided the user with much greater control than was achievable with just a neural headset.

After lunch, Jackson reentered the virtual world, the break having done his mind some good. The team spent the next several hours coaching him and steadily increasing his abilities.

Professor Kensington had her own CRP implant, and she demonstrated for Jackson how to take what he learned and apply it to more advanced forms. First, she made a spider, showing him how she was able to make all eight of the limbs move, and even using it to climb up the wall of the room.

Jackson was impressed but also worried that the task would prove too difficult to master in the limited time he had, knowing that while he was working with the team, the admiral was already prepping for him to catch a ride on the *Severus*.

The professor then showed Jackson how to rapidly morph the spider construct back into a ball, then have it roll around the room before seamlessly changing shapes once more into a small bird, which took flight.

The professor landed the bird on the back of her hand, looking at Jackson through the construct, his mouth still slightly open in awe.

"Yeah, I get that a lot." The professor smiled. "It's actually not that difficult. The key is to break down the barriers in your mind that tell you that you *can't* do it. We're not that different, genetically speaking, from a spider, a bird, or a variety of other animals. When you compare genomes, you see that given a different set of circumstances, we could have evolved along any number of different evolutionary paths. Just look at the variety of humanoids in the GCH. Different heights, skin colors, sexual orientations, placement of organs, and attributes, such as speed, strength, metabolisms, bone structures, and different visual ranges. The list goes on. The diversity is astounding.

"The key to mastering constructs is breaking down the barriers that tell you you're only humanoid. Don't think about who you are. Think about *what* you are, or, more accurately, what you want to be. You are a life-form that comes in a variety of shapes, sizes, and other attributes. In this virtual world, you can be whatever you want to be if you concentrate. Now, just focus, breathe, and project the self that you want to see onto the RC."

Jackson took a deep breath and focused, trying to let go, pushing the limitations of his body from his mind as he became what he saw in his imagination, projecting it into the Remote Construct. He closed his eyes in the virtual world where his consciousness stood. It wasn't exactly the same as closing your eyes in the real world (in which they were closed already), but it made it harder to see the virtual representation of the construct before him.

He focused his thoughts, blocking everything else out and pulling back a vivid memory, feeling the RC transform, though not daring to look lest his vision betray the image in his mind's eye.

Suddenly, he heard a faint gasp, nearly causing him to lose his concentration, uncertain whether the sound was from him failing or succeeding. Finally, after a moment, the professor spoke in a soft voice, so as not to startle him from his focus.

"Will," she said, barely a whisper, "open your eyes."

He did, and there before him in the virtual world sat a baby dragon, the details incredible. He turned the dragon in a slow circle, its body covered in scales, spikes, and horns, its wings so thin that the virtual light penetrated them.

The professor moved to stand beside his virtual form in the shared VR world. "How did you do that?" she asked. "I've never seen someone achieve that level of detail after such a short time."

"I don't know," he said honestly. "I just thought about a book my mother used to read to me many years ago when I was a child, where a baby dragon was born. The writer painted such a vivid picture of the creature, and my mother added to it with the way she read it so that I could see it in my mind as though it was in front of me. I never forgot it."

"Well, I must say, I'm very impressed. Can you make it fly?"

"I don't know. But I'd love to find out!"

Now, as he lay on the bed in his small quarters on board the *Severus*, he thought back to that moment, reassuring himself that he was ready.

He took a moment to orient himself, shaking off the feeling of falling that accompanied entering the VR environment. An empty white space surrounded him while he waited as Bits activated the RC, flowing it into the center of the room from half a dozen locations in his quarters and belongings where he'd hidden it. As it came together, the RC's sensors began fleshing out the surrounding room while he waited.

"All right, buddy, let's run through a series of diagnostics," he said as Bits took on the role that Dr. Devesh had trained him for, monitoring Jackson's neural connection and the transmission between his CRP implant and the construct.

Jackson took his time, recalling the team's advice that he needed to have the construct fully calibrated and operational before venturing out.

He moved from form to form, following the diagnostic protocol that Professor Kensington had instructed him to use. Bits monitored the nanites' operational status with the diagnostic and reporting programs that Maraleh and Whitson had developed. At the same time, he kept an eye on the metrics Dr. Davesh had uploaded to ensure that the implant was transferring Jackson's consciousness according to normal parameters and that there was no neural feedback.

"Status?" Jackson asked.

"All systems operating at optimal levels. The neural link is strong, quantum tunneling protocols are active to keep the signal from being detected, and the remote cognitive transfer is at one hundred percent efficiency," Bits informed him.

"All right, let's get this done. Start the clock," he said, forming the construct into a spider, then creeping up the wall and into the ship's air ducts.

As he moved, Bits projected a map of the ship in the VR environment for Jackson to navigate while he quickly made his way to the cargo bay in the real world. Once there, he initiated a low-level scan to ensure that the coast was clear. As the results came in, the world around him changed from a limited area of visibility with a sea of white beyond to a larger area, where the definition was grainier at the edges but the reach of his "vision" had extended greatly.

Jackson watched for a moment, spotting Mara working below, prepping a container to be off-loaded, while just outside the ramp, he could hear Desnik through the auditory sensors.

Confident the coast was clear, he slowly maneuvered the spider along the ceiling of the cargo bay, concentrating to keep its form together while it gripped the small imperfections in the otherwise smooth metal. Bits worked in the background, ensuring that the nanites were in a translucent state to hide the construct's appearance. It wasn't as efficient as cloaking technology but required only a fraction of the power and complexity.

Jackson kept moving, exiting the ship, then proceeding along the top of the *Severus* until he reached a point far away from the cargo ramp and close to one of the station walls. The spider leapt into the air towards the wall of the hangar bay, shooting a nanite web ahead of it. The tiny machines latched onto the imperfections in the metal while Jackson quickly scuttled the spider up the wall. Once at the top, he stopped, surveying the hangar for a moment to get a better lay of the land.

From his perch high above, he had an excellent vantage point, allowing the optical sensors to run through various display modes while he scanned the rest of the bay with passive scans.

A vast area came into view, rendered inside Jackson's virtual world. Dozens of possible exit points appeared as Bits processed the data, including power conduits, small duct-like tunnels, and many other structural spaces behind and between the walls highlighted in the view before him.

He moved the spider towards the station's duct system. Once there, he morphed into a liquid form, slipping inside the vent, then into a ball, silently rolling and picking up speed as he went. The ball moved swiftly and quietly deeper into the system of vents, the virtual world becoming smaller once more, now just the duct system and a few feet around the RC appearing in varying degrees of resolution as it navigated the dark confined space.

The nanites' sensors included a variety of scanning modes, such as infrared, ultraviolet, thermograph, magnetic, bio-scanners, and power sensors. These, combined with the optical sensors, created a diverse and detailed picture that was relayed back to Jackson's virtual environment, reminding him of being in a nano-suit with the HUD and scanners appearing before him. The only major limitations of the construct were the sensors' range and the need to keep the power levels low.

As the ball continued to explore, more and more of the station revealed itself, while Bits continued to build a larger map around them to track their progress. It was a somewhat disorienting process where the edges of Jackson's vision were always somewhat blurred, with everything before him white space until it entered the sensors' range. It reminded him of video games he'd played as a child, where he had to explore a map hidden under a fog of war, which only lifted as he made his way to each new area.

Bits overlayed a rough map of the station, based on covert scans that had been taken over several thousand trips by different ships and crews, but these simply gave a patchwork of the overall layout and provided no actual detail aside from general direction finding and suspected locations of key areas based on a structural and power analysis.

Jackson continued to roll the ball along, morphing into a spider once more at several key junctions and scaling the RC upward, trusting that his AI would find the way while he focused on getting them into the general area where the station's critical systems were believed to be housed, thirty-seven levels up and halfway across the station.

He'd been at it for several minutes, having taken a few wrong turns already, but still was making progress as he made his way deeper into the heart of the station, focusing his mind on the task at hand while pushing away any doubts or fears as he continued forward.

The structure itself, while resembling a GCH station somewhat on the outside, was a classic Insectoid design on the inside, which essentially meant that most conventional humanoid thinking was out the window and that everything was seemingly random. Twice so far he'd run into bulkheads while weaving his way down a duct where it made no sense for a bulkhead to be. Frustrated and forced to double back, he pressed on, trying his best to remain positive while the clock continued to count down.

Finally, after nearly fifteen minutes of navigating his way through the station, he'd made some progress.

"William, I'm detecting a scanning system ahead. I believe that this is an entry point to another part of the station."

"Understood," Jackson replied, quickly bringing the ball to a stop while Bits initiated a passive scan, carefully examining the detection system from a distance.

"I believe that it is a simple bio-scanner with a motion detector."

"If we go slow and I make the construct translucent, do you think we can slip by it?"

"Uncertain. The bio-scanner should not be a problem; however, the motion sensor is a different challenge. One moment," Bits said, running dozens of potential scenarios through his processors. "I believe I have a working plan. If you can flow the nanites into a thin stream and run it along the bottom corner of the duct, keeping them tightly compressed, I believe the sensor will not detect the motion. Its scanning range appears spherical, focusing on the center of the duct."

"Do I even want to know the probabilities on this?" Jackson asked warily.

"Need I remind you of the Han Solo rule?"

"Ha, nice one. You're right. I probably don't want to know anyway."

"Probably better that you don't get distracted and instead focus your mind on the task at hand."

"Copy that," Jackson sighed, morphing the ball into a puddle, then flowing the nanites into a long, thin stream, moving it to the corner of the duct where the floor met the wall.

"Slower," Bits cautioned. "And I recommend making it thinner. Once under the scanner, if you harden the top layer for half a meter on either side of the scanning field, you can flow the nanites beneath the surface more rapidly."

"On it," he said, carefully stretching the stream out, making it longer and thinner until it was nearly three and a half meters long and just a few millimeters wide.

Slowly and carefully, he approached the edge of the sensor's range, inching the forward edge of the RC slowly under the scanning field. Jackson moved as delicately as he could while still maintaining the form, seconds passing while he focused his mind, keeping the surface smooth and solid and the bottom liquid as it moved at an agonizing pace past the detection field's range.

Finally, he'd moved the RC out of the scanner's range, taking a break and letting out a breath, the tension from his body releasing as he cleared his mind once more. After a moment of reprieve, he reformed the ball and began moving once again, hoping he was making some progress and not just lost in the dark.

CHAPTER 7
NEEDLE IN A HAYSTACK

Forty-eight minutes passed while Jackson continued to explore the station, a mix of luck and intuition guiding him as best they could. He stopped to study the map while Bits ran another series of passive scans from the RC's sensors.

"What do you think, buddy?"

"Based on my analysis of the distance that the construct has traveled, I believe you are in the general vicinity of what we are looking for. I suggest you move down from the duct system to ground level and explore from there, as it holds the highest probability of us reaching our target in the time remaining."

"Good idea. How are we doing for time anyway?" he asked, not entirely certain as to how long he'd been searching.

"Approximately sixty-three minutes have passed since you initialized the construct. The *Severus* is scheduled for departure in one hour and thirteen minutes."

"How long will it take us to get back?"

"I've plotted a direct route based on our current position. At present, it will take us eighteen minutes and seven seconds."

"Okay, we'd better hurry up then."

Jackson rolled the ball to the nearest exit point, peering through a small grate into the room below. It appeared to be a medical station of some kind, although, as with most things Insectoid, it was often difficult to be certain. He scanned the room, finding it empty and the exterior door closed. "Bits, increase power to sensors and cycle modes. Let's see what's beyond that door."

"Increasing power by ten percent. Any higher and we risk detection."

"Understood," Jackson replied, watching as the sensors increased their range and began cycling through infrared, ultraviolet, thermal, and several other modes. "Looks clear."

"Agreed."

"All right, here we go," he said, liquifying the construct, then flowing it through the narrow slats in the grate and down to the floor in a gentle, slow-motion waterfall.

Once on the ground, he reformed the RC into a pool of liquid, carefully flowing it through the tiny crack between the doors and out into the hallway, keeping it translucent to maximize stealth. As he moved, he realized how strange the perspective was, seeing the world as a tiny insect must, the experience somewhat surreal as he tried to push it from his mind.

The corridor came into focus in his VR world as the scans came back, the walls and floor a pristine white, running off in both directions. "That's weird. I've never seen the Imperium make anything like this. I guess the Mantises have a different sense of aesthetics," he commented, switching back to the ball and quickly making his way down the hallway to his right, passing the next door and stopping just off to the side while Bits initiated another scanning cycle.

A long room took shape, the scanning modes fleshing it out one layer at a time before him. Jackson's heart skipped a beat as a dozen ant-like creatures suddenly appeared inside. He quickly decided to put some distance between them, rolling the construct for several more minutes past door after door while Bits scanned them in turn, Jackson beginning to lose hope. "Okay, I'm officially lost here, buddy. Any idea where we are?"

"I believe we may finally be close to locating our target. As we've moved throughout the station, I've been using a variety of techniques, as we discussed in our planning with the admiral, such as using known Imperium design elements to look for clues. This station appears to be significantly different on the inside from any known designs, possibly the result of a retrofit to accommodate its role as a trade hub."

"Makes sense."

"With that in mind, I began running scans in an attempt to map the energy and data conduits. It is a slow process, requiring various points of reference and to measure the electromagnetic signatures flowing through the conduits to determine where they are stronger and weaker."

"So, you can map them back to the source, where they'd be strongest?"

"Precisely. I believe that I am close to being able to triangulate the source of the data flow. We need to perform several circular sweeps of the immediate area on this deck, and possibly the level below. Once we complete these scans, I believe I should have a bearing we can follow."

"Sounds good to me, but that may take a while if I continue with the ball."

"Agreed, we'll need to pick up some speed in order to cover the area more quickly."

"All right," Jackson said, taking a deep breath as he focused his mind, reforming the RC into a lean catlike shape resembling Razor in nearly every detail, a smile creeping across his face as he looked at the representation of the RC in his virtual world. "Ready to run, Raz?" he asked, the thought of his friend filling him with a mix of emotions as he wondered where he was now and if he was happy.

He quickly pushed the thoughts aside, knowing that now was not the time to get lost in emotion.

He took another deep breath, focusing once more, Razor taking off like a shot, galloping down the corridor with silent speed and agility, bounding around the corners while Bits monitored the sensors, attempting to triangulate the source of the data signals.

Jackson made his way around another corner and down another long corridor, passing dozens more rooms as he went, reveling in the joy of being a cat and simply running free.

As he approached the next corner towards what appeared to be a wider, longer main corridor, the RC's sensors triggered an alarm.

A Mantis was heading in his direction.

Jackson quickly leapt Razor towards the closest wall, splashing down into a puddle as he landed, then quickly altering the construct to form a paper-thin coating along the bottom of the wall.

Just as he finished making it translucent, a three-meter-tall Mantis came into view, swaying as it moved upright on four legs, towering over him from his low vantage point. The long, lean body resembled a Mantis from Earth, but its anatomy was considerably more evolved, with a rounded head, recessed spikes on its arms, and an almost humanoid face, aside from the eyes.

"Looks like a female," he whispered, the bright, shimmering wings and beautiful coloring on her body disguising the hidden deadliness she possessed.

"Confirmed," Bits replied as the creature continued past the construct, its body moving with an unnatural grace before pausing mid-stride.

The Mantis twisted her neck, angling her head to the side while her body remained stationary, her eyes silently scanning the corridor behind her.

"Shit, Mantises have excellent vision, don't they?" he asked, fairly certain he already knew the answer.

"Yes, most species have very high visual acuity. I would recommend that we power down the nanites and leave only the transparency mode active. Even with the construct stationary, the nanites still move, forming new links and connections for greater power distribution and communication as part of their basic coding. The Mantis may be able to detect the subtle variations, even though they are too small to see."

"All right, do it."

Bits powered the nanites down while the Mantis continued to look in the general direction of the construct, her antennae twitching slightly while her mandibles moved almost imperceivably, as though she was puzzling out what she was searching for, sensing that something was off.

Jackson didn't dare to breathe, keeping his mind focused on maintaining the construct and praying that she wouldn't see it.

He stared up at the representation of the towering creature in his virtual world. If she discovered the construct, it was all over. The *Severus* was the only humanoid vessel docked at the station, and it wouldn't take long for the Insectoids to determine it was them. They would be captured, tortured, and either killed or kept as prisoners of war.

There was no chance of escape.

A wave of guilt washed over him for bringing the crew of the *Severus* into this. For risking their lives along with his.

Just as he was losing hope, the Mantis turned her head back and continued swaying down the corridor at the same leisurely pace she was before, seemingly dismissing the oddity she'd sensed.

Jackson let out a relieved breath, deciding to hold his position for the next minute to be sure that the coast was clear before proceeding again.

Finally, after what felt like an eternity, he reformed the construct into Razor, quickly bounding around the corner and down the corridor, Bits scanning each room as he passed.

"I believe we are getting close," Bits informed him. "Turn right at the next junction."

Jackson ran harder, faster, galloping as he completed the circuit, a red X appearing on the map seconds later as he headed towards it.

"I believe we are here," Bits said, Jackson pulling up just outside a wide set of doors. "The door to this room appears to have an advanced security field in place. We'll need to find another way inside."

"All right, keep scanning while I make my way back up top," Jackson said, morphing the RC into spider form and quickly climbing the wall. Once at the ceiling, he located the nearest duct, then liquefied the construct, reentering the air vent system.

Jackson moved cautiously as he made his way through the duct into the space above the room, while Bits ran a series of scans. "I believe we can create a small opening and stream the nanites through the hole without risking detection," Bits suggested.

Jackson formed the ball, silently rolling into position. Once there, he focused the nanites on a tiny spot, the machines burrowing a pinhole through the metal a few seconds later. "Okay, I'm going to create a thin stream the width of a spiderweb and feed it down."

"Acknowledged," Bits replied as Jackson streamed the translucent thread of nanites a few centimeters through the hole, their visual sensors bringing the space to life in his virtual world.

"Holy shit," he said, staring down in awe at the room below.

Two large data cores sat three meters apart from one another, each with heavy power and data transport cables running between them and out to the station, the entire room crawling with small cockroach and spiderlike insects skittering over every surface. The cores themselves resembled huge hive-like structures, each glowing with a different color.

"What are they doing?" he asked, zooming in on a cockroach.

"Unknown. Each core has different organic compounds built into its structure, acting as a hive of sorts," Bits inferred, running through a series of scans.

"I've never heard of anything like this," Jackson said, his frustration after coming so far getting the better of him as the mental toll of piloting the RC began to take hold. "Can we even interface with it?"

"I cannot be certain, but I believe that these insects have been modified to act as data carriers," Bits said, bringing up a scan of one of them in Jackson's virtual world. The roach hung in the air, the scan showing its body embedded with nano-circuitry. "I've analyzed the pattern of the roaches' and spiders' movements," Bits continued, as he displayed a projection of the paths from individual creatures moving between the cores in an intricate web.

"They're a data transfer system, moving information between the cores," Jackson said, awestruck.

"Yes, I believe so."

Jackson thought for a moment, trying his best to remember Captain Delgado's lessons on the Insectoids. "Okay, let's take a step back. So, the Mantises have a seat at the table of the Imperium Council, but the rest of the ruling species really hold the true power in terms of the overall empire, right?"

"From what we know, yes," Bits replied. "They have sovereignty over their own space, aside from the Gateway, which is run in collaboration with several other species."

"Right. So perhaps there're two cores: one for the Mantises and the other core for the Imperium. The roaches and spiders could be agents for each side, facilitating requests for data between the two while keeping them isolated."

"It is a viable theory, and the data, although limited, that we have now appears to corroborate it based on the patterns of interactions between the spiders and roaches."

"Can you tell which core is which?" Jackson asked, considering how to go about their task.

"I would infer that the core with the blue light belongs to the Mantises, as it's hardwired into the station, spreading out in various directions. There are far fewer connections to the yellow core, and they run beyond the scanning range of the construct. Based on their direction, I would surmise that they lead towards the edge of the station to a transmitter where they uplink to the Imperium central network."

"All right, so we need to access the yellow core, but how do we get down there with thousands of these things crawling all over? Could we mimic one and climb down?"

"I do not believe so. Based on my scans, the roaches and spiders, while primitive, would likely be able to identify any construct as a foreign entity."

"Hmm. Could we hijack one?" Jackson asked, a plan forming in his mind.

"I believe so. However, without knowing the protocols, we risk becoming exposed. I recommend targeting a single roach – which appears to be the carrier species for the Imperium – one that is already en route to the core, injecting it with a small nano-payload. I can then access the roach's internal nano-system and covertly monitor the data transaction."

"Okay, let's try it," he said, taking another breath, then concentrating on morphing the thread of nano-material to form a tiny needlelike shape a few millimeters in length. "I'll focus on holding the construct's form while you target a bug and release the payload, then you take it from there."

"Acknowledged," Bits replied, severing off a sliver of his own consciousness into the nanites, then releasing the needle seconds later. The tiny nanite construct fell from the darkness towards the mass of crawling roaches. Bits's aim was perfect as it landed on the back of one of the tiny roaches, penetrating its shell and injecting it with nanites.

Bits quickly went to work targeting the roach's cybernetic systems to erase any trace of the injury occurring, then accessed the control matrix, easily taking over the rudimentary interface while keeping the creature unaware of his presence. Seconds later, it approached the towering Imperium data core, following the stream of roaches ahead of it and crawling inside. Bits powered down the nanites to minimal levels, keeping just a few active to maintain his connection while they waited, interfacing with the roach's data access circuitry, ready to inspect all the traffic going through the interface.

The roach made its way into the core, Jackson watching on the sensors as it crawled deeper, quickly realizing that what they could see of the core was just the surface. Like an anthill, it ran far deeper below the deck than it appeared from above, going down at least another level, if not two.

It really is a hive, he thought.

Finally, the roach moved into a small alcove, artificially created pheromones drawing its primitive biology to the designated access port. The nano-systems initiated contact with the core while the roach ate a small ration, all while Bits silently monitored the transaction.

Minutes later, the roach emerged from the hive and back towards the spiders. Bits waited patiently until it was at the fulcrum between the two cores, then initiated a full uplink, focusing a tight-band data stream up towards the tiny thread hanging above to avoid detection.

"How did it go?" Jackson asked.

"Very well. I now understand the hive access protocols and how to initiate a data request. Unfortunately, we will be limited in how much data we can retrieve at a time, and I will need to break the requests into pieces to remain undetected," Bits replied, running the calculations.

"How's our time?"

"We have forty-three minutes remaining before we need to start making our way back to the ship."

"How much buffer will that leave us with the time you need?"

"Approximately five minutes."

"Okay, let's focus on what we came here for first. If we have more time, we can try to get more, but if we can't get back to the ship, then this is all for nothing, as we can't upload the data across the neural link. I'll keep the construct together while you get the data."

"Very well. Based on my calculations, I will need to use approximately half of the RC's nanites in order to infect the required number of hosts," Bits informed him.

"Take whatever you need. Let's just get this done."

CHAPTER 8
COUNTDOWN

Thirty-nine minutes passed while Bits worked diligently, infiltrating a hundred and thirty roaches with tiny nano-payloads and compromising their systems, then accessing data from the Imperium core and transmitting it back to the RC once clear of the hive.

"How are we doing, buddy?" Jackson asked, having kept mostly quiet and watching while Bits worked, realizing, not for the first time, how incredibly skilled and intelligent his companion was.

"Nearly done," Bits replied. "I have been piggybacking my data requests along with those from the Mantis core. I nearly have all the data segments for the information we need. I've also intercepted several incomplete data fragments, which may have strategic value. I believe I can complete harvesting the rest of this information; however, I will need more time."

"How long do you need?" Jackson asked, the fear growing in his mind that they might not make it back in time and that all of this will have been for nothing.

"Approximately six minutes."

Jackson's mind raced, considering the risks versus the rewards.

"Do it," he said decisively, knowing that this would be their only shot and that anything Bits identified as being valuable was likely worth the extra time and could make a difference in the war.

Minutes passed while Bits continued to work, Jackson studying the map of the station they'd compiled thus far, attempting to memorize the fastest route back like tracing a finger through a maze. A moment later, a small chime sounded.

"Data harvesting complete," Bits informed him.

"All right, let's get the hell out of here," Jackson said, reforming the remaining nano-material into a ball, just under half the size it was before due to the nanites they were forced to leave behind inside the roaches. He moved quickly and carefully for several minutes before unexpectedly coming across a dead end. "What the hell?"

"Curious," Bits replied, initiating a scan and finding an alternate route. Jackson quickly got back on track with no time to waste, and several minutes had passed when, once again, an unexpected dead end appeared in their path. "The station appears to have altered the duct system," Bits said. "This would explain some of the difficulties during our initial trip and why certain corridors were inexplicably blocked. I would infer that it is a security measure designed to shift at specific intervals to prevent any unauthorized access."

"Damn, that makes sense. They need the ducts to move air around, but since the Insectoids don't even trust each other, they'd need to secure the system to keep other creepy-crawlies out, preventing exactly what we're trying to do," he said, frustrated he hadn't thought of it earlier.

"Agreed."

"Options?"

"We can attempt to find another route; however, our timeline is highly constrained at this point. I recommend using your dragon form to quickly descend to the hangar bay level, then switch to Razor's form and take a direct route through the corridors to save time."

"Are you sure that's a good idea?" Jackson asked.

"I don't believe we have any other choice," Bits stated plainly. "Our margin for error is rapidly shrinking, and we need to make up for lost time."

"All right," he said hesitantly, altering course and heading for the nearest shaft down, then forming the dragon and diving into the blackness.

Jackson opened the wings, slowing the RC down and using them, along with the tail, to control the dive, the feeling of flying natural, like something out of a dream.

"Two more levels to go," Bits informed him, highlighting a junction off to the side of the shaft ten meters ahead in Jackson's VR.

Jackson banked the dragon, maneuvering into the duct and gliding for nearly a minute before Bits detected a barrier in their way, just beyond the next junction. He landed the dragon, forming into the sphere once more, then moved it into a nearby vent, scanning the corridor below.

"Shit, there's a lot of action down there!" he said, the scans showing dozens of Insectoid life-forms moving through the corridor.

"Double back seven meters, then go left. There is another route we can try that should lead to a series of smaller side passages."

"Copy that," he said, rolling back the way he came and following the map Bits projected before him, the tension in his body growing as the seconds ticked by.

"There is another vent just ahead on your left," Bits informed him.

Jackson stopped, watching as the data from the scans came back. "Okay, I'm dropping down now."

A moment later, he was on the floor, taking on the form of Razor once more and galloping down the hallway at top speed, the doors and side passages passing by in a blur.

Bits upped the sensors' range slightly while Jackson focused all his attention on keeping stride, the tiny cat racing along the floor, keeping tight to the walls should the need arise to hide.

Jackson whipped past a side corridor, scans showing three Insectoid life-forms not far from the junction, sending a jolt of adrenaline through him. "Do you think they saw us?"

"Negative. Visual scans show that they were facing away from us. However, they likely detected the vibrations and disturbance in the air, though it is unlikely that they will realize what just happened."

"All right, fingers crossed," he said, shifting the RC's form to appear translucent, hoping that if they ran into any more Insectoids that they'd only appear as a blur at range, buying them precious seconds to hide.

Bits navigated as they continued to race forward, pushing Jackson's mental ability to keep the construct together and run on four legs to his limits. Precious seconds ticked by as they grew closer, Jackson doing his best to block out everything else and trust his AI.

Bits redirected him several times to alternate corridors to avoid Insectoids as they entered his scanning range, the frequency increasing as they entered what appeared to be the busier part of the station. Twice, Jackson was forced to stop and hide as they ran out of options, waiting nervously as a Mantis and two Wrenthari bodyguards, a humanoid-like Insectoid species he'd encountered before, passed by.

"How's our time?" he asked through gritted teeth, the mental stress and exhaustion taking hold, knowing he'd reach the breaking point soon.

"Four minutes, fifty seconds until scheduled departure," Bits replied.

"How far out are we?"

"Three minutes, eleven seconds. However, I'm detecting a security checkpoint up ahead. We will need to find a way through."

"Shit! This is gonna be close. Any ideas?"

"I'm working on several possible solutions. I believ— William, a door is opening ahead!"

Jackson collapsed Razor's form instantly. The RC hit the ground and liquefied, forming a transparent puddle of nanites as a squad of Insectoids emerged a moment later. The four-and-a-half-meter-tall, six-armed, heavily armored creatures filed out of the room, standing upright on two powerful legs, their knees bent backwards. A rapid series of clicks filled the hallway as they trudged past.

Jackson looked up, recognizing them immediately as Skifters, a species that excelled in heavy combat operations and were typically used for black-ops assignments, along with Yilen fire ants and Wrenthari. The Imperium deployed them as elite troops in ground and boarding operations, and their reputation was well-known throughout the GCH as powerful, deadly foes.

Jackson slowly flowed the liquid construct towards the wall. As he moved, one of the Skifters turned, its antennae twitching, its keen senses detecting the slightest movement. Jackson froze as the Skifter leaned over, examining the liquid. Six sets of eyes moved over the puddle, studying it intensely.

"Bits," Jackson whispered, uncertain what to do.

The Skifter leaned in closer, dipping its finger in the liquid, then rubbing it between its two clawed nails.

It brought it closer to its olfactory glands, suddenly pulling its hand back in revulsion.

Jackson's heart skipped a beat, realizing that the creature must have smelled a humanoid scent on the nanites. "Oh shit!"

The Skifter stood back up, Jackson ready to reform Razor and make a mad dash, when it suddenly shook its hand in disgust, turning and wiping its fingers on the wall, before speaking in a series of clicks and moving off.

Jackson felt as though he'd just escaped from the jaws of a predator, the adrenaline rushing through his veins while his heart pounded in his chest. If the construct wasn't already a puddle, it would have been now, his legs feeling weak both in his virtual world and the real one as he tried to shake off the feeling.

"What the hell just happened?" he asked, dumbfounded. "I thought we were done for!"

"I used the chemical processors on the nanites to replicate the smell of ant urine," Bits replied.

"Ant pee!" Jackson laughed, feeling the tension drain somewhat. "Seriously? You never cease to amaze me, buddy!"

"I suggest you be amazed later. We have less than two minutes and thirty-eight seconds remaining to get back to the ship."

"Oh shit! Can we make it?"

"I believe so. We are less than twenty meters from the security checkpoint leading to the cargo section of the station. Take the door the Skifters came out of."

Jackson reformed the construct into Razor's avatar, darting through the door. Once inside, he rushed through the room, taking in the odd furniture. "Looks like a briefing room," he said, sliding to a stop. "Bits, quickly, we've got to document everything," he stressed, a display on the wall showing various tactical information.

"Got it. Continue forward eight meters, then turn left," Bits instructed, Jackson crossing the distance in seconds. "Go straight for nine meters, then right when you reach the far wall."

He followed the instructions, weaving through a large room with what he could only describe as furniture made from some type of natural resin, then entered another small room. "Looks like a dead end!"

"Use your spider form to climb to the top. There's a vent in the left-hand corner. Once inside, go left. This will take you back to the original vent leading to the cargo bay, two hundred and thirty-seven meters away. Be careful, though; there is a scanner eighty-four meters ahead."

Jackson moved quickly, entering the vent system, then carefully slipping past the sensor the same way he had on the way in, all the while conscious of the seconds ticking by. Once past the sensor, he formed the dragon once more, knowing that time was short as he took to the air.

He reached the vent to the bay moments later, landing the RC and peering out towards the ship, spotting Desnik just outside, handing a pad back to a tall Mantis standing before him. "Pleasure doing business with you," he said, turning to enter the ship.

Jackson liquefied the construct, slipping through the vent and falling towards the floor, reforming into the dragon as he fell and pulling up at the last second. The RC slipped beneath the ship, weaving and dodging just under the hull, hoping that any cameras in the bay hadn't caught the blur of motion.

He maneuvered the tiny dragon form as fast as its wings could take it, making his way towards the rear of the ship.

A noise filled the bay as the ramp began to close, Jackson's heart pounding in his chest as he pushed the construct as hard as he could, bending it to his will and racing towards the back of the *Severus*. He twisted around the aft landing pylons and pulled up sharply, making a beeline for the top of the ramp, knowing that he had just seconds until it sealed shut.

He pulled up over the top edge of the ramp, then dove inside the ship, the ramp narrowly missing the dragon's tail, while praying that they'd remained undetected.

Once inside, he pulled up from the desperate dive, the bay full of crates blocking his path and forcing him to dodge several times before finally running out of space with nowhere left to go.

The dragon crashed into the side of a crate with a thud, Jackson liquifying it upon impact and dropping to the floor.

Desnik stopped, looking back over his shoulder, then shrugged and continued moving towards the door to the forward section of the ship, exiting the bay while Jackson stowed the RC, forming it into the shape of a small data pad, then severing his connection.

Bits shut down the implant, bringing Jackson's consciousness out of the virtual world, his mind suddenly becoming fully aware of his physical body once more, his jaw and fists clenched and his head pounding from the intense concentration.

"Howlett, where the hell are you?" Turner called angrily over the speakers.

"Sorry, sir, had my headphones on while I was sleeping. Must have missed my alarm," he replied, attempting to play dumb.

"Well, hurry the hell up and get to your post. We're ready to depart, and I, for one, want to get the hell out of here!"

"Understood. I'm on my way," he replied, attempting to get to his feet, the feeling of walking on two legs suddenly foreign to him as he struggled for a moment to push past the disorientation and make his way to the bridge.

CHAPTER 9
GAMBIT

Jackson stepped onto the bridge, his mind still reacclimating to the limitations of his body after the freedom of the construct. Turner and Desnik each gave him a sharp look as he walked past, making his way to the Ops station, still feeling slightly off.

"Hey, Howlett, have a good nap while the rest of us were doing all the work?" Desnik jeered.

"Slept like a baby," Jackson replied smugly. "I should have signed up for a gig like this years ago," he added, enjoying rubbing it in his face.

Desnik was about to say something in response when Kaspar cut him off. "All right, you two, that's enough. You can have a pissing contest on your own time. For now, let's get out of here. Any objections?"

The crew was silent.

"That's what I thought. Howlett, navigational sensors only. Turner, start spinning up the hyperdrive and give me thrusters. How's our cargo, Mara?"

"All tucked away and tidy, sir," she replied cheerfully.

"Okay, let's go. Howlett, open a channel," Kaspar said, waiting for the chime to indicate the channel was open. "Ulpharisha Station, this is the GCH transport *Severus* requesting permission to disembark."

A moment later, a reply came granting them permission. Kaspar maneuvered the ship around with the thrusters, slowly exiting the large cargo bay and moving it farther away from the station. Once they were two hundred meters out, he switched to sublight engines, setting a course back towards the Wall.

They entered through the doors into the Wall station, Desnik transmitting the code that the dock master had provided a moment later, and the doors on the far end opened, allowing the *Severus* to pass through.

Kaspar set a course for the jump point, turning to face Jackson. "Howlett, activate full forward sensors once we're ten thousand klicks out."

"Copy that," he replied, watching while they pulled away from the Gateway station, the weapons on the Wall easily enough to take out a ship the size of the *Severus* a hundred times over if they suspected that something was amiss.

Once farther out, Jackson activated the forward sensors, and Kaspar began running astrometric scans to plot their course back to the Lkarus System, watching the computer's progress as they approached the waypoint, the calculations taking longer than normal.

"What's the problem, Cap?" Mara asked, sensing something was wrong.

"I'm not sure. Looks like there's been some activity in the region, possibly from one of the nearby neutron stars. The computer's having a hard time plotting a jump solution."

Jackson pulled up the readings on his console, taking a look. "You're right; it looks like one of the neutron stars is throwing off some serious electromagnetic and gravitational interference along our flight path."

"What can we do?" Turner asked.

"Not much," Kaspar admitted. "We hold here until it clears."

"How many hours do we have left before our window closes to cross the border?" Desnik asked, saying what was on all of their minds.

"About fifteen hours left, I think," Kaspar replied, checking the countdown. "Yeah, fifteen hours and twenty-two minutes."

"What happens if we don't make it back in time?" Jackson asked.

"They'll activate the hyperspace defense grid in that sector as a precaution. In case the ship was captured and the bugs sent it back as a bomb," Kaspar explained. "Protocol says we have to drop out of hyper on the bugs' side of the border in that case, then make contact with GCH Traffic Control. After that, they'll force us to jump into a quarantined system, where we'll get boarded by an armed party of very unhappy marines. Then, once they do a full sweep, they'll grill us for hours as to why we're late. We had it happen once before, and let me tell you, it's not fun."

"Won't the bugs have ships patrolling their side?" Desnik asked.

"They will, and they probably won't bother to ask if we're supposed to be there before simply destroying us if we're discovered," Turner added, drawing a glare from Kaspar.

"Well, let's hope it doesn't come to that. Howlett, any idea how long the interference will last?" Kaspar asked.

"It's hard to say, but based on these readings, I'd say it's slowly dissipating. Probably six or seven hours, though, till it's safe. Maybe a bit more," Jackson replied.

"We'll just have to wait it out then," Kaspar said.

Jackson sat back in his chair, trying to act calm and natural while keeping watch on the Gateway and the ships patrolling nearby, nervous that traces of his activities might still be discovered.

Eight hours and twenty-seven minutes later, an alarm went off at the helm, snapping Jackson and Kaspar out of their respective tasks.

Kaspar shot Jackson a look, and he double-checked the readings, giving Kaspar a nod in return. "All hands to the bridge," Kaspar said over the ship's speakers. "We're ready to jump!"

Turner, Mara, and Desnik quickly made their way to the bridge, taking their seats, the *Severus* disappearing in a flash of light a moment later, the crew relieved to be back in hyperspace, while silently dreading what almost certainly awaited them in the Lkarus System.

Just under an hour and twenty minutes later, they approached the Lkarus System.

"Dropping us out of hyper in thirty seconds. Look alive, people!" Kaspar called, the ship appearing back in normal space moments later.

Turner's hands moved quickly, powering down all but the critical systems, while Jackson began scanning the area for enemy contacts.

"What have we got?" Kaspar asked.

"Scans coming in. So far, so good," he reported. "Hang on… I'm detecting an ion trail not far from our position. The decay rate suggests that the ship that left it passed by here only moments ago and…" Jackson trailed off, studying the readings in more detail.

"And what, Howlett? Out with it," Turner snapped.

"Based on these readings, I'd say it wasn't a raider… The trail's way too wide. The ion dispersion pattern is definitely from something larger." He paused. "I think it was a Scorpion destroyer," he said, his voice grave.

"Shit. Just what we don't need," Turner said.

"All right, I'm plotting our jump back. It shouldn't take more than a few minutes, and we'll be out of here," Kaspar said.

Jackson looked around the bridge, the crew clearly rattled by the discovery of the ion trail. Raiders were bad enough, but a destroyer would make short work of an unarmed cargo ship like the *Severus* in no time. Jackson focused on the sensors, hoping that they might be able to outrun the enemy if he picked them up far enough out, while suspecting there would most likely be several raiders nearby, all of them hunting together as they swept the system. Typical Imperium tactics.

"Come on. Come on," Mara muttered quietly, rocking slightly in her chair, vocalizing how they all felt while Turner hunched over his console, cycling through the engineering systems. Desnik, for his part, remained cool and calm, surprising Jackson without so much as a snide comment while he waited for the nav computer to finish its calculations.

The Ops console beeped. Once, twice, then rapidly in a steady sequence, and the crew turned towards Jackson.

"They found us!" he said, his voice grave as he pulled up a tactical display showing the *Severus* and the surrounding space. "No sign of the destroyer yet, but there's a frigate three point four million kilometers to port, and I'm also detecting two—damn, no, make that three—raiders approaching from starboard…and three more from above. They're still over half a million kilometers out but heading this way fast. I'm raising shields to minimum and rotating the magnetic signature; it'll make it harder for them to lock on to our exact position, but we don't have a radiation pocket nearby like we did last time to hide in."

"The computer still needs at least two and a half minutes to complete its calculations!" Kaspar interjected.

"Can we outrun them?" Mara asked, the fear in her voice sharp like a knife.

"Maybe. They're cutting us off, spreading out and coming at us from several angles. We'll never outrun them all, but I can buy us some time, and with Howlett's shield trick, it will be harder for them to lock on until they're much closer," Kaspar said, piloting the *Severus* on a vector away from the enemy ships.

The raiders altered their course a moment later, increasing their speed, the small ships—twice the size of a fighter—closing rapidly while the frigate approached from behind.

"They're gaining on us! I think they've locked on," Jackson reported.

"Shit, the change in course caused the nav computer to restart its calculations!" Kaspar replied, his face turning ashen as he realized with a deadly clarity that the enemy ships would close on them before they could jump out. He turned back to his crew, his eyes wide with horror. "I'm so sorry."

The crew looked at one another, terror and despair written on their faces as the Scorpion ships slowly boxed them in.

"I'm sorry too, Captain," Jackson said.

"You've got nothing to be sorry for," Kaspar replied, his voice nearly cracking. "I just wish I hadn't let you down. That things could have turned out differently. That we could have made a difference."

Turner was silent, meeting Jackson's eyes as he nodded, agreeing with his partner's sentiment as his heart fell in his chest, knowing that they were finished, while Mara and Desnik looked at one another, uncertain what was happening.

"Thanks, but I'm actually sorry about *this*," Jackson said, a slight smirk appearing on his face. "Bits, activate Archangel protocol."

Bits's voice resonated over the ship's speakers, startling the crew. "Acknowledged. Archangel protocol activated."

The crew's consoles suddenly went dark, all systems transferring to Jackson's station. "Initiating subspace ping," Bits said, a look of horror crossing the crew's faces as a high-frequency broadcast emanated from the ship, echoing inside the hull, then spreading out in an invisible subspace wave at several times the speed of light in all directions.

"What the hell are you doing?" Turner shouted, knowing that the ping would bounce off anything metallic, just like sonar in an ocean, lighting it up on sensors, the *Severus* included. "Now they can triangulate our exact position. They don't even have to wait until they're within targeting range to get a lock. What the hell were you thinking?"

"Bits, activate the comm. Full-spectrum broadcast. Maximum power," Jackson said, ignoring Turner's comments.

"Channel open."

"Operation Archangel is a go!" Jackson called over the open comm, flipping the viewscreen to show a 360-degree view of the space around the ship.

"What the fu—" Turner cut himself off, his jaw dropping as a brilliant flash of light lit up the main viewscreen, a GCH warship appearing out of nowhere.

"Bits, engage visual and sensory tracking on the main viewscreen. Oh, and shields to *full* power," he added smugly, a hum echoing throughout the ship as six hidden shield generators came online, tripling the power of their defenses seconds before one of the raiders opened fire.

Jackson took evasive action, maneuvering the ship, the enemy fire narrowly missing them while two more raiders locked on, the shields absorbing the impacts.

The crew watched on the screen as the GCH warship darted forward, quickly picking up speed and closing on the closest group of incoming raiders. A devastating volley of weapons fire appeared seconds later, destroying three raiders with ease, the ship banking around and setting a course for the next closest group.

The crew continued to watch on the *Severus*'s optical sensors and the tactical view in the top corner as the battle unfolded.

"Holy shit, that thing is fast!" Desnik said, watching as the sleek warship weaved and dodged, evading several waves of incoming fire, then banked like a bird of prey, swooping in for the kill, diving right towards a pack of raiders and picking them off one by one before swinging back around towards the incoming frigate.

The Scorpion ship opened fire, the GCH warship maneuvering back and forth, evading most of it, while lining up an attack run and opening fire with its plasma cannons, hammering the frigate's shields.

A brilliant streak of white light lanced out from the front of the GCH ship, striking the frigate dead center along the port side. The enemy ship tore in half from the impact of the mass driver, and the warship swung around, following up with another barrage of fire, pummeling the stricken vessel, the hull exploding in a blaze of light seconds later.

"Holy shit!" Turner said. "I've never seen anything like that. What the hell type of ship is that?"

Jackson smiled. "Spartan class."

"*Algeron* to *Severus*, do you copy?" a woman's voice said over the comm.

"*Severus* here. Nice to see you, *Algeron*," Jackson replied, the image of Captain Olivia Michaels appearing on the main viewscreen. "You're right on time."

"You're not," she said, folding her arms across her chest. "You were due back almost nine hours ago. My ship's paint started to bubble from sitting so close to the damned sun. I'm adding that to your bill, Jackson," she said jokingly, then looking away for a moment. "Hang on… Full burn on a heading of 285 mark 117. There's another group of incoming raiders a little further out and a Scorpion destroyer coming into range. I don't want them to get any lucky shots off at you. Run like hell and jump as soon as you can. We'll mop up here."

"Roger that, moving off at best speed. Good hunting, *Algeron*!" he said, the image of the captain disappearing and the visual display reappearing as the *Algeron* sped past.

Jackson altered course, taking them away from the incoming enemy vessels, and the crew watched as the two larger ships engaged one another, the destroyer throwing up a heavy field of fire with its broadside while the raiders attempted to close and flank the *Algeron*.

"Can they actually take on that many ships at once?" Mara asked, the concern clear in her voice.

"Just watch," Jackson said, unable to hold back his smile as the *Algeron* lined up a strafing run, lobbing a few gamma torpedoes ahead of it to soften up their prey, then bringing to bear the full force of its forward batteries, including the deadly mass driver once more, devastating the destroyer in a single pass.

The *Algeron* swung around, setting a course to chase down the raiders, now in too close and hopelessly outgunned with the destroyer out of the fight.

"What the hell just happened?" Turner called out, the destroyer listing to one side, Bits zooming in the long-range visual image while they watched as multiple decompressions emanated from the shattered vessel's hull.

The *Algeron* closed on the raiders, the ships scattering as they tried to run. Less than a minute later, only one remained, the *Algeron* letting it go, then turning back towards the crippled destroyer.

The Spartan class warship closed on the enemy ship, evading the last of its weak counterattack and lining up another run.

The crew of the *Severus* sat awestruck, watching as the destroyer exploded seconds later, the *Algeron* twisting and turning as it evaded the debris, its shields absorbing the brunt of the shockwave.

"Whooo!" the crew of the *Severus* cheered as the *Algeron* sped past them once more, reducing its speed, then circling back around to pull into a parallel formation with the cargo vessel.

"Nice shooting, *Algeron*," Jackson said. "The crew of the *Severus* owes you a debt of gratitude."

Olivia Michaels appeared on the viewscreen once more, a mock scowl on her face. "Now you really owe me a new paint job, Captain," Michaels said, her frown quickly replaced by a smile. "You certainly have a knack for attracting trouble, I'll give you that."

"That I do. Thanks for the assistance, Captain. I owe you a bottle or two for this one," he said, happy to see his old friend after so many years.

"A bottle? Hell, you owe me a whole case for this one, Will!"

A voice spoke in the background, just off the viewscreen, muffled slightly over the comm. "And Lieutenant Morgan says you owe her a box of that good chocolate you brought with you last time as well." Michaels looked away for a moment, then looked back to the screen. "Better make it two boxes."

"Tell the lieutenant that I'm on it. I'll treat you both to dinner the next time I see you."

"You're on, Captain."

Just then, an alarm beeped on both ships, drawing their attention.

"Looks like we've attracted a few more raiders and another frigate. Poor bastards still think they're actually the ones hunting out here." She smiled a wicked smile. "You'd better jump out while we mop up. My crew's been itching for some payback since the Scorps jumped our convoy a few months ago at Kentaris V. We'll make sure that their little operation here is fully out of commission before we leave."

"Copy that, Captain."

"See you around, Jackson. *Algeron* out," Michaels said, her image disappearing as the *Algeron* powered up its engines and sped forward once again. The crew of the *Severus* watched as it made short work of the raiders before changing course to intercept the now fleeing and outclassed frigate.

"Everyone always underestimates the Spartan class because it's small," Jackson commented, the crew staring at him. "They always seem to realize too late what they're up against," he added, checking his console, noting that the nav computer had long since finished plotting their course back to the border. "Bits, stand down from Archangel," he said, the other bridge consoles coming back to life a few seconds later. He looked over at Kaspar. "It's your ship, Captain. Would you care to do the honors?"

"Gee, thanks," he replied.

"Who the hell are you?" Turner asked, staring at Jackson while Mara and Desnik sat silently, still in shock at what had just happened.

"Come on, Turner, haven't we already been over this?" he said, raising an eyebrow and flashing a wicked smile. "I'm Captain William Fucking Jackson, and this is your lucky day," he said, feeling that he was finally, truly back to himself for what felt like the first time in years.

CHAPTER 10
FRESH START

The *Severus* exited hyperspace in the Delconia System just over nine hours later, their journey back across the border having been uneventful and the crew visibly relieved to see the Hub as it appeared on the screen.

During the journey back, Jackson explained that he was a GCH officer on a covert mission, thanking them for their service but giving them little more than that, enjoying the air of mystery.

The *Severus* docked at the station moments later, and he said his goodbyes to Mara and Desnik, then walked back to the cargo hold, retrieving the RC and heading down the ramp with Kaspar and Turner to greet the station's cargo and logistics officer.

"Welcome back, *Severus*," the officer said cheerily as they approached. "How was your journey?"

"Eventful," Turner said flatly.

"Just glad to be back in one piece, Commander. All cargo is present and accounted for," Kaspar added.

"Excellent work, Captain. A few dozen more runs like this, and you'll clear your ledger and own your little ship here," he said, smiling and handing Kaspar a pad for him to approve the final paperwork.

"Actually, I'm just going to borrow that for a second," Jackson said, intercepting the pad and taking a step back with it.

"Hey, you can't—" the commander began, Jackson cutting the officer off with a glare and pulling the pad in close.

"Bits, authorization code: Jackson-tango-three-beta-four," he said, watching as the display changed, then handing the pad back to the commander. "I believe you'll find that the *Severus* is now the joint property of Captain Kieran Kaspar and First Officer Evan Turner."

The commander examined the pad, clearly confused, looking back up at the equally stunned Kaspar and Turner. "I...uh...I believe that your...*friend* here is, uh, correct. My apologies, gentlemen."

"Oh, and a couple of other things," Jackson said. "You'll note that the crew are owed a year's back pay for their brave service to the Confederation." He paused, meeting the commander's eyes. "They'll also need a new route. I was thinking...Delconia to Archon," he said flippantly.

Kaspar and Turner gave each other a look, knowing that the route was one of the most sought-after in all of civilian shipping—the journey between the two core systems a short, safe, and very lucrative one. Most crews had to wait years, if ever, to get a shot at a premium route like that.

The commander looked up at Jackson, stupefied.

"It's all on *your* pad, Commander," he said, a slight hint of superiority in his voice.

"Uh, yes, uh, sir?" the commander asked, a look of confusion on his face.

"Captain," he replied cordially. "And please make sure that my friends here are upgraded to full citizens, as per the terms of completing their contracts."

"Uh, of course, Captain," the commander responded.

"As you were then. Keep up the good work, Commander," Jackson said, patting the man on the shoulder, then walking off towards the lift.

Turner and Kaspar stood with their jaws agape, neither one believing what had just happened.

Jackson spun as he entered the lift, flashing them both a smile before the doors closed, each waving back awkwardly as the commander passed them the pad once more to get their thumbprints on the updated changes.

The doors to the lift closed, and Jackson disappeared from their sight, his smile lingering as he rode the lift up, feeling reinvigorated while he thought about what was to come next.

Two hours later, Jackson exited a shuttle, stepping out onto the landing fields on Archon.

He paused, the gusting wind flowing through his hair while the waning heat from the late-autumn sun warmed his skin.

Season's changing, he thought, savoring the sensory experience as he allowed himself a moment to breathe in the clean air and enjoy the simple pleasure of being outdoors.

Minutes later, he arrived at the entrance of the GCH Command complex, excited to see the admiral and show him the data they'd recovered.

He located Admiral Valentyen a few minutes later in the central GCH Intelligence room, his new clearance, courtesy of his former CO, giving him access now without an escort. They quickly moved off to one of the unoccupied briefing rooms to review what Jackson had found.

"I'm glad to see you're back in one piece, Will. I take it the mission went well?" the admiral asked.

"A few bumps along the way, but all in all, I'd take an op like that over some of the shitshows I've been on any day."

The admiral smiled. "Did you end up needing our little surprise?"

"I did. I just filed the report before I landed. The Scorpions were waiting for us when we got to the Lkarus System. Fortunately, the *Algeron* was right where it was supposed to be, and it made short work of them." He smiled devilishly. "They even stuck around to mop up the system after we jumped out. I received a coded transmission from Captain Michaels about an hour ago that they took out seventeen Scorpion raiders, one destroyer, and two frigates in total," he said, proud of his friend and his former crew.

"I'm glad I was able to pull them from the front lines. That was a good idea. Nothing like a Spartan class to lead a hit-and-run strike. So, what were you able to find out?"

"Quite a bit, actually," Jackson said, waving his hand to dim the lights. "Bits."

Bits took over, activating the holo-display, a map of the Imperium appearing as shown from the enemy's perspective, with the GCH represented on the opposing side.

"As you can see, this shows the positions of three large Imperium fleets highlighted in red. This one here"—Bits zoomed in on one of the fleets Jackson pointed at—"appears to be significantly larger than the other two and is the Insectoid's primary presence in the region, at over fifteen hundred ships strong. There are also two dozen small patrols of around ten to fifteen ships each, spread out in half a dozen other systems. We were able to acquire their patrol routes and schedules for the next six days. The map also shows two key logistics stations that are keeping the bulk of these forces supplied. There are large convoys coming from deeper within the Imperium that restock them every fifteen days."

"Excellent work," the admiral said. "We can put this to good use and should be able to hit them hard with several coordinated attacks, catching them off guard."

"My thoughts exactly, sir. If we take a small fleet of a few dozen cloaked ships and we wait here"—Jackson pointed at a navigational marker on the map—"in this system, I think we could ambush and destroy the next convoy that comes through."

Bits chimed in. "My analysis indicates that the supply convoys must pass by this waypoint en route to the largest of the supply stations. The navigational beacon in the system is a safety net which they use to ensure that their destination is secure, stopping and waiting for a confirmation before the convoy proceeds closer to the front."

"If we can hit them fast and hard," Jackson said, a tinge of vengeance in his voice, "we could cripple their largest fleet's ability to function at full capacity for at least a week, maybe more."

"Any idea what's in the convoys?"

"That's the best part; it's mostly food."

"Food?"

"Yes, sir. Bits pulled the cargo manifests, and that fleet is already well stocked with weapons and fuel. In fact, it hasn't moved in almost a month. It looks like they're preparing for something. Staging for a big attack, possibly. But while they sit there, they still need to keep all of their soldiers fed, and from what we've gathered, the Imperium is having some supply issues, particularly with food at the moment. Our best estimate is that they only have rations for a force of that size for a few days."

"So, we can cut off their food supply..." the admiral said, considering. "It won't necessarily ground their fleet, but it will certainly limit their ability to respond."

"That's our thinking as well, sir. And if we can take out those resupply stations, we could really impact their operational effectiveness. I'm also thinking that if we can take out these smaller patrols, and maybe even hit one of these other smaller fleets and take them by surprise, it will have a ripple effect along the front lines," Jackson said enthusiastically.

"Forcing them to redeploy and weaken that larger fleet, while also thwarting whatever attack they've been staging for," the admiral said.

"Exactly. Bits was also able to get the supply schedules for two other regions, one along the border, farther down the Holt Line, and another, a key staging system deeper inside the Imperium. That one, we think, based on the huge amount of traffic and shipping manifests tied to it, appears to be a major manufacturing center for their war machine. If we can disrupt their front lines in a few areas, then we could send a strategic strike force in to hit that system, causing significant logistical and supply problems."

"We'll still have to deal with the Shroud."

"Yeah, that's the trickier part. We'll need to have multistage attack plans for each target system to scout it out first, then take out their Shroud generators before we can move in with the Fleet and hit them in force. I figure we'll need at least a few dozen cloaked scout ships to precede each assault. There is also some data on a handful of systems where it shows the approximate location of some of the Shroud generators, giving us an edge if we attack there. Unfortunately, we ran out of time, and the list is far from complete."

The admiral studied the map thoughtfully for a moment, the master strategist considering it from all angles and looking at the data in detail while Jackson suddenly worried that he may have gotten too excited and a bit ahead of himself with his strategy.

"Your plan has a lot of merit, Will, and the intel you've come back with should prove extremely valuable. I have a few ideas though."

"Of course, sir."

"I'll need to bring some more people in on this, but we should be able to come up with something that we can act on quickly, based on this intel," the admiral said, nodding slightly as he turned, ready to lead them out of the conference room.

"Agreed, sir. There's one more thing though," Jackson said, pausing for a moment, smiling while the admiral turned back. "And this might change all of our plans, depending on how we decide to act on it. Bits, show the admiral what we got him for Christmas."

The holo-image changed, displaying a larger map of the Insectoid Imperium. "We believe we have located the primary sites that control the Shroud of Darkness," Bits said.

The admiral moved in closer to study the new map. Tens of thousands of small green dots appeared across a vast area of space, along with twelve larger blue ones, each deep inside Imperium space, all save one.

Bits continued, "We believe that the green points indicate the devices that are generating the Shroud of Darkness and that the blue ones are the command-and-control centers. These enable the Shroud to function, coordinating Imperium fleet movements while allowing them to navigate safely through the sensor blackout the Shroud casts."

The admiral studied the map for several moments, begrudgingly admiring the impressive web the Insectoids had created. "That system"—he pointed to the one inside what was formerly GCH space, nodding slowly—"is that..."

"Yes, sir," Jackson chimed in. "It's Stornoway."

CHAPTER 11
STORNOWAY

The admiral continued to stare at the map, deeply immersed in thought, his brow furrowing as his gaze focused intensely on the Stornoway System.

Jackson watched in silence, looking at the holo-projection while he tried to follow the various windows the admiral pulled up, comparing and analysing the data. Finally, he broke the silence after several minutes.

"Can I ask you a question, sir?"

"Of course," the admiral replied, still focused on the holo-display and pulling up another window, the fourth he was now referencing.

"I remember when the war started, and you gave us all a briefing on what happened during the Imperium's first strike back at the Hideaway. You indicated back then that it was a big deal when the Imperium took Stornoway. I recall you mentioning that it was highly strategic, with lots of resources and a shipyard, but there's clearly more to it than that. What's so special about it?"

"Do you want the long answer or the short answer?"

"I'm always up for a good story, sir."

The admiral turned, smiling. "You'd better get comfortable then."

Jackson nodded, taking a seat, eager to hear the admiral's tale. The admiral remained standing, opening up a new window showing a map of the galaxy.

"The best place to start is around seventeen hundred years ago, when the GCH and Insectoid Imperium were in the midst of a long and bloody war during one of the Imperium's overpopulation explosions, what we call today a Great Expansion. After years of conflict, the GCH finally turned the tide of the war, winning a series of key battles and striking several blows to the Insectoids' war machine in the process. The Imperium, still licking its wounds but far from defeated, unexpectedly switched tactics. Instead of continuing to fight, they fortified their positions along their border, then struck out, pushing into new areas of the galaxy, searching for unclaimed worlds to conquer.

"The GCH watched and waited for several months, the war seemingly over as little more than a scout ship from their side crossed into GCH space. We still hit them hard a few times, especially in the first few weeks, hoping to bring a formal end to the war. But oddly, they didn't retaliate. Instead, the Imperium just pushed farther and farther into unknown space along the frontier, perplexing GCH Intelligence as to what they were up to."

Jackson nodded attentively, his experiences in the current war making it clear that this was far from standard Imperium military protocol.

"Initially," the admiral continued, "they followed a straight line beyond the border, expanding along it but not crossing over into to what was implied to become future GCH territory, and only taking systems on what would have been their side. Again, something very unlike them. After several months, however, our worst fears were confirmed, and they began to spread out once more, taking systems on what would have been our side and effectively blocking any future expansion. Days later, the Admiralty met for an emergency session at GCH Command on Archon. The debate was heated, with two of the five Fleet admirals favoring holding the current border and fortifying our position, grateful that the war was effectively over. They argued the Insectoids would eventually come back in force, once their populations and fleet had recovered, and wanted to hold on to what we had, rather than expand and spread ourselves too thin.

"The other two Fleet admirals, however, feared that if the Imperium got too far ahead and continued expanding on what would be considered our side of the theoretical future border, then they would outflank us and could eventually surround the GCH on two, possibly even three sides, creating multiple potential fronts for future conflicts and an impossible area of space to defend."

"This is the same fear you mentioned after the attack on Kuteria," Jackson interjected. "That the GCH might pull back and eventually be surrounded."

"Exactly," the admiral said gravely. "As the emergency session wore on, Fleet Admiral Rickard Holt was the swing vote and had remained mostly quiet while his colleagues debated the options. After hours of back-and-forth in the Fleet Admiralty chamber, he rose unexpectedly, silencing the room. He then moved towards the map displayed on the wall and drew a line across it. 'There is no choice,' he said decisively. 'We have a duty to defend the Confederation now, yes...but also for generations to come, and we cannot lose sight of that, or it will be our undoing. I've listened carefully to what you all have said for the past few hours and know that I have the deepest respect for each of you, all of your years of service, and the vast experience and wisdom you all bring to this hallowed hall. But I've considered my position, and the ramifications of it, extremely carefully...and I've come to a decision.' He paused, meeting each of their eyes. 'We *must* keep the Insectoids on this side of this line at all costs. The risk of them taking more systems unchallenged, of their having access to vast amounts of potential resources unfettered, and giving them that much room to grow and breed is simply too great. They could come back at us with a hundredfold their current strength, crushing us in their path. Therefore, we have no choice but to match their expansion along this line, wherever it may take us,' he said, thus sealing the decision for the GCH to continue expanding."

The admiral paused for a moment while Jackson nodded slowly, considering the turning point in history and where they were today because of it. "The Holt Line," Admiral Valentyen continued, "as it became known, set the stage for one of the greatest interstellar expansion races in galactic history."

Jackson leaned forward, knowing the Holt Line well from his time at FoxBlind, where he'd crossed it entering enemy territory many times, but he had never known the full story.

"With the GCH Fleet repaired, restocked, and fully ready for combat, we regrouped, shoring up the existing border, and then moved forward, staking claim to systems the Imperium left alone on our side first. Next, the Fleet pressed forward, taking systems by force that the Imperium had claimed on what was our side of the Holt Line, one by one."

Jackson watched as the map updated, a red line indicating the border and a dotted line extending out to represent the path of the Holt Line. A time-lapse continued to update the image, and he could see the Imperium expanding farther ahead, while the GCH moved forward, taking system after system, but only on the GCH side of the line, as they slowly caught up.

"Command also sent in large construction fleets," the admiral explained, "the largest logistics and building project ever undertaken by the Confederation, following the massive assault fleet of nearly six thousand warships. As systems of value were taken, the construction fleet quickly entrenched our presence, building defenses to secure these new prizes. Some of the systems the Imperium had taken were simply cleared, even though they held no value for us, with worlds that couldn't even support humanoid life. The goal was to ensure that the Line was intact above all else. Meanwhile, covert forward scouts catalogued everything, and Command prioritized systems based on habitability, resource potential, and strategic value."

The admiral paused, the images fast-forwarding as the Line continued to grow and grow before their eyes. "The expansion continued, with each side claiming hundreds of systems along the border, which grew from just under thirteen hundred light-years in length to a staggering eight thousand seven hundred light-years in just two years' time! More than double the size of all our borders combined, including with the Reptilian Empire and the Oceanic Union." He paused, the map showing a view of the galaxy with each of the borders of the different galactic powers outlined.

"As both empires continued to stretch farther and farther out, the fleets driving the race on both sides grew thinner and thinner, and it became almost a staring contest, with neither side willing to blink first. The GCH, however, became more and more strategic, focusing only on the best systems, while the Insectoids focused on taking anything they could populate. This forced the GCH to leave gaps, sometimes dozens of light-years wide between systems, weakening our overall defensive ability. And the rapidly expanding border became an ever-increasing mess, to be candid, creating an inevitable scenario for future conflicts and strategic challenges.

"The Holt Line ultimately worked, however, ensuring that the GCH grew in parallel with the Imperium, giving neither side the advantage, at least not at that time, and preventing us from being boxed in. Unfortunately, it also set the stage for a huge, volatile region of space, which remains to this day."

"I'd heard bits and pieces of this before, but now it all makes so much more sense," Jackson said. "I didn't really know how it all came together."

"How it ended is equally important," the admiral said, and the display updated, showing the once mighty GCH expansion Fleet, now down to a mere five hundred ships, with the rest now stationed at various key systems along the Holt Line. "As the expansion continued, Command made the decision to permanently double the size of the Fleet, with ship building becoming a huge priority. The creation of twenty-seven new fleets was outlined, with the goal of having them all built and operational within a decade. This dramatically changed our military structure, adding over a million new officers and tens of thousands of ships and stations to the Fleet. We colonized hundreds of new systems, our population shifting dramatically, giving us more resources than we knew what to do with and creating opportunities for tens of billions of citizens to settle on new worlds. The expansion along the Holt Line essentially laid the groundwork for the modern GCH we know today, and over the past seventeen hundred years, our overall population has grown tenfold or more. We went from being one of the smaller powers, with the Imperium, the OU, and the Reptilians all being bigger than us at that time, to being the second largest in size, second only to the Imperium. The trade-off, however, was that while the Imperium didn't make out as well as we did in terms of strategic resources and systems, what they did gain, which is critical to where we are today, is hundreds of habitable worlds. And since that time, their overall population has increased nearly a thousandfold, based on our best estimates."

"Wow, yeah, that makes sense. We know they breed at exponential rates, and having all of those new worlds to colonize would certainly give them room to grow for centuries," Jackson commented.

"Close to seven centuries, to be exact, before the next major expansion in their population growth took place, but by then, they had hundreds of systems still to explore on their side of the line farther to the galactic north, as we did with ours to the south. This averted another potential war, and a fragile peace lasted for nearly another hundred years, with no real reason for conflict on either side," the admiral said. "But back to the story. With no end in sight to the expansion, and often only a few ships left to hold systems along the line, Command considered the possibility that they may be forced to concede defeat in the race to expand, consolidating our border and holding on to the riches we'd claimed. After months of debate, Command finally halted our advance, focusing instead on building colonies, orbital and ground defenses, and deploying vast mine fields and sensor nets to protect each system along the frontier. The Imperium, however, continued to push forward, undaunted.

"Weeks passed while GCH Intelligence continued to monitor the enemy's expansion," the admiral said, the map updating once more. This time, the GCH side remained static while the Imperium continued to grow farther to the galactic west. "The Imperium, sensing that we were no longer keeping pace, shifted the focus of their expansion, confirming the Admiralty's worst fears as they slowly turned once more, moving into space on our side in an effort to stop our expansion and claiming multiple systems as they went. Command rerouted dozens of ships to hold our outermost systems, shoring them up and waiting for what they feared was an inevitable attack while the enemy swung around our flank."

He paused, his voice growing quieter as he continued. "Weeks passed, however, as reports of Imperium fleet movements grew scarcer and scarcer. Finally, Command deployed dozens of cloaked scout ships, sending them out into enemy space in an attempt to locate their fleets. Several days passed before one of the scouts reported in, having located the remains of a massive Imperium fleet, all of it destroyed. Hours later, a covert-ops team was deployed, tasked with boarding one of the wrecks and salvaging its data core. Two days later, the heads of GCH Intelligence met with the Admiralty to present their findings.

"As the Imperium pushed farther out along their side of the border, they encountered a populated system, quickly discovering a highly territorial, xenophobic, and technologically superior race. The Insectoid ships were mercilessly destroyed, but not before sending a message back to the Imperium. Several days later, another Insectoid fleet arrived, engaging this new enemy again. Despite their superior numbers, they were soundly beaten once more and forced to retreat. The Insectoids pulled back, licking their wounds and pulling more ships from along the Holt Line to challenge this new enemy and defend their new territory. But…they were completely unprepared for what happened next.

"The enemy, rather than sitting back and letting them come, counterattacked! Weeks passed, while this unknown force took system after system from the Imperium, annihilating their ships, stations, orbital defenses, and even wiping out entire colonies. The assault continued as weeks turned to months, pushing deeper and deeper into Insectoid space, showing no signs of stopping. As the conflict expanded near where we'd abandoned our expansion at the end of the Holt Line, Command issued an order to all GCH captains to not engage these ships should they encounter them, fearing that we may suffer the same fate as the Imperium. Several weeks later, a large unknown fleet entered the Kalath System, one of the farthest GCH outposts along the line."

The holo-display changed, showing a top-down view of the system. "A lone GCH vessel, the *Mayfield*, was out on patrol nearby and cautiously approached the incoming fleet, opening a channel. 'This is Captain Nagato of the GCH starship *Mayfield*. We have no quarrel with your people and are no friends to the Insectoid Imperium. We wish only to live in peace,' she said as the armada continued to approach, bearing down on them.

"The captain ordered her crew to hold their position with no shields, no weapons, and no scans of any kind to possibly provoke the huge battle fleet. She knew that they were the only thing standing between the unknown ships and Kalath III, a planet with over nine thousand civilian colonists. Their only chance, she hoped, was to show that they posed no threat and to pray that these creatures, whoever they were, could be reasoned with.

"The fleet continued to approach, their massive ships dwarfing the tiny frigate as they moved closer and closer. They were less than five kilometers away when they finally stopped." The admiral stopped, and the holo-display zoomed in. "The fleet held position menacingly before them as a single ship broke formation and approached to within five hundred meters. Captain Nagato knew that at that distance, there would be no time to raise their shields if an attack came, gambling that if they wanted to destroy them, that they would have done it already. She stood fast, her crew holding their collective breath until, a moment later, the ship initiated a powerful scan, sweeping the *Mayfield*.

"Finally, the vessel sent a response. A message appeared on the main viewscreen with no text, no audio, just a map which showed their current position along with a small region of space, highlighted in red. The image held on the screen for several seconds, the ship powering its weapons, then opening fire at a nearby comet, completely obliterating it in a show of force."

The holo-display changed to show a recording from the bridge of the *Mayfield* as Captain Nagato spoke over the open comm. "We understand," she said, clearly having to fight to find her voice through the tightness in her chest. "The GCH will respect your borders. You have nothing to fear from us."

An inhuman laugh echoed over the comm a moment later, the hairs on Jackson's arms standing on end as it filled the bridge of the *Mayfield* and echoed in the meeting room. He watched as the holo-display split, showing an exterior view from the *Mayfield* on one side as the armada powered its weapons, firing on a small moon half a million kilometers away. Seconds later, the moon shattered, splintering to its core. A deep, menacing voice followed, speaking in perfect Archonian, "You do!"

"The ship then turned and headed back to the rest of its fleet, all of them jumping out seconds later. They were never seen again," the admiral concluded.

"Holy shit!" Jackson said, finally taking a breath as he contemplated the power needed to shatter a moon, let alone from that distance. "What happened next?"

"The captain of the *Mayfield* quickly contacted GCH Command, and after a thorough debriefing and review of the visual and limited sensor logs, a strict general order was issued to all GCH captains, which still exists to this day, to never approach the area indicated on that map. In fact, GCH Stellar Cartography and Navigation have marked the entire region as unstable, due to 'dangerous anomalies,' in the hopes of keeping all civilian ships away, and all navigational arrays manufactured in the Confederation won't even allow a course to be plotted there. After the incident, the GCH decided to give this new civilization some space, abandoning the Kalath System and pulling back nineteen light-years to the next populated system along the Holt Line in an effort to extend the buffer zone. Even today, that sector is only sparsely populated, and we ensured that any future expansion steered well clear of the area marked on the map."

"Did we ever find out who they were?"

"Over the next several months, GHC Intelligence focused intensive resources on attempting to monitor this new threat as they continued their push into Insectoid space. Finally, after nearly three months and sixty systems, based on our best estimates, along with tens of thousands of Insectoid ships being destroyed, their assault abruptly ceased. The Imperium had been soundly beaten, losing considerable territory, and their fleet lay in a state of complete disarray. They also pulled back, abandoning all of the systems they'd lost to this new enemy and consolidating their forces back along the Holt Line in an effort to hold what they still had. Years later, an intelligence operative, working through the Mantises, actually, learned that the Insectoids named the aliens the Cyir'Alar. The rough translation means Abyss of Death."

"So, how does all of this relate to Stornoway?" Jackson asked.

"Sorry." The admiral smiled. "I got a little caught up there. Just trying to give you some context. During the years that followed, the Insectoids slowly began fortifying their positions and never returned to any of the systems that the Cyir'Alar had taken from them, even though scans indicated that they were uninhabited. It was speculated that this race had sent a similar message to the Imperium that should they ever approach their space again, this time they would not stop until all of their kind had been eradicated.

"These events, while dramatically reducing the Insectoids' numbers and military capabilities, also fundamentally changed the way that they approached expansion in the future. At first, they moved away from us, finding ample systems along their side of the Holt Line to colonize, as I'd mentioned, for the next seven centuries. Unfortunately for them, that region of space contained several vast nebulae and stellar nurseries, leaving limited room for growth in many regions. Centuries passed while they colonized what they could, before their attention turned to our borders once again, hoping to take a few systems from us. Stornoway was the first of these."

"What's so special about it?"

"Well, for starters, it contains a vast asteroid belt with considerable quantities of hydricite ore, daramite, palladium, promethium, isilium, phosphoric magnesium, yttrium, and astatine. These alone make it worth fighting over, as many of these extremely rare elements are critical components essential in the manufacturing of quantum cores, hyperdrive tech, and nano-circuitry, among other things. On top of that, it has a large L1 and medium-sized L3 class planet, ideal for humanoid or Insectoid life, along with ample terrestrial fresh water, minerals, and indigenous flora and fauna. Not to mention four habitable moons in the system, all of which fall into the L-class spectrum."

"Yeah, that would do it. That's a heck of a rare combination. The Imperium would do just about anything to get its claws on a system like that," Jackson commented.

"Indeed. But that's not all. It's also located at a key point, two-thirds of the way along the Holt Line, where the GCH discovered a treasure trove of seven other bountiful systems, all with similar resources, but farther back on our side of the line. Our scientists speculate that several massive supernova events billions of years ago created this rich pocket of systems full of resources, similar to the GCH core worlds. As a result, our primary defensive strategy focused on Stornoway, the closest to the border and the crown jewel of them all. During the period after the Cyir'Alar had ended the Great Expansion along the Holt Line, the GCH focused heavily on Stornoway, building shipyards, a huge supply hub, and a massive ground-based center of operations into the side of a mountain. Command also permanently stationed the 39th and 52nd fleets there, along with deploying thousands of weapons platforms and hyperspace defense grid satellites to protect the system.

"By taking Stornoway at the beginning of the war, however," the admiral continued, "the Imperium knew that they could cut a swath into our territory, cutting off vital supply lines to systems farther out along the Holt Line and crippling our main military presence in the region. In the past fifteen hundred years, give or take, the Imperium has tried to take Stornoway an astonishing twenty-nine times. As a result, the surrounding region has become one of the most militarized and volatile in the galaxy. Time after time, the Insectoids launched assaults on Stornoway, and time and time again, they were repelled by the massive arsenal they faced when they arrived.

"At the start of the current war, however, the Insectoids made it a priority to capture the system. And during the first hours of the conflict, they launched offensives into several nearby systems, weakening our defenses in the region while they drew out small forces from our two fleets to respond. Then, a massive fleet of over thirteen thousand vessels, their movements cloaked—we suspect by using the Shroud of Darkness with ships in their fleet to generate it—arrived to capture the system. The 39th and 52nd fleets were almost completely destroyed, with only forty-three vessels managing to escape.

"The Insectoids paid an immensely heavy price as well, losing over three-quarters of their ships, but in the end, it was a major strategic victory for them, putting the GCH on the defensive in the entire Capsia, Benthar, and Gathalan Sectors. And, by controlling the Stornoway System, it provided them with a foothold into GCH space, allowing them to threaten dozens of other systems in the region. This, in turn, forced Command to commit thousands of ships to the defense of these systems, many of which have vital shipbuilding, research, and mining operations, leaving other regions along the Holt Line weakened as a result. Since that time, the Insectoids established a vast military presence in the system, using it as a spearhead into GCH space."

"And now we know that it also provided them with an ideal location to house one of the control centers for the Shroud of Darkness, extending it into GCH space," Jackson concluded. The admiral nodding solemnly.

The two of them sat for several moments in silence, each pondering this information. "We've gone through a lot of the data we recovered, sir, and based on everything I've learned, I think that Stornoway is the key to winning this war," Jackson said. "And I think, using the other intel we recovered, we can take it back!"

CHAPTER 12
MENACE

The Insectoid convoy dropped out of hyperspace in the BC-193 System precisely on schedule.

Forty-nine ships in total—forty-four supply vessels and five escorts—all held position at the waypoint while they initiated scans.

At the start of the war, at least twenty-five escorts would have guarded a convoy this valuable, but having gained confidence over time, the Imperium began directing more and more ships to the front instead, assured by the protection of the Shroud to keep their precious cargo safe.

The supply vessels contained parts, power cells, and, most important of all, food.

The Insectoids were voracious eaters, and the need to keep their soldiers fed was one of the most critical. If the food supplies ran out on a large ship with a diverse crew, the cycles of predator and prey would begin – something that could not be allowed to happen.

The convoy signaled the Imperium fleet in the YD-252 System, their main staging area in the region, that they were on schedule, while waiting for a response to proceed. The stop in BC-193 was part of the route, a necessary waypoint to make adjustments for the Bynard black hole, a large navigational hazard in this region. But the Imperium was also cautious, holding back the convoy until the fleet confirmed that all was clear.

YD-252 was close to the humanoid border, and while the GCH were thus far not aware of their fleet's presence there, the Insectoids were always cautious to ensure that their food supplies, above all else, were maintained.

Twenty-four light-years away, all was quiet in the YD-252 system. The command ship was preparing to issue the convoy its jump authorization when suddenly, a flash of light appeared just fifteen kilometers from the idle fleet, a small GCH scout ship registering on their sensors.

The battlecruiser immediately ordered the three closest ships to engage, each moving quickly as they broke formation, eager for the kill.

Stupid humanoids. They have no idea what they're jumping into, the Insectoid commander thought.

Suddenly, the small ship registered a massive power spike, exploding seconds later. The detonation created a massive disruption in subspace, stretching nearly three million kilometers in all directions.

The Insectoid commander's blood ran cold as he suddenly realized what had happened: The humanoids had discovered how to duplicate their subspace disruption weapon. Their fleet was now trapped, unable to make the jump into hyperspace until they were clear of the affected area.

The commander screeched in rage, ordering all ships to form up.

They had to leave. Now!

Other targets would almost certainly be under attack, and they were the primary response force in the region. They had to get back into the war, and quickly.

The massive fleet of fifteen hundred ships formed up and began moving at full speed towards the edge of the affected area. As they did, the command ship's alarms blared.

Five hundred GCH warships jumped into the system, just beyond the edge of the disrupted area, partially surrounding the Insectoid fleet as they formed up a battle line, cutting off their escape.

Seconds later, another warning sounded as dozens of the satellites maintaining the Shroud went offline, small GCH strike craft appearing near the locations where they once were.

The Imperium commander looked over at the viewscreen, staring at the enemy fleet, knowing what was about to happen as time seemed to freeze for an instant.

A second later, the GCH ships unleashed a massive volley of torpedoes.

Thousands of them.

The commander ordered the fleet to scramble, taking evasive action as another wave of torpedoes followed the first. Then a third. Then a fourth.

The GCH ships then turned and jumped away. All but one. It alone remained to watch the carnage unfold.

The first wave of torpedoes approached the Imperium fleet seconds later. The Insectoid ships attempted to take evasive action but were too close together as thousands of spatial disruption torpedoes detonated at close range. Chaos followed as the onslaught unleashed massive waves of kinetic energy, causing dozens of ships to collide. Thirty-four Insectoid ships were destroyed outright, with nearly a hundred and twenty others suffering moderate to heavy damage.

Many of the ships now turned, attempting to flee the next wave as the second volley detonated all around the fleet. Hundreds of gamma torpedoes erupted in a dazzling display of light, creating massive pockets of deadly radiation that overwhelmed the shields of nearly all but the largest battleships.

Their defenses down, the third wave of torpedoes closed on the helpless Imperium fleet. The deadly projectiles locked on to their targets, and another four hundred ships were reduced to shattered wrecks in less than a minute by the onslaught as a mix of explosive and kinetic warheads slammed into them relentlessly.

The final wave approached seconds later, the torpedoes targeting systems hunting for active power readings as hundreds more Imperium ships blinked off the map.

The few surviving ships took evasive action, many engulfed in explosions or hit with massive chunks of debris from the other vessels as the fleet was torn to pieces all around them. Those that remained turned and attempted to escape in the opposite direction, thankful to be alive.

Minutes passed, and the Imperium ships were nearly at the edge of the disrupted area on the opposite side from where their fleet lay in ruins when suddenly, the GCH Fleet reappeared, cutting off their escape once more.

Another massive wave of torpedoes launched forward at close range, then a second, then a third, before the Fleet jumped out again.

The commander of the once mighty Imperium fleet cursed the humanoids with his last breath as the final wave hit, all fifteen hundred ships destroyed in less than eighteen minutes.

Admiral Valentyen stood on the bridge of the stealth ship *Exeter*, watching as half a million kilometers of space burned before his eyes with the shattered hulls of the enemy fleet, fighting to keep the smile from his lips.

Meanwhile, the Arachnid captain of the lead convoy ship had waited long enough. Something was wrong. She ordered the convoy to turn and set a course back, deeper into Imperium territory. If the fleet had been engaged, then they needed to protect the convoy at all costs.

As the ships began to turn and power up their engines, thirty-one small vessels decloaked, spread out along the line of the convoy. Before the captain could give the order for her escorts to engage, the small ships opened fire.

The close-range assault pummeled Insectoid supply vessels, their hulls torn to pieces within seconds from the intense fire, the ships venting atmosphere, their precious cargo destroyed or blown out into space. The GCH ships continued to pour on the barrage, ignoring the Insectoid escorts entirely and focusing their fire on supply ships, until the last one of the massive three-kilometer-long vessels tore in half.

The Imperium escorts, enraged at the loss of the ships they were charged to protect, closed on the line of GCH ships, ready to open fire.

Before they could unleash their deadly weapons, the small ships jumped away, leaving only a single ship remaining—the farthest from the convoy, where it sat, unmoving.

The escorts quickly turned, setting an intercept course while the small ship stood its ground, taunting the fast, well-armed protectors to avenge their fallen charges, if they dared.

Just before the Imperium ships entered weapons range, dozens of flashes appeared behind the lone stealth ship, as a task force of twenty GCH warships appeared and mercilessly rained death upon the approaching escorts, annihilating them in seconds.

Jackson stood on the bridge of the stealth ship, *Decius*, beside the command chair, looking at the main viewscreen as the last of the escort ships erupted in a massive ball of fire. "What's our final count, Ensign?" he asked the officer at the ops console.

"Forty-nine out of forty-nine ships destroyed, sir," the officer said with a smile.

"Nice work, people," Jackson said, turning to the look down at the command chair. "Well, Captain, do you think your recruits learned something today?"

"I would hope to hell so," Captain Delgado responded. "I'd say history learned something today, Captain."

"Yeah, payback is a bitch!" Jackson said, eliciting a cheer from the crew.

Captain Delgado allowed his crew to celebrate for a moment. He was hard on them all, he knew that, but if even one of them turned out to be half the operative that Jackson was, well then, he'd have a reason to cheer as well.

"All right, knock it off, everyone," Captain Delgado gently chided. "Our work isn't done yet."

Fifteen hours later, the *Decius* exited hyperspace at the edge of the Stornoway System, cloaking and initiating scans. The crew sat in silence, having spent the rest of the day delivering one devastating blow after another to the Imperium using the data Jackson and Bits had stolen to hit the enemy where they were weakest and clear out thousands of Shroud generators in over a dozen systems.

Jackson stood on the bridge next to Captain Delgado, studying the map of the system, watching as passive scans filled in areas of the holo-display, while hundreds of small cloaked probes moved through the system, providing more data in real time and cutting through the blackout created by the Shroud. The probes were tasked with providing intel, while also locating the satellites generating the Shroud and holding position near them. Once in position, they continued to feed what sensor data they could, while standing by for their final objective, taking them down when the time came.

Just hours before, a large GCH armada led by Admiral Janus hit a major enemy system twenty-three light-years inside Imperium space, annihilating all of their ships, manufacturing installations, and infrastructure. Meanwhile, Admiral Easton and Admiral Valentyen each commanded smaller assault fleets that continued running targeted incursions, hitting dozens of patrols, outposts, and convoys. Their hit-and-run attacks decimated the Imperium's defenses across a wide area along the Holt Line while the armada focused on hitting key systems and driving deeper into enemy space.

Captain Delgado was right, Jackson thought. It had been a day for the history books indeed.

"There they go," Jackson said, watching as hundreds of ships jumped out, rerouting to shore up key systems within striking range of the GCH assault armada just over two-hundred light-years from Stornoway.

"Looks like they made their choice," Captain Delgado said. "The Imperium Council can't risk losing any more key systems, and we've already dealt them a massive blow today. They know that if we keep coming, we'll cripple their operations along a quarter of the Holt Line within days."

"Too bad at least one more of their systems will be in ruins by the time they get there and Admiral Janus's armada is done with them," Jackson said coldly.

"Indeed. We've also got more ships coming in from as far away as the frontier with the Canids to provide reinforcements once we unleash hell here."

Jackson nodded, a wave of adrenaline mixed with fear washing over him as he thought about what was to come next.

The Imperium had now redeployed nearly two-thirds of the sizable fleet in the Stornoway System, leaving only five hundred and eighty ships remaining. Unfortunately, it was still far from defenseless. The Insectoids were prepared to hold their crown jewel, having deployed more than a thousand weapons platforms and sensors in the system, ready to fight to the death.

Admiral Vincenze was staging an assault force that would arrive shortly, and Admirals Easton and Valentyen were on their way to meet up with them soon.

Jackson's heart beat faster as one of the probes grew closer to the Imperium lines. He let out a short breath as the data came in showing the vast defenses in their path, his chest tightening at the immensity of the task ahead of them.

If it worked, it could be the strike that would break the Imperium's back and turn the tide of the war.

And it was just hours away from beginning.

CHAPTER 13
ASSAULT

Hundreds of flashes of light appeared against the blackness of space as a fleet of seven hundred and fifty GCH warships dropped out of hyperspace in the Stornoway System. The flagship, the dreadnought *Vengeance*, commanded by Admiral Easton, held position while the rest of the ships quickly formed up into battle groups and the armada moved forward, approaching the Imperium defenses.

The Insectoid fleet remained in a defensive formation near the planet, staying well behind the lines of weapons platforms, ready to intercept any ships able to get through. The commander of the Imperium defenses held fast, knowing that the Shroud would force the enemy ships to close to dangerous ranges in order to target them through the sensor interference. He watched as they moved closer, confident that the defenses would hold.

Just then, dozens of Shroud generators went offline as the cloaked probes powered up and crashed into them, taking them out. Two dozen stealth ships decloaked seconds later as Captain Delgado gave the order, and they targeted more of the generators, the Shroud suddenly dropping over a vast area.

The GCH ships advanced, targeting the weapons platforms with long-range ion cannons and torpedoes. While ion blasts lost most of their charge from the extreme distance, they were still effective in reducing the weapons platforms' capabilities and disabling some of them entirely as the Fleet pressed forward, continuing to soften the enemy's defenses as they closed, taking advantage of their superior weapons range.

The lead ships in each formation, all Icarus class frigates, pulled away from their battle groups, taking point several dozen kilometers ahead. Each ship was crewed entirely by mechs, while an advanced holo-projector system maintained the appearance that they were a dreadnought seven times their size, barreling towards the enemy as they led the assault. The ships' incredibly powerful shields, along with multiple quantum cores to power them, convinced the Imperium sensors of the threat they posed as the ominous vessels quickly closed the distance.

As the battle groups approached the front line of weapons platforms, the Icarus frigates drew most of the enemy fire, allowing the rest of the ships to attack at will, decimating the defenses while taking minimal return fire.

Within minutes, the Fleet broke through the first line of weapons platforms, quickly pressing forward and engaging the second line.

The Insectoid commander tightened the blockade, cursing the humans, along with his own hubris. With the Shroud down, he knew that once their second line of defenses fell, they'd be quickly overrun and severely outgunned; the tables suddenly turned. Still, he could make them pay dearly and ordered his ships to hold the line at all costs, their duty to keep the enemy from reaching the surface no matter what.

The GCH Fleet closed on the second line of weapons platforms, launching a volley of gamma torpedoes to blind their sensors.

Admiral Easton ordered all ships to fire, then sent an encoded signal, and sixty more ships emerged from hyperspace several million kilometers behind the GCH formation.

"Blockbusters, the door is open. Proceed to target, maximum speed!" Admiral Easton called over the comm, his voice hard. "Good luck and Godspeed! Give 'em hell!" he added, eager to take the fight to the Imperium after responding to the attack in the Kuteria system and witnessing the destruction there firsthand just weeks ago.

The Blockbusters responded, each ship engaging its powerful engines and accelerating rapidly, spreading out for their runs. The Blockbusters' massive triangle-shaped bows protected their smaller aft sections while powerful forcefield generators created a barrier ahead of each ship, allowing it to take a massive amount of head-on punishment as it drove straight towards the enemy line. Each ship held room for up to seventy-five soldiers, along with fifteen suits of armor, and also carried a complement of a six-fighter craft, ready to deploy at a moment's notice.

The Blockbusters continued to accelerate, scanning for gaps in the enemy lines as the Fleet ahead of them broke through the last of the weapons platforms.

Jackson sat at the rear of the bridge of the *Katana*, along with Chief Henrick Johansen, Lieutenant Kelara Quentarus, and Admiral Valentyen. Farther back in the ship, in the deployment bay, sat thirty-five soldiers from GCH special ops, along with fifteen tech specialists and engineers, several suits of armor, and two squads of mechs. Each of the Blockbusters had a similar complement of either soldiers, mechs, or armored units as they rocketed forward, quickly gaining on the Fleet, just a few million kilometers ahead.

"Just sit tight, everyone," Captain Azraya Brighthawk said, turning to look over her shoulder with a smile. "This is the fun part!"

Jackson and Johansen both smiled nervously, while Quentarus and the admiral remained stone-faced, having been through these types of deployments before.

Despite their outward appearances, each knew that running a blockade was a dangerous business.

You either made it, or you didn't.

If your ship lost its forward shields or took too many hits, you were dead. And in this case, even if you made it, that was just the first danger. Then it was time to worry about surviving what came next.

Still, Jackson was happy to be back with his friends.

At least if I die today, we'll be together, he thought as the acceleration pinned him to his seat.

The admiral had tried several times to dissuade him from coming, his argument the same as before: that he was too valuable to lose and that the Confederation needed him if things went wrong. Jackson insisted that his experience with Ancient tech and unique abilities would give them the best chance at success, and in the end, the admiral acquiesced to his request to be part of the mission—but with the promise that he wouldn't take any unnecessary risks.

The soldiers on board the *Katana* were some of the best close-quarter combat experts in the Fleet, most of them handpicked by Quentarus herself. They, along with two other elite units on other ships, were the linchpin in the entire plan. All part of Admiral Valentyen's newly minted GCH Advanced Weapons and Tactical Operations Unit.

"Tactical, full power to shields, ready countermeasures. Engineering, stand by with auxiliary power. Ops, coordinate with our designated ships in the 5th battle group to clear the way. All right, people, this is what we do. Helm, take us in!" Captain Brighthawk ordered.

The *Katana* rapidly approached the rear of the GCH formation. A volley of shockwave torpedoes detonated just over a million kilometers directly ahead, hitting the enemy lines in a coordinated strike. The powerful directed waves of energy rushed forward, heavily damaging several ships in close proximity while pushing others back, opening a gap.

"There's our window. Helm, punch it!" the captain ordered. The ship initiated a micro-jump, disappearing into hyperspace for an instant, then emerging once more, thousands of kilometers ahead, its speed doubled.

The Blockbusters jumped again, reappearing seconds later, their speed rocketing them forward at incredible velocities and making them nearly impossible to target as they shot through the heavens like a bat out of hell.

More shockwave torpedoes detonated all along the Imperium lines, clearing a path as the Fleet battle groups moved quickly, pressing the attack while the Insectoid ships scrambled to close the gaps.

"Ops, hail our escort," Captain Brighthawk said. "Tell them to engage."

The ops officer sent a signal, and dozens of ships suddenly appeared, jumping out of hyperspace all along the forward lines, the assault force commanded by Admiral Vincenze. The escorts split into pairs and spread out ahead of the speeding *Katana* and its sister ships, laying down a barrage of covering fire while the Blockbusters rocketed past seconds later. The maneuver repeated all along the enemy lines as the rest of GCH Fleet hit the Insectoids with the full force of their assault.

The *Katana* was rocked by enemy fire as it approached the Insectoid line, the bugs knowing the threat the ships represented and throwing everything they had at them.

"Shields holding, Captain," the tactical officer reported. "They're firing blind, trying to throw up a screen of fire."

"Our gap is closing, ma'am!" the helm officer warned as a large Insectoid cruiser farther back in the Imperium formation blanketed the space ahead with heavy fire.

"Signal our heavy hitters to target that cruiser!" Captain Brighthawk called.

A moment later, two deadly beams of energy shot past the *Katana,* slamming into the broadside of the Imperium cruiser, the mass drivers from the *Vengeance* tearing through its shields and shredding holes in its hull, large plasma fires erupting from the gaping wounds. The enemy weapons fire ceased instantly as the crippled cruiser listed to one side, the *Katana* closing rapidly.

"Detecting heavy debris ahead from the flak and damage to the cruiser," the ops officer warned.

"Engineering, fire a grav-wave pulse on our current heading and clear our path. Tactical, stand by to pick off anything that's left over," the captain commanded.

The *Katana* approached the wreckage of the Insectoid cruiser, rocking as the remaining debris impacted the forcefields, and the gravity-wave pulse shot forward, clearing their path.

The officer at the helm chimed in, "We're through the blockade, Captain!"

"Good work, everyone," Captain Brighthawk said. "Ops, how many other ships made it through?"

"Fifty-one Blockbusters made it, Captain, but we lost six escorts, and a dozen more had to fall back and regroup with the Fleet."

The captain nodded gravely. Some ships were always lost, but fifty-one out of sixty was considered a very good day. "Signal the nearest escorts that made it and have them form up with us to provide cover," she said to the ops officer. "Tactical, any bugs on our tail?"

"No, ma'am, and our path to the planet is clear. Scans indicate that ground defenses are mobilizing, but I'm not detecting any more ships or weapons platforms in our way."

"Ops, signal the other ships to prepare their fighters for launch and alert our own pilots to stand by. Let our troops know that we'll be landing in a few minutes. How are you and your team doing, Admiral?" the captain asked, turning to face her guests.

"Just enjoying the ride, Captain," the admiral replied with a brief smile. "Thanks for the lift."

"Anytime, sir. My crew and I are always happy to serve."

"Slowing for atmospheric entry," the officer at the helm reported as the ship shook from the reverse thrust. "Deploying subspace anchors. Inertial dampeners to maximum."

The inside of the ship was bathed in a green light as the inertial-dampening field activated, protecting the crew from the intense deceleration. The *Katana* generated six spheres of subspace energy around the hull, bubbles that penetrated the fabric between normal space into subspace, creating a drag effect on the ship as it interacted with both layers simultaneously, slowing it rapidly for orbital insertion.

"Just hold on to your lunch for a few more minutes. We'll have you on the ground soon," the captain said, the strain from the intense gravity making it hard to speak despite the field compensating.

"Captain, I'm showing a large concentration of enemy troops and heavy defenses at our landing site. They don't appear to be deploying the way we'd hoped," the tactical officer reported.

"Hmm, tactical, have the remaining escorts form up with the fighters once we reach launch altitude. Helm, have the rest of our BBs pull back once we launch our fighters. Let's give them time to pound the hell out of those ground forces before we land."

"Yes, ma'am," the tactical officer said with a smile.

"Acknowledged," the officer at the helm replied.

The Blockbusters reached the stratosphere seconds later, further reducing speed as dozens of small fighters launched, forming into attack wings. Four of the escorts, much larger than the fighters, formed up in the center, opening fire as they approached the enemy ground positions moments later, strafing them with a powerful bombardment.

Two remaining escorts veered off with the Blockbusters, covering them in the event that any other surprises came up while they waited high above. After several minutes of watching on the viewscreen and circling two hundred kilometers away, the captain requested a status update.

The tactical officer responded a moment later. "We've lost twenty-eight fighters and one escort, but the enemy anti-aircraft defenses are completely down, Captain. The bugs are taking heavy losses now, and most of their armored units and defense turrets have been destroyed."

The captain gave the admiral a quick look. He nodded as she turned back to her crew. "Ops, signal our ships to land at their designated coordinates and begin the ground assault."

The rest of the Blockbusters broke off, heading for the designated landing zones while the *Katana* and the two other ships remained in formation with the two remaining escorts.

Minutes later, the Blockbusters landed, rapidly deploying their forces to launch an assault on the main entrance to the base of the mountain, while the remaining fighters and escorts continued to pound the enemy defenses.

Six fighters broke off, strafing the compound's main sensor array and crippling the Insectoids' ability to monitor the battle outside, then turned back and continued to support the main assault force.

"*Saber*, *Lance*, you're up," Captain Brighthawk said, opening a channel to the two Blockbusters in formation with them. The ships broke off, landing in a clearing near a valley at the far side of the mountain, twelve kilometers from the main entrance. Troops and armor deployed from the ships seconds later, quickly securing the area.

The *Katana* followed shortly after, surveying the scene before setting down beside the other ships to ensure the area was secure.

"Good hunting, Admiral," Captain Brighthawk said.

"Thank you, Captain. Get clear and stay safe. We may need a fast pickup."

"Copy that, sir."

The rear doors of the *Katana* opened, and the soldiers quickly filed out from the deployment bay, securing the clearing before splitting into three squads. Eight suits of armor lowered from the sides of the ship, forming up to provide cover while Jackson, Johansen, Quentarus, and the admiral exited a moment later.

The admiral activated his comm, moving towards a cluster of trees with the rest of the team in tow. "Squad leaders, report in."

"Alpha ready."

"Gamma ready."

"Delta ready."

"Copy that; push towards the auxiliary entrance. Gamma squad, take the left flank; Delta, the right. Alpha will follow up the center and cover the rear. Move out!" he barked, the teams quickly springing into action.

The soldiers on foot moved swiftly despite being heavily armed and carrying an array of weaponry, ready for nearly any situation. The side of the mountain grew closer as they moved through the cover of the forest, the armor on point followed by groups of soldiers, with the engineers and the admiral's command group bringing up the rear.

The squads each had a team of engineers equipped with advanced computing and technical capabilities as part of their tech-suit configuration, and each member carried a plasma rifle and pistol, ready to assist or defend themselves if necessary.

Johansen moved with his squad—Alpha—breathing heavily as he tried to keep up. They stopped at a cluster of trees, the chief clutching his rifle tightly and looking around nervously.

Quentarus stopped, looking back to check on him, noticing right away that something was wrong. She opened a private channel as she turned to face him. "Hen, you okay?" she asked.

"Just not used to this, LT. I'll be fine," he lied, hoping he could fake his way past his fears.

"Are you sure?"

"I'm good," he said unconvincingly, the anxiety in his voice betraying him.

"Just stay close to me and watch my back. I've got you."

He nodded, staying close as the formation moved again, making a direct line for the entrance on the side of the mountain just a few hundred meters ahead.

The squads moved quickly as the Blockbusters dusted off in the distance, throwing up a powerful wind which carried loose soil and leaves in all directions. Once off the ground, they fired their primary engines, the sound deafening even inside the suits, while the squads held their position once more, scanning ahead for any signs of enemy forces.

As the echo of the Blockbusters faded from his ears, Jackson could hear the fighting kilometers away near the main entrance.

The distance from the landing zone to the base of the mountain was only a few hundred meters further, but it felt longer as the squad moved, stopping to take cover every fifty meters or so before pushing forward again.

Moments later, they approached the wall of rock that formed the base of the mountain. The squads and armor took up a defensive position, while Johansen moved forward with a team of techs, quickly going to work and lowering the holo-projection that concealed the massive doors.

The admiral pulled up a live feed of the battle at the main entrance on his holo-display while Johansen's engineers continued working. Jackson watched the view from the tactical drones overhead showing the devastation. Insectoid body parts and shattered pieces of technology lay scattered over an area several kilometers wide. Craters nearly five meters deep scarred the landscape where the bombardment had struck. The Insectoids had put up a good fight, but against the firepower of the fighters and the escorts combined, they hadn't stood a chance.

"Looks like they've pulled back into the complex," the admiral said. "There's only a small contingent left outside, and our forces are mopping them up."

"Smart," Quentarus commented. "Forces us to fight in close quarters and takes away our air support as a factor. Even with the number killed outside, they still have God knows how many more lying in wait inside."

They watched as waves of GCH troops and mechs dropped the last of the Imperium soldiers defending the main entrance, then poured into the complex.

The base had been built with two auxiliary entrances. Scans showed that the Insectoids had discovered one of them, but the structure inside the mountain was vast, and the second entrance was well hidden, with cloaking technology concealing the passageway both inside and out. The hope was that they could enter through the hidden passage without the bugs knowing they were inside or behind their defensive lines until it was too late. If not, they faced being overrun before the main assault force could reach them. It was a risk, but time was of the essence if their plan was to succeed.

Quentarus turned, scanning the area, while watching over Johansen, Jackson, and the admiral, her assignment to protect her crew above all else.

The doors opened with a hiss a moment later, the outside air rushing into the complex.

"Nice work," the admiral said to Johansen and his team.

A dark ominous hallway stood before them, ten meters high and fifteen wide. Two soldiers stepped forward, opening large cases and tapping controls on their wrists. Hundreds of small spheres launched into the air, cloaking as they rose. The drones darted forward into the darkness, activating specially calibrated shields allowing them to pass through the advanced holo-projectors and force-fields that kept the side entrance hidden. They entered into the main complex and spread out, flowing silently into the corridors, mapping enemy positions and power signatures as they went.

"I didn't realize the corridors would be so big," Jackson commented as he stared into the blackness of the massive entrance, watching on the admiral's wrist holo-display as the map of the complex grew larger by the second. "It's a bit counterintuitive, isn't it? It lets them deploy larger assets inside, unlike most GCH bases, which have smaller corridors to prevent exactly that."

"When it became clear that the Imperium would keep trying to take Stornoway, the GCH decided to take a different approach with the base here and designed it this way both to allow for heavy suits of armor—such as Gate Keepers and Door Crashers—as well as to spread out any enemy advance if the complex ever came under attack," the admiral explained. "The idea was to allow our superior weapons to have more room to operate while keeping the combat at a distance where possible. The GCH Corps of Engineers carved over a dozen long, wide corridors like this one, interwoven with smaller ones, which are designed to be fallback positions and choke points, which can be used for defense or to limit the number of larger enemy units that can stream through at a time. There's also a number of barricades and a command center that is too small for the Imperium's heavy hitters to enter. These tactical positions are designed to hold off large contingents of enemy forces, with good lines of sight and dedicated firing positions. Unfortunately for us, we're coming at them from the wrong side this time. But once we take these positions, we'll have a good place to hold while our teams work," he said, pointing to several areas on the map.

Jackson nodded, recalling how the admiral explained that the Imperium had tried nearly thirty times to take the system before, failing each time except the last.

"The soldiers stationed here when the Imperium attacked at the start of the war gave the bugs one hell of a fight," the admiral continued. "It took the Insectoids four days to break through to the command center, and the reports that got out indicated that the men and women who died here made them pay for every millimeter of ground they took."

The Alpha, Gamma, and Delta squad leaders stood gathered around, each nodding at the admiral's sentiment. "A good death," one of them commented, knowing that the same thing could happen to them if things went south on this mission.

"There!" Johansen called, breaking the group from their thoughts and pointing to a heavily fortified area of the complex, the readings on the display spiking with power and radiation signatures. "It looks like they built a secondary power core. Scans show it's nearly twice the size of the original one, which powers the base itself. This has to be what we're looking for, sir."

The admiral studied the readings for a moment. "Looks like they fortified the entrance. Where is that?"

"It's in the main cargo bay. The scans show large power conduits that run from there in a straight shot across the complex to here." Johansen pointed to a smaller heavily fortified area.

"That's the main command center," the admiral said. "Any contact with our primary force yet?"

"Nothing yet, but the complex is vast. They may not have broken through the main defenses yet, or the probes simply may not have gotten that far," Johansen replied.

"How much resistance is there between here and the command center?"

"It looks pretty heavy, sir. At least three to four hundred enemy troops and several defensive checkpoints. The power core in the cargo bay, however, is much closer and has only about half of that. If we can break through, we might be able to interface with the Shroud controls from there."

The admiral considered for a moment, knowing that time was of the essence. Once the Imperium knew about the incursion in Stornoway, they would redeploy every ship possible within thousands of light-years to retake the system. If the Fleet could hold when the inevitable Insectoid reinforcements arrived, then they would have a good chance of completing their mission.

If they couldn't, then they would be forced to pull out or risk being trapped. And if that happened, they would have to hold until another group of GCH reinforcements could retake the system once more – something they all knew was likely a death sentence.

GCH Command had other ships already en route from across the Confederation, while Admiral Janus's armada and other smaller battle groups continued to stage hit-and-run attacks along the Holt Line in an attempt to limit the Imperium's response. But the admiral knew all too well that Stornoway was a prize they valued above all others, and with the risk of exposing the secrets of the Shroud of Darkness, he knew they would come at them with everything they had.

"All right, we push for the power core," the admiral finally said. "We move carefully, deploying snipers and drones where possible to hit them before they know we're there. Our goal is stealth for now. I don't want this whole damn place knowing we're here and coming down on top of us! Once we reach the cargo bay, we move hard and fast, hit them with everything we've got. We need to break through and get to the power core before they can reroute troops from elsewhere and come at us from behind. Once we take the core, we'll deploy to hold our position, while our engineers work to figure out their systems and attempt to take control. Questions?"

The group was silent. They all knew the jobs they had to do.

"Chief," the admiral said, looking to Johansen, "activate blackout protocol."

Johansen pressed a button on his holo-display, and the probes spreading throughout the complex activated a powerful jamming field, preventing the Insectoids from communicating with anything other than hardwired connections. "Blackout protocol active, sir. Our encrypted comm frequencies will still work, but only at a range of fifty meters unless we have a line of drones to relay the signal."

"Acknowledged. Gamma, take the lead. Delta, you're on support. Alpha will cover our backs as we reach each junction. You all know what to do. Let's move!"

CHAPTER 14
THE CORE

Forty minutes passed while the squads worked their way through the dark corridors of the sprawling complex, going as quickly as possible while still being cautious and maintaining stealth protocols.

Since the war began, the Insectoids had been busy, making considerable changes, forcing the squads to trust the route the probes mapped, rather than relying on the old schematics, and remain ever vigilant for traps or ambushes.

The hidden entrance brought them deep into the complex, behind several enemy checkpoints, allowed them to get the drop on the pockets of resistance they encountered using cloaked tactical drones and snipers to pick them off before they knew what hit them.

With the enemy comms jammed from the blackout protocol along with the cloaked probes scouting ahead and sonic dampeners to mask the sounds of the heavy armor, they had managed to remain undetected by the rest of the Insectoids as they moved closer to the core. The deeper they got, however, the greater the risk that if they were discovered, they could be overrun from multiple sides if the Imperium forces were able to get the word out.

Jackson stayed close to the admiral, flanked by Quentarus, with Johansen close behind. He'd also noticed the change in the chief since they'd first boarded the *Katana*. The dash through the enemy blockade and walking into what could easily become a massacre had clearly rattled his friend, along with several of the other engineers who rarely, if ever, saw combat.

They were nearly to the cargo bay when the Gamma squad approached a T intersection, stopping while the wave of drones scouted the corridors ahead of them, sending back an alert.

"Scans show something's off, sir," Johansen said, studying the readings and having Foxy check the sensor data again. "I can't say for certain what it is, but there's something there for sure in the corridor to the right. The one that leads towards the cargo bay."

"All right, let's be cautious. Commander Johnston, send in a mech to check it out," the admiral said over the comm to the leader of Gamma squad. "Delta and Alpha squad leaders, hold back to give them some space, but be prepared to support them if needed."

Johnston signaled to his team, and a lone Talon stepped forward, approaching the intersection, rifle ready. The mech stood just over two and a half meters tall, scanning the area and moving steadily forward. An advanced combat model, it was quick and agile, with personal shields and an array of weapons, allowing it to scout ahead and respond in force if necessary.

Jackson watched the feeds from the nearby drones showing the Talon moving ahead in the long corridor towards the intersection.

“All clear,” the Talon reported in a nearly humanoid voice after sweeping the area.

“Copy,” Commander Johnston replied. “There’s still something weird, though, on the scans.”

“Commander, send in a team, shields and scanners to maximum. Whatever it is may only react to bio-signs. Tell your team to use extreme caution,” the admiral said.

“We’re on it, sir,” Johnston said, signaling to his team. A moment later, one of the huge heavily armored Door Crashers came around the corner at the T intersection, stopping just behind the mech. The two spread out, dozens of probes flanking them and scanning ahead as they continued forward, four soldiers in heavy tactical gear following them ten meters back.

Another group of soldiers moved to the intersection, covering the long, dark corridor to the left, the scans there still showing it was clear.

The squad moved forward down the right tunnel with practiced precision, each soldier knowing their role, sweeping every grate, alcove, and air duct both visually and with their sensors while keeping their weapons ready.

As they made their way closer to the next junction, the Door Crasher checked the probes before stepping out, the feed jumping several times.

“What the hell?” the officer, Ensign Landry, said.

“What is it?” a nearby lieutenant called, signaling the squad behind the Talon and Door Crasher to hold position.

“Something’s wrong with the probe’s feed, sir. Scans are showing some kind of interference.”

“I’ll call it in,” the lieutenant said, opening comms to his squad leader and the admiral. “Sir, it looks like we’re getting some interference just ahead.”

"Hold your position, Lieutenant. Let's proceed with caution. Landry, take your armor and the Talon farther ahead to check it out, full power to forward shields," Commander Johnston said while the admiral brought up the feed from the probes on his display.

"Roger that, sir," Landry replied.

A moment later, the Door Crasher stepped forward around the corner, following half a dozen meters behind the Talon, each taking slow, measured steps.

"The corridor appears to be clear, sir," Landry reported. "It looks like one of our old defense points that's been cleared out. The readings might be from the power conduits that used to power the defenses here. There's another bend just ahead. This looks like one of the choke points. The corridors are much smaller here. I'm proceeding forward."

"Copy that," Commander Johnston replied, signaling the rest of the team to follow, but stay well behind the towering armor. "We'll move up to provide support if you need it, but stay twenty meters back," he said, motioning to the rest of Gamma squad to move out.

The Talon approached the next junction, the Door Crasher close behind, weapons ready. The mech stepped out, peering around the corner into another larger corridor and sweeping with its rifle. Landry followed, watching the scans from the probes showing that the interference was slowly subsiding.

"All clear," he called. Then, suddenly, weapons ports hidden in the walls activated, bombarding the armor from all sides with a deadly assault of plasma fire.

The Talon dodged the first few volleys, the mech moving rapidly and returning fire as it managed to stay just ahead of the blasts for a few seconds. More weapons ports revealed themselves, the torrent of fire cutting it down a moment later in a cross fire while soldiers farther back returned fire, attempting to take out the weapons ports.

"I'm taking heavy fire! Fall ba—"

Landry's transmission ended abruptly as the powerful weapons breached the shields and penetrated the armor of the Door Crasher, the concentrated fire peppering it with hundreds of bursts in a matter of seconds.

The soldiers nearby scattered as the automated systems turned on them, the smoldering wreck of armor going down hard, the weapons ports cutting them down like blades of grass.

The rest of Gamma squad, farther down the corridor, fell back, each of them looking around at the walls, uncertain if they were about to open and deliver the same fate as befell their comrades.

"Shit!" Johansen yelled, quickly pushing aside the fear that had been lingering in his mind and pulling himself together, running through the readings to look for a weakness in the defenses.

"Sir," Commander Johnston called to the admiral over comms, "I've got six units down! We need some help up here to get past this junction."

"Understood," the admiral replied, signaling to Johansen, who was studying the display projected from his wrist, relaying the signal from one of the cloaked probes that survived the assault.

"Sir, I've got something. Chambers, Suzuki, launch a few more cloaked probes. Have them run EM scans, full spectrum."

The two engineers moved forward, each launching their own cloaked drones and running extensive scans while Johansen watched the results appear on his display. "Damn, that's why the probes' visual signals were disrupted. There's a carefully crafted holographic image along with a dampening field coming from within the walls, hiding the weapons ports," he explained, grudgingly impressed with the technical design while his mind worked to find a solution. "Looks like they installed dampeners for nearly thirty meters to make it look like a sensor anomaly, so we would dismiss it and move forward right into their trap. Exactly like we did," he said, shaking his head in frustration. "Chambers, can you confirm these readings?"

"Confirmed, sir," Chambers replied. "Are you thinking it's a polarity inversion?"

"Exactly," Johansen replied. "You and Suzuki move your drones to the center of each wall. " Johansen turned to look at the admiral. "The drones have mapped out the locations of each of the main power matrices, but we'll only be able to take the dampening field and the shields down for a few seconds before they adapt."

"What do you need, Chief?"

"I need the closest three Sentinels to charge out into the junction on my signal and target each of the ports with heavy fire. I've got targeting solutions for the two power matrices and each of the weapon clusters mapped. All they have to do is not miss," Johansen said, realizing that he was risking their lives if his calculations were off.

"All right, Gamma leader, ready your three best Sentinel shooters and prepare to execute the chief's plan," the admiral said. "Talons two through ten, follow and provide additional supporting fire.

"Copy that, sir," Johnston replied. "Edwards, Valasic, Barrie, you're up. Don't stop shooting till every last weapons port is down. Talons, follow their lead. Ready on the chief's mark."

Johansen brought up the control to activate the polarity inversion, the three Sentinels and nine mechs standing ready at the front of the company, metal ready to move on a moment's notice. "In five, four, three, two, one, *now*!" Johansen called, activating a field from each of the drones that created a burst of oppositely charged electromagnetic energy, disrupting the shield and dampening units concealing the weapons ports, while interfering with the power flow momentarily.

The Sentinels darted out into the open, firing as they moved, their targeting systems picking off the concealed enemy weapons and power matrices before the scrambled sensors could lock on and return fire. The group of Talons followed, the agile mechs moving into flanking positions to support the heavy suits and laying down a barrage of fire.

Seconds passed, the sounds of battle echoing throughout the corridor, thick smoke filling the air.

A few blasts of return fire could be seen through the haze as they impacted the Sentinels' shields, glowing arcs of energy spreading out and lighting up like distant lightning strikes at night.

Several seconds later, the battle ended as quickly as it began.

"All enemy targets destroyed," one of the Sentinel pilots called over the comm.

"Confirmed," a second chimed in.

"Good work, people," the admiral said, staring at the destruction all around the armor and Talons, knowing they didn't have time to properly deal with the fallen soldiers and that they had to keep moving. "Now we know what to look out for. Talons, move our fallen off to the side. Let's keep pushing ahead and honor our dead by getting the job done."

Ten minutes later, the squads reached the final blockade, having lost seven more Talons, two more soldiers, and one Sentinel in the process. Several other officers had also suffered minor wounds but remained with their squads, rather than being left behind and risk being overrun.

The forward scouts sent another cluster of cloaked drones to venture around the corner towards the final blockade protecting the power core. Jackson, Quentarus, and Johansen stood with the admiral, watching as the enemy defenses came into view and several Insectoid forces appeared on the display, skittering behind the large barriers, the sounds of battle having reached them while they stood ready to defend their positions.

Commanders Johnston, Lydan, and Ellis and squad leaders of Gamma, Delta, and Alpha, respectively, joined the admiral and his team a moment later, the group huddling to devise an attack strategy while studying the scans in detail.

The huge cargo bay lay at the end of a long, wide corridor, which was protected with several staggered rows of fortified positions on both sides, ranging in height from lower at the front to higher at the back. Automated turrets in the ceiling provided heavy weapons fire, while the barricades gave the enemy troops long clear lines of sight, making any assault a dangerous endeavor.

After several moments of discussion, the admiral decided on a plan, giving the order to attack.

The squads quickly moved into formation, their commanders briefing each of them as to their roles. A minute later, two Door Crashers rounded the corner, each carrying a large energy shield that created a protective barrier ahead of them, taking the lead as they began their charge. Four more Door Crashers fell into formation directly behind them, all of their shields linking to provide maximum protection for the lead pair. The heavy armor thundered forward, a massive onslaught of Insectoid fire coming at them in return.

The Door Crashers continued unabated, roaring towards the Insectoid lines while cloaked tactical drones activated, attacking the enemy from behind and creating a break in the fire aside from the automated overhead cannons.

Dozens of Imperium soldiers dropped to the ground as the drones swept the lines of the barricade, striking with deadly precision.

The reprieve was all the Door Crashers needed.

Despite their size, the bulky armor was surprisingly quick, propelled by swift legs and boosted by thrusters, providing rapid acceleration. As they charged, the six suits rotated formation; the two at the front moved out to either side while the next two in line increased their speed, taking up the center position, helping to distribute the damage and wear on their shields.

The enemy fire intensified once more as the last of the tactical drones went offline, but it was too late.

Seconds later, the Door Crashers bridged the distance, reaching the barricade, where they began to smash and batter the enemy defenses without mercy. The lead two suits, assisted by their thrusters, leapt for the overhead turrets. Several concentrated bursts of point-blank fire hit the first armor, causing heavy damage, and it fell to the floor, a smoldering hole in its chest. The second, however, reached its turret, grabbing it with two huge powerful hands and ripping it from its mount. The armor landed on the ground and threw it at the second turret, which was already turning to target it.

The rest of the Door Crashers moved quickly, picking up the debris and using it as devastating weapons, crushing enemy troops within range before finally throwing it towards the enemy lines. The heavy metal hit the solid barricade, echoing throughout the corridor, crushing several troops in the process.

Less than twenty seconds after the Door Crashers reached the barricade, a dozen Sentinels and fifty Talons were on the move behind them, providing covering fire and taking out dozens of other enemy targets while they closed.

Moments later, the last remaining Insectoid troops were down, smoke filling the area.

The Talons shouldered their rifles, then got to work dragging the bodies of the fallen Insectoids away from the barricades and out along the corridor, off to the sides. The rest of the squads arrived shortly after, Gamma and Delta taking up positions along the Insectoid barricades to hold their position, while several teams of engineers attempted to open the doors to the cargo bay, with Alpha covering them.

"Status?" the admiral asked.

"All enemy combatants neutralized," Commander Lydan said.

"The Door Crashers are pretty banged up and took a heavy pounding," Johnston added. "Only one of the units will be of any use for another assault. The others can still provide some defense and close-quarter support, but that run took a toll, and we lost O'Neil, sir."

"Understood," the admiral replied, keeping his voice level. "Chief?"

"We're on it, sir. We should have the doors open in a minute. Two at most."

"Any life signs beyond?" Commander Ellis asked over the comm, his team ready to respond once the doors were open.

"Negative, but our scans can't penetrate the bulkhead; it's too thick," Johansen replied.

"Be ready for anything," the admiral cautioned. "Once the door is open, I want another wave of tactical drones to sweep the room and eliminate any threats."

"Copy that, sir," Commander Ellis replied, nodding to several of his drone techs to be ready to deploy.

A moment later, the huge doors slid open, revealing the room beyond: a massive space the size of a hangar bay. Cloaked tactical drones flooded into the room, set to search-and-destroy mode, the dark ominous space appearing in more detail as their scans relayed information back.

A moment later, Alpha squad followed, taking up defensive positions and sweeping the vast space with their rifles, then checking the smaller alcoves and the spaces between equipment.

The engineers launched half a dozen spheres, which quickly filled the room with light and began mapping the cavernous space for access panels, power conduits, and radiation signatures while documenting the technology and locating points of entry or exit. After several tense moments of waiting with no enemy response, the tactical drones completed their sweep.

"Admiral," Commander Ellis called over the comm, "the room is secure."

"Scans show three other entry points on the far side of the room, Admiral," Johansen offered, pulling up the data on his display.

"Sentinels, deploy and cover those entry points. Alpha squad, back them up," Admiral Valentyen said.

Three suits of armor thundered across the room a second later, with several dozen soldiers and Talons in tow. "Johansen, deploy some engineers to weld those doors shut and see if we can barricade them."

"On it, sir."

Jackson, Johansen, Quentarus, and the admiral entered the room a moment later, accompanied by another group of Johansen's best engineers. As they stepped inside, the spectacle of the room spread out before them.

At the center stood the immense power core, at least six stories high and twenty meters wide, humming with raw energy. The core was shaped like a giant dome with dozens of interface panels spread out along it. A larger display in the center showed the power readings, the quantum fusion core generating massive amounts of energy.

Johansen activated the holo-display on his wrist, studying the scans and dividing the engineers into teams to investigate several access controls and other systems that the probes had identified. He took two engineers, quickly moving to the main control station, with Jackson, Quentarus, and the admiral close behind.

Once they reached the station, Jackson took up a defensive position, while the admiral and Quentarus huddled and checked in on the progress of the main assault force.

"How are we doing, sir?" Jackson asked over his shoulder.

"The probes have mapped most of the complex and made contact with our primary attack force that entered through the main entrance. They've broken through the defenses inside and appear to have divided up into smaller units to search and destroy enemy positions throughout the base."

"So far, so good," Johansen said absentmindedly, listening in on the conversation while he worked.

"Don't get overconfident, Chief," Quentarus said pointedly. "It looks like a large number of enemy troops have congregated at the command center and are setting up in the corridors with staggered firing positions and ambush points. Scans show at least ten thousand life signs!"

Johansen swallowed hard at the thought of ten thousand Insectoids bearing down on them, turning back to his work while the admiral contacted several of the unit commanders from the main force, directing them to continue their sweep and instructing a group of several dozen soldiers to meet them at the cargo bay to reinforce their position.

Jackson watched their backs while Bits brought up reports from the primary battle group. Despite taking the entrance and breaking the enemy lines, they'd sustained significant losses and were down to just over sixty percent strength from the initial force of forty-three hundred troops, mechs, and suits of armor that had landed. Fortunately, the majority of the forces that were lost had been mostly mechs, and the loss of humanoid life had been limited thus far to a hundred and eighty-six soldiers. Still, he knew they'd need everything they had to take the command center or repel an enemy force of that size if the bugs decided to go on the offensive, hoping that the blackout protocol was doing its job and limiting their sensors and ability to communicate.

After discussing it with the other commanders, the admiral ordered the bulk of the primary force to move forward and take the command center under the command of Captain Conroy, ensuring that the enemy stayed holed up there rather than risk them counterattacking with the GCH forces divided. While the main battle group moved to the command center, a few smaller, specialized units continued to search the rest of the complex, rooting out the remaining pockets of Insectoids.

The squads held their positions at the core for the next hour while Johansen and his engineers worked. Several small forces of enemy troops attempted to retake their position but were easily repelled or wiped out by Gamma and Delta squads as they held the barricades with the new reinforcements. Shortly after the last of the fighting died down, the admiral approached Johansen for an update. "What have you got, Chief?"

"We've figured out the main power control systems, Admiral," Johansen responded. "We should be able to cut off power to most of the remaining enemy defenses. However, we'd like to leave the Shroud operational. I only have limited access from here, but it's like nothing I've ever seen before, and we need it powered up to study it properly."

"Do it," the admiral replied decisively.

"One more thing, sir. It appears that the main controls and the technology that generate the Shroud are housed in a separate area, beyond the main command center. My team has confirmed that massive amounts of power are being routed to a large chamber in that section of the base. My best guess is that it's something the Insectoids created, digging deeper inside the mountain to create a new chamber, as there's nothing there on the original schematics. Unfortunately, the command center appears to be the only way to access it, and we can't learn as much from here about the Shroud as we'd hoped. I did, however, find something interesting: The technology in this power core is not Imperium tech; it appears to be Ularan, sir!"

"Ularan? How the hell would the bugs have gotten hold of something like that?" the admiral asked, knowing that it was unlikely that the Imperium would have attacked the Ularans and taken one of their systems without the GCH knowing about it.

"I don't know, sir," Johansen said. "Perhaps they were able to capture a Ularan ship and reverse engineer its technology, or maybe they're trading with them. I can't tell you how they got it, but I can say for certain that the technology is Ularan in origin and highly advanced."

"Interesting," the admiral said, considering for a moment. "All right, we've got several large combat groups converging on the main command center as we speak, and it appears that we'll have to take it rather than just bottle up the enemy there. Leave who you need here to continue the analysis. I'll have Gamma and Delta squads remain to cover them. We'll bring the rest of the engineers and Alpha squad with us to the command center. Hopefully the main battle group will be able to break through by the time we get there."

"Yes, sir," Johansen said, quickly reassigning his teams, leaving nine engineers at the power core to continue to learn what they could. He instructed them to keep the power on at all costs to ensure that his team could study the Shroud once they reached the room beyond the command center. "Chambers, you're in command of the team here. Delta and Gamma squads will watch your backs. Be sure to listen to them. If they can't hold, then your orders are to blow the core. Work with the squad demolition techs to place the charges at key areas to make sure the job is done right. Then haul ass for the far side of the bay and take cover behind the rows of storage crates there and power up the portable force-fields. You don't need the core to go critical; you just need to damage it enough that it will shut down and cripple its ability to power the Shroud. That should minimize the blast radius. Hopefully it won't come to that though."

"Copy that, Chief. We won't let you down," Chambers said.

Johansen put his hand on his engineer's shoulder. "I know you won't," he said, the thought hitting him that he was possibly leaving these people here to die, the burden of command weighing heavily on him. "If you have to blow the core, just lie low and hide afterwards. The bugs will have bigger problems if that happens, so hunker down and wait for help."

"Got it."

"All right, the rest of you with me," Johansen said, the remaining thirty-six engineers falling into line with Alpha squad a moment later and proceeding out of the cargo bay, while Gamma and Delta dug in to hold the area.

As Alpha squad moved out, Jackson turned, looking behind while the troops took up the positions formerly occupied by the Insectoids, hoping he'd see them again.

Little did he know, the battle had just begun.

CHAPTER 15
FIGHT OR FLIGHT

Twenty-five minutes later, Alpha squad moved through the vast complex of tunnels and corridors, making their way towards the command center. The main force of just over two thousand five hundred GCH troops, mechs, and armor had arrived ahead of them and had hit the enemy positions hard, the sounds of the battle echoing throughout the fortress.

They arrived at a staging area near the long, wide corridor that led to the command center, the sounds of fighting diminishing to just small pockets of controlled fire as they approached. As they rounded the corner into the huge corridor leading to the command center, the devastation spread out before them. Hundreds of shattered mechs littered the path ahead, along with the thousands of bodies of fallen Insectoids and suits of heavy armor, collapsed to the floor in ruins. The rest of the assault force was past the barricades and already inside the command center, clearing out the last pockets of resistance.

Quentarus wasted no time, taking point and signaling for five other special-ops soldiers to form up and follow her as she scouted a path through the chaos and destruction. The rest of the squad quickly fell into line, carefully picking their way through the debris, the aftermath of the battle brutal and costly for both sides.

Quentarus moved carefully, her trained eyes methodically scanning the wreckage while her tactical mind pieced together the engagement as it unfolded. The distance to the barricades was still several hundred meters away, but despite the corridor being thirty-five meters wide, it was difficult in places to find an unobstructed route forward through the endless sea of bodies and debris.

She passed by the remains of a fallen Sentinel, rounding the crushed frame, then pausing for a moment as the first of the humanoid bodies appeared. The rest of the squad caught up seconds later, many of them turning away as the remains of their fallen comrades stretched out across the landscape ahead.

Thousands of small centipede-like creatures littered the floor, a wave of enemy troops that likely came in low while the other Insectoid forces behind the barricades picked off the soldiers, mechs, and armor as they were forced to deal with the up-close threat.

Quentarus pressed through the maze of fallen bodies, taking in the scene while she looked downfield towards the barricades, noticing the shattered remains of several heavy suits of armor ahead. She took a step forward, the floor slick with fresh blood, moving carefully to maintain her balance.

"Helo, run a scan for survivors," she whispered, keeping her comm off.

Outlines of broken bodies appeared in her HUD as Helo swept the area while she continued to press forward, her AI searching for any signs of life. She focused her mind, pushing down the anger she felt as the bio-signs showed only cold, lifeless husks. It was a sight she'd tragically grown too accustomed to, but one which never failed to elicit a powerful emotional response despite years of training and combat experience.

She pressed on, making her way towards the remains of several heavy suits of armor, which lay among the devastation, like black-and-gray metal islands in a sea of red. She stopped to examine a hole cut clean through the thick armor of a Devastator, noticing another in a nearby Door Crasher with the same wounds.

"Looks like heavy weapons fire, sir," she said over comms. "An IL-90 if I'm not mistaken. The bugs must have taken some of the base's outer defenses and moved them in here as a last resort. Our people never stood a chance against that kind of firepower."

"Let's keep moving," the admiral replied calmly, knowing they needed to reach the command center as quickly as possible.

"Roger that," she replied, moving on from the fallen armor and taking the lead once more.

As she approached the barricades, a sea of Insectoid bodies appeared in vast numbers, too many to count. The troops stationed there were some of their best: Fire Ants, Hydrax, Arachnids, Wrenthari, and Scorpions, along with several other species which couldn't be easily identified. Many of them were sizable, requiring considerable force to take down.

As she moved beyond the final barricade, the door to the command center came into view.

"Life signs detected ahead," Helo said in her helmet.

She froze, raising her arm with her fist tight. The squad behind her reacted immediately, taking cover while she signaled for a group of Talons to move ahead. Once in formation, she led the way, her AI scanning ahead as they approached the entrance.

She peered around the corner. A hallway seven meters long bridged the gap from the massive corridor to the command center. The long, wide room with a low ceiling spread out as she moved inside, the space littered with corpses, both humanoid and Insectoid. A group of about fifty GCH soldiers, along with two battered Sentinels, stood in a loose formation near the middle of the command center.

"This is Alpha squad to the survivors in the command center; do you copy?" she asked over comms.

The soldiers at the far end of the room twitched slightly at her voice in their helmets, turning and raising their weapons on instinct, snapping them out of their collective shell shock momentarily.

"Copy, Alpha," a woman replied, her voice hollow as she signaled the group to lower their weapons.

Quentarus rounded the corner into the command center, the Talons with her breaking off and sweeping the room while she proceeded towards the group ahead. "Admiral Valentyen is coming up now, and he'll want a full report, Commander..." She looked down at the name bar on the soldier's suit. "Winters..." she said, stopping short, her heart skipping a beat.

"Quentarus?" Winters said, reading her name bar in return, each woman giving the other a nod, surprised to see one another and standing in silence while the rest of the squad approached the command center.

The admiral called out orders as they passed the barricades, splitting the squad into teams and sending the medics to the command center to check for survivors and to tend to the wounded, while the rest of Alpha squad stayed back to take up defensive positions.

The Talons filed out of the command center after completing their sweep and began working to clear the bodies from the barricades.

Jackson and Johansen entered the command center just behind the admiral, hurrying past the clusters of soldiers to the far end of the room to examine the door to the chamber beyond. Jackson stood back while Johansen worked, examining the entrance, the secrets of the Shroud suddenly so close that it filled them both with a nervous excitement.

The horrors of the previous room held fast in Jackson's mind, the inescapable thought that ten thousand Imperium soldiers had just given their lives to protect what was now nearly within their reach. The feeling that the fate of the war was within their grasp was suddenly dampened by the knowledge that the enemy would do *everything* within their power to get back control, no matter the cost.

He took a slow, deep breath. The thought was a sobering one, sending a chill down his spine.

Farther back, the admiral moved to where Quentarus stood near Winters and a group of officers, while many other soldiers sat with their heads in their hands or stared at the walls, lost in thought after the intense battle. Others stood with their helmets retracted, blood in their hair and on their faces, and at least a dozen more wounded lay near the side of the room.

The admiral lowered his own helmet, nodding to each group as he passed, several officers moving to stand or salute. "As you were," he said softly. "Who's in command here?"

"I am, sir," the officer standing next to Quentarus responded shakily, stepping forward, retracting her helmet. "Commander Winters."

"I'm sorry that you all had to fight through such hell to break this position, Commander. Can you tell me what happened here?"

"I'll tell you what I can, sir, but it was chaos, so it's hard to say exactly. My battle group approached the main corridor from the south, forming up with three other groups led by Captain Conroy. His scouts had sent in dozens of drones, but the bugs had a powerful EM field ready for them. As the drones moved forward, they literally just fell out of the air, leaving us mostly blind to their defensive capabilities. The captain sent out another group of drones, keeping them farther back and tasking them to run full-spectrum scans. He knew that the EM field would block most of it, but he figured some intel was better than nothing. We were able to get a partial scan, enough to form a rudimentary battle plan. From there, he followed standard combat protocols, sending in a wave of remote-piloted Door Crashers to break the enemy lines. I was with his command group watching on a holo-display," she said, brushing a strand of hair from her face, the blood on her fingers leaving a small streak along her forehead in its wake.

"The Door Crashers rounded the corner, nine of them in a wide formation, full shields forward and linked. Two Devastators followed, ready to unleash the might of their arsenals once the path was cleared. They began their charge, gaining ground quickly as they thundered down the corridor. The bugs reacted immediately, hitting them hard but exposing their positions to our snipers while the DCs' shields took a pounding. They were halfway to the barricades when suddenly they were hit with heavy weapons fire. I'm not sure what the hell it was, but it tore through them like they were made of paper, sir. After the first few fell, the others scrambled, but they quickly picked off the rest in a matter of seconds. The Devastators got off some good offensive strikes, letting loose with all they had before they were taken out, helping to soften up the enemy, at least, but we lost eleven suits of heavy armor in just under two minutes."

"Likely the IL-90s we passed, sir, heavy antiaircraft plasma cannons," Quentarus interjected. "Looks like they affixed portable power generators to them, which is why they were still online even after our team in the core cut the power to the rest of the base's internal defenses."

Winters nodded. "Our scans hadn't detected them…a dampening field or something. I… I'm not sure, but they ripped the armor to shreds. The captain quickly changed tactics, sending in three two-person teams in stealth suits with bunker-buster rockets. Once in place, five of our Sentinels entered the corridor to provide covering fire while the stealth units decloaked and fired. The bunker busters hit the 'sects hard, the destruction creating a smoke screen. Captain Conroy quickly mobilized the mech battalion to move in, and they charged forward. They were just past the wreckage of the armor when the big guns, the IL-90s, resumed fire, taking out pockets of them at a time. The bugs were also ready for them with some kind of ion weapon, picking them off in droves. Still, the mechs did their job, pressing the attack and thinning their numbers somewhat.

"In the smoke and chaos, the bugs sent a massive wave of smaller creatures forward. They waited in huge numbers in the debris, lying in ambush. From what we could tell, though, about a hundred or so of our mechs made it through, close enough that the heavy fire couldn't target them. They then hit the enemy positions hard, taking several of them out and disrupting their lines as they engaged their forces at the first and second barricades. Unfortunately, there just weren't enough of them, and the bugs' resistance was too heavy, but they weakened their forward lines and took down the heavy guns enough to give us a window.

"Captain Conroy had sixteen more bunker-buster rockets on point, and this time it was enough to knock out a large portion of their defenses. Once they were down, he ordered twenty Sentinels, along with our remaining Devastators, to engage. They quickly took the fight to the enemy lines. But the bugs had a lot of troops entrenched to hold the barricades, including some heavy hitters like Lacartan Arachnids and some species of – I don't know what the hell they were – huge armored centipedes or pill bug things or something. They took on the Sentinels pretty well at close range, keeping them occupied while the Arachnids' razor-sharp legs cut through the weak points in their armor, and the centipedes, or whatever they were, constricted around them, crushing them.

"With their defenses engaged, the captain ordered the rest of us to move with our few remaining Sentinels and Door Crashers leading the way. That's when we ran into the smaller bugs waiting in hiding. They got the drop on us in the smoke and chaos and… I don't know how many people we lost, but a lot," she said, shaking her head slowly as the memory faded.

"Once we cleared our way through, I took a squad with me along the right side, and we ran like hell. There wasn't much fire at first, and, as I'm sure you saw when you came through, there was a lot of wreckage from the mechs and heavy armor that provided some initial cover. The enemy fire increased as we grew closer, but it was pretty random. Their lines were in chaos, still attempting to repel our heavy armor. Then the frag grenades came. Hundreds of them. Likely an automated defense. We lost over three hundred soldiers in a matter of seconds.

"I was pretty close to one when they went off. Knocked me down for a minute and shell shocked me before I recovered and got back into the fight. By the time I got there, most of the Sentinels were down. I could hear a few of the pilots screaming from their broken shells, crushed and…mangled inside," she said, a tear escaping her eye as the sounds echoed in her mind. "All of that happened in a matter of twenty or thirty minutes. Over seventeen hundred dead on our side and thousands on theirs. I… I have no idea how many. I've been in some intense battles, Admiral, but nothing like this…" she said, trailing off, shaking her head in disbelief.

Jackson turned, listening from across the room while the commander recounted what happened. He recalled the destruction they'd passed in the corridor, now knowing why there were so few remaining from the force of over twenty-five hundred mechs, soldiers, and armor.

"It's all right, Commander, take a moment," the admiral said gently, placing a hand on her shoulder. He had seen more than his fair share of combat and had been where she was right now more times than he wished to remember.

Winters turned her head, wiping one eye, a small patch of dried blood visible on her temple, near her hairline. As her side profile became clear, Jackson's heart skipped a beat, his stomach falling in his chest.

Amy.

She looked exactly like his wife, Amy.

He stood, staring at her in stunned disbelief, his mind reeling, a feeling as though he couldn't breathe washing over him.

Winters turned back, nodding at the admiral, appreciative of the moment he gave her while she composed herself, then continued. "From there, we just concentrated our fire on the enemy troops. Most of the centipede things were easier pickings for us, and our flamethrowers made short work of them. The Arachnids, however, were a damned nightmare. They hit us from all sides, dropping down from the shadows above. Must have had another dampening field, as our sensors didn't see them at all until they were right on top of us.

"I had my unit pull back, knowing that if we tried to engage them up close, we'd be done for. We filed into one of the channels between barricades and made our stand there. As we held them back, waves of Ants and a few dozen Scorpions filed out of another side pocket between the last barrier and the back wall of the tunnel, some hidden space for their reserve troops, likely the ones in command, based on the species. They nearly overwhelmed us. Nearly turned the tide, routing our forces and taking out at least another couple hundred of us, before we knew what hit us. It was a bloodbath, sir.

"We'd have been dead if it wasn't for these guys here," she said, gesturing to the two battered Sentinels behind her. "They were part of one of the hunter-killer crews sweeping the rest of the complex. After completing their area sweep, they heard the call for reinforcements and came in hot, ten Sentinels rushing forward with weapons blazing, breaking the enemy press and giving us time to reorganize and counterattack.

"I can't say exactly what happened next. It was…a few minutes, maybe more, of intense, close-quarters combat. Honestly, I don't know how we did it. I guess we were all just fighting for our lives. In the end, we finally broke through the last of their defenses, taking the barricades and finishing off any of their wounded troops. After that, the captain arrived with a small group of reinforcements and engineers. The techs went to work while he reorganized the survivors, and within a few minutes, they were able to open the doors to the command center.

"A hundred and eighty-three of us, including the captain, entered this room." Winters looked around the command center. Rows of consoles lined the middle, while smaller alcoves dotted the walls along the sides, housing substations and storage and providing defensive firing positions. The bodies of GCH soldiers and Insectoids lay scattered, scorch marks visible everywhere from the intense combat. "We're all that's left," she said solemnly, her eyes dropping to the floor as she let out a breath.

"You did well, Commander," the admiral said. "You all did," he said, addressing the rest of the group of survivors. "Get some rest. We'll secure the area, and the medics will attend to you all momentarily."

"Yes, sir," Winters replied. "Thank you, sir."

The admiral gave her a nod, then moved off with Quentarus to speak with Johansen, who was still working on a way to open the doors to the next room. After checking in, they headed back towards the barricades to confer with the Alpha squad leader.

Winters walked over to a nearby console, retrieving her rifle from where it had been leaning, the weapon having overheated as the battle ended. She turned back to see

Jackson staring at her intensely from a few meters away, freezing her for a moment as she met his eyes. "Can I help you, sir?" she asked.

"I..." Jackson struggled to find the words, still unable to believe what he was seeing. She looked and sounded like Amy. Even her mannerisms were hers. "Uh...sorry, I—"

"Wait...do I know you from somewhere?" she asked, a spark of recollection hitting her.

Jackson and Winters both stood for a moment, locked in each other's gaze. Just as Jackson searched to find the words, an explosion shattered the moment.

"We've got incoming!" came a call from outside the door to the command center as several more explosions echoed through the hallway along with the sound of weapons fire.

"It's okay," the admiral called, addressing the room, everyone clearly on edge. "There's a small force out there, nothing Alpha can't handle. But more will come, and we may not be able to hold off the next waves, so we need to work quickly."

The admiral approached where Jackson and Winters stood just a few meters apart from one another, Quentarus flanking him.

Jackson looked at the admiral, nodding towards the hallway back to the barricades. "Sir, I could—"

The admiral shook his head. "Not yet. We need to get into the next room now and get access to the Shroud technology. There could be another force waiting for us in there, so we need to be ready for anything. I've sent out an all-call to any GCH forces left in the base to head for our location or the power core, but for now, we're on our own and need to move quickly."

"We've tried to get through, sir, but the console there..." Winters pointed to a smashed station. "The bugs took it out themselves. We believe it opens the doors, but we couldn't bypass it."

Two of Johansen's engineers broke off, examining the wreckage of the console and shaking their heads to let him know it was a lost cause.

Johansen stood before the doors, taking several steps back and tilting his head to one side as he stared at it quizzically. He moved forward, spreading his arms out in front of him as he approached the doors, his fingers splayed as he pressed them against the smooth metal. "All right, Foxy girl, show me what we've got. Run deep-level tactile analysis and full-spectrum scans," Johansen said, his suit flowing across the doors, coating an area six meters wide and twice his height in a thin layer of nanites.

The admiral waited while Johansen and Foxy worked, the sounds of battle inching ever closer in the distance. "Chief?"

The suit pulled back, reforming around his body a moment later, and he stepped back, activating the holo-display from his wrist.

"Scans indicate that the doors are made of an advanced alloy and have a sophisticated locking mechanism," Foxy said over the suit's speakers. Jackson, the admiral, Quentarus, and Winters gathered closer, studying the scans. "The locking mechanism cannot be bypassed. The control module appears to be consistent with known Imperium designs and can only receive authorization from a trusted command source."

"All right, so we can't hack it, but we might be able to melt it or break through it. The problem is that the alloy appears to be extremely dense, and either of those will take time we may not have. But we may be able to go around them," Johansen said, rubbing the stubble on his chin as he considered.

"One moment," Foxy said, picking up on his line of thinking. "There are two pockets in the wall where the doors retract. The alloy is the same as the rest of the walls in this room – not the same advanced one the doors are made of. This appears to be the weakest point and is thinner to allow the doors to slide into it. A particle beam from a Sentinel at full power should be sufficient. However, if we cut through the wall, there will be no way to seal the door behind us," Foxy warned.

Johansen looked at the admiral, who gave a nod. "One problem at a time," the admiral said. "Commander, do either of your Sentinels have an intact particle beam?"

"Yes, sir, I believe Lieutenant Veshoff's Sentinel does," Winters said, quickly tapping her wrist. "Veshoff, we need you back here ASAP!"

Seconds later, the Sentinel armor lumbered towards them, its left leg dragging slightly, the outer shell of the armor looking like hell. Veshoff stopped just short of the group and spoke through the armor's audio system. "How can I be of service, Admiral?" he asked.

"We need a way in *there*," the admiral said.

Johansen flicked the image hovering over his arm, and the holo-display jumped to overlay the wall, mapping out a targeting grid just beside one of the doors. "A particle beam at full power in a rectangle along these lines should do it," Johansen said.

"All right, everyone, get back and take cover," Veshoff said, moving into position. "Once this wall is down, we don't know what will come out from the other side."

The admiral, Quentarus, Johansen, and his engineers moved to an alcove on the far wall, taking up a firing position, the sounds of the battle from the main entrance fading in the distance. Johansen left a small piece of his suit on a nearby console, projecting the outline for the door on the wall.

"Report," Admiral Valentyen said over the comms.

"All clear here, sir," Commander Ellis, the squad leader from Alpha, said. "No casualties and no signs of additional enemy contacts."

"Good work. Do what you can to dig in. We're proceeding with the next phase of the plan and opening the last chamber. There's the possibility that we could be opening a literal hornet's nest, so be prepared to move and back us up if I give the order. I've also sent out an all-call to any available units in the complex to rendezvous here. Hopefully we'll have some pockets of reinforcements coming soon."

"Copy that, sir," he replied.

Veshoff went to work in the Sentinel, the blinding beam slicing through the wall while he slowly moved along the path Johansen's suit projected.

While the Sentinel worked, Jackson stood in an alcove with Winters, the two having gravitated to one another as they moved off to the other side.

Veshoff ceased fire a moment later, moving forward and striking the wall with a swift kick from the Sentinel's good leg. Thick gray smoke wafted from the hole, and the armor reached inside, ripping out the various gears and motors that controlled the door, then cutting again, this time through the other side of the wall leading into the next chamber.

Winters looked down, and Jackson suddenly realized that he had his hand on her wrist. She looked back up, meeting his eyes and giving him a questioning look.

"Sorry," he said, pulling his hand away, unaware until that moment that he had instinctively reached for her, bringing her closer for protection as they huddled in the alcove.

"It's fine," she replied.

"Just not sure what's behind that door, that's all..."

"No need to explain. And thanks. It's nice to have someone looking out for me." She smiled.

Jackson smiled back as time seemed to stop, his head spinning while he tried to convince himself that this wasn't Amy. That it was just someone who looked like her...and talked like her...and smiled like her. He stopped himself mid-thought, turning to look away, watching the Sentinel work while trying to block everything else from his mind, knowing that any distractions now could get him killed.

The Sentinel kicked down the second piece of metal, and the room beyond came into view. Veshoff moved closer, his forward shields set to maximum as he bent down and peered into the opening. "Looks clear!" he called. "Nothing on any of my scans," he added, stepping back to allow the others access.

Jackson and Winters moved quickly towards the opening, weapons ready. He stepped through first, Winters following, both sweeping the room with their rifles. Quentarus arrived seconds later, forming up beside them and throwing a dozen small spheres into the air, the drones taking off and sweeping the large open space.

Quentarus lowered her helmet and shot Jackson a scolding look, saying more than any words could have.

While she was often sparing with her words, the lieutenant seemed to have nonverbal communication down to an art. It was only then that he realized he'd entered the room without raising his helmet or shields, his mind unfocused, still half thinking about the mysterious woman beside him and not the mission.

He tilted his head, raising his helmet and activating his shields a second later. Winters flushed for a moment before quickly doing the same, and Quentarus reactivated her helmet as well.

Jackson and Winters followed Quentarus's lead, the three of them sweeping the area and moving to a better tactical position behind a large bank of processing cores while the drones continued their task. As they rounded the huge data cores, an immense machine took shape before them.

"Clear," Quentarus called, the drones having completed their sweep, confirming that the room was unoccupied, aside from them.

Johansen entered, followed by his engineers, with the admiral close behind. Johansen waved his hand in the air in a sweeping motion, his suit instantly collecting the data from the drones.

He held his arm out, and a holo-map of the room appeared, the group of engineers huddling around him.

"There." He pointed to one location, directing two of his team, then did the same for another location, and another, quickly assigning them points of interest to investigate, the group of thirty plus spreading out across the vast space, encircling the machine. He and another engineer walked over to what appeared to be the main control console, a long, wide panel off to the side of the room underneath a metal overhang with banks of displays filling the walls and containing active systems readouts along with a wealth of technical information.

The sound of shots firing pulled the admiral's attention away, and he stepped aside, opening his comm to the commander of his squad. "Alpha One, do you copy?"

"Ellis here, sir. All clear. We're still holding. We moved to clear the area and lost two of my team, with one more wounded, sir. A couple of Arachnids still had some life in them and ambushed us."

The admiral looked to Quentarus, who already had her own holo-display up. Since they'd arrived at the command center, she'd been in active contact with several other squads throughout the complex and was redirecting them to their position.

"The first group is two minutes out, sir," she reported.

"Friendlies inbound in two mikes, copy," the admiral said.

"Copy that, sir," Ellis responded, quickly passing word along to the defenders that reinforcements were en route.

"There'll be more coming. We've made contact with seven other squads. They'll all be here soon. You're in command of the overall defense. Hold that position at all costs, understood?" the admiral said. "We've found what we're here for," he added, letting Ellis know what was at stake.

"Acknowledged, sir. Alpha *will* hold this position."

"I know you will, son. Valentyen out."

Meanwhile, Johansen stood at the command console, working feverishly while Foxy translated the controls, providing a holographic overlay for his fingers as they moved, while the other engineer, Gilmore, studied the readings on the screens behind her.

Twenty minutes passed, the rest of the team keeping their

distance, watching for any signs of Insectoids in hiding while the engineers worked.

The final squad of reinforcements reached the barricades moments later.

"Looks like our final count is eleven Sentinels along with one hundred and sixty soldiers and forty-three mechs, a mix of Talons and Enforcers," Quentarus said.

"Focus our resources on the main entryway and the barricades, but have two teams in reserve – one to hold the command center and another to hold this room," the admiral said. Jackson and Winters moved closer, looking on as Quentarus brought up a display of the main defenses with the two rooms behind them.

"Agreed. Ellis's a good officer, but his deployment could use a bit of tweaking to maximize the firepower they have," Quentarus commented.

"Go help him tighten things up and see if the Sentinels and mechs can clear more of the bodies and debris from the barricades first, then focus on the center of the corridor to give them better lines of sight."

Quentarus nodded. "I'm on it. Once I get back, I'll lead the team holding the command center, with your permission, sir. I've got some ideas on setting up an effective multilayered kill box to take down anything that gets through the hallway."

"Agreed," the admiral said. "Commander Winters, you and half your team will stay with us in here. We'll focus our defense on the entryway we cut and take up positions around the room to create a cross fire. The rest of Alpha squad and the reinforcements will stay out there. Get your wounded and any officers who you think are still too shook up to fight into the farthest alcoves. That will give them more time to rest and recover. We'll do the best we can to shelter them if the enemy breaks through."

"Thank you, sir. I appreciate that. I think most of them will be okay. They just need time after what happened," she said, studying the room for points to set up her team and thinking about who to put where.

"Will, I want you ready if we need you, but I'm keeping you in reserve for now," the admiral said.

"I'll be standing by, sir," Jackson responded, Winters noticing the unique insignia on each of the admiral's team's suits for the first time, a pair of daggers crossed over the image of a sleek starship pointing upwards.

"Admiral, I think I have it," Johansen called from a few meters away, the team moving over to stand beside him. "We've got a rudimentary understanding of the Shroud's controls and how it works. I think I can lower it, sir!"

"Do it," the admiral said. A moment later, he opened a channel to the Fleet in orbit. "Admiral Vincenze, Admiral Easton, this is Admiral Valentyen; do you read?"

"I read you," Admiral Vincenze responded. "Admiral Easton took the *Vengeance* along with a small battle group to hunt down the remaining pockets of Imperium ships that escaped. He's farther out in the system."

"Understood; secondary objective achieved. Primary objective still underway."

"Acknowledged. Stand by for confirmation," Admiral Vincenze said. A moment later, he returned. "Secondary objective confirmed. Our long-range scans from GCH recon stations are now detecting an enemy fleet amassing near their orbital station in the Kelus System, right where we expected them to be. Smart move leaving that base intact, Admiral. Told us exactly where to look for them. The

27th Fleet is en route and is around ten hours out and will engage them there, keeping them from sending reinforcements our way."

"What about our other scouts?"

"One moment. I'm getting reports now from Captain Delgado and our stealth ships along the Holt Line. The Shroud is down over an area nearly eight hundred light-years across!"

"That's good news, but it's not enough. We'll see if we can take it down entirely, but we'll need time."

"Agreed. More reports are coming in now. There's another enemy fleet gathering farther down the Holt Line. About fourteen hours from here. Looks like it's around seven hundred ships strong based on the data from our scouts."

"How many ships are amassing at Kelus?"

"Approximately twelve hundred ships… Stand by. Damn it, they're jumping out. They must have detected that the Shroud was down. Shit, our other scout just reported the second enemy fleet farther down the Line is starting to jump out as well. The Imperium must be rerouting all available units here. Based on our estimates, the fleet from Kelus will be here in just under four hours and thirty-three minutes."

"Acknowledged. Can you hold?"

"Not for long against a force that size, and definitely not once those other seven hundred ships arrive. We paid a heavy price to take Stornoway, and we're down to just under three hundred ships that are combat ready. I spoke with Command about an hour ago, and they've got more reinforcements on the way, but it'll be at least twenty-seven hours before we can have a sizable-enough force to take on both of those enemy fleets and hold the system for good."

"Understood. We're continuing with our primary objective. We'll transmit what we have in two hours and proceed with fallback scenario Bravo."

"Understood. Good luck, Admiral. I'll contact you if anything changes. Vincenze out."

The admiral turned back to Johansen. "What do you think, Chief?"

"I don't think that two hours is going to be enough time, sir. This system is… Well, it's remarkable. I don't know how they did it, but it's an incredible piece of engineering. It could take us days, weeks even, to fully understand it."

"Can you use it to shut the whole system off?"

"No. Each control station appears to have dominion over a vast area, but as best as I can tell, they're independent. We can turn this one off entirely or destroy it, but the rest of the Imperium will remain shrouded. If we do destroy it, however, there's the possibility that they could regain control over the Shroud satellites this station controls if it goes offline for good. Like a fallback."

"Thoughts?" the admiral said, turning to Quentarus first.

"We'd be able to take the fight to the bugs," she said plainly. "It's not going to win the war, but giving us back eight hundred light-years' worth of sensors, combined with the gains we've made in the past few days, should give us an advantage to keep hitting them hard while they're unprepared. At least if we keep pressing the attack in the unshrouded regions."

"Captain?" he said, turning to Jackson.

"It might be enough… We could hit them pretty hard after the holes we punched in their defenses, but they likely have thousands of other ships they can reroute from more distant parts of the Imperium if they need to. If they decide to do that…if they become that *desperate*… I don't know.

And even if we destroy this site, they might figure out a way to take over the Shroud satellites from another site, like the chief said, making this all for nothing unless we take them all out as well. Our goal was for this to be the decisive blow that would win the war. We can do some decent damage, but I don't think it's enough, sir."

The admiral turned to Winters. "Commander, any thoughts?"

"I've been out of the frontier for the past few months, so I'm not exactly sure what all of this Shroud stuff is, but I think that after the price we've paid to take Stornoway back from them, we need to make this worth it and hit them as hard as we can, whatever we do, sir."

He turned to Johansen. "Chief?"

"I hate to say it, but we can only do so much here in the time we have if we have to pull out in two hours. And if they take Stornoway back, which we know they'll do once those two fleets arrive, then we're left with two choices. One: destroy their system here, crippling the Shroud for eight hundred light-years and take the win, or two: we stay and finish the job. I've learned a lot about the system already, and if I can break their encryption and hack in, then there's a chance I can gain access to their full command and control system and take it all down for good."

"Is that even possible?" Quentarus asked.

"Yeah, I think so," Johansen said. "The different Shroud sites, while they each appear to independently control their own areas, they also appear to work together overall and are connected to a specialized central network. If I can gain full command-level access to that network, then I could figure out a way to take them all down. The Shroud technology is impressive, but the Imperium's security and command systems are standard designs. I suspect they never figured anyone would get into it, as you have to be at one of these sites to do so. But I really think we can do this. We just need time."

"Do you think we can hold that long?" the admiral asked Quentarus.

"I don't know, sir. I don't think so, not unless we're willing to make this a one-way trip."

"Sir," Jackson interjected, "I agree with the commander. This is why we're here: to hit them as hard as we can. This is *the* moment, sir. The key to winning this war is taking down the Shroud of Darkness. If we can knock it all offline, and the Fleet can hit them where it hurts the most *now*, while they're not ready for it, we can end this war for good." He paused, looking at the faces around him. "I want to live as much as the rest of you, but this is it. *This* is our shot. I think we have to take it!"

"Yeah," Quentarus said quietly, nodding. "Will's right. We can do some damage by taking part of the Shroud down, but the bugs will just shift tactics. The Fleet is in too much disarray, and we've lost too many ships to mount the kind of offensive we'd need to break them with just this section of the Shroud down. If we could take it all down, however, I'm guessing we'll catch them with their pants down, like we did over the past several days when we hit them where they weren't expecting it. The Shroud has made them overconfident. If we can take it out of the equation, then we could target them where they're weakest all along the entire Holt Line and really strike a decisive blow. One they can't recover from."

"What do you think our odds are of being able to hold here long enough for the chief and his engineers to finish their work?" the admiral asked.

Quentarus thought for a moment. "We could make it work, but only for so long. The Fleet's going to have to get back here *soon*, as we can't hold indefinitely."

"What do you think, Commander?" the admiral asked, looking at Winters. "You took this position. Can we hold it?"

"I don't know if I'm qualified to say, sir."

"It's all our lives on the line if we stay. I want your opinion on this."

"Well, sir… with what we have now, even with the other hunter-killer teams joining us, I don't think it'll be nearly enough to hold for more than half a day at most with the sheer numbers they can throw at us. I think the captain is right though. If we can hold, we can win this war. I-I think it's worth the risk. We have to do whatever it takes, sir. If we have to hold, we'll hold."

The admiral stroked his chin thoughtfully. "All right then, we hold. Let's get to work. Lieutenant, have the probes in the rest of the base do one final sweep and reroute every remaining solider, mech, and armor we can, aside from Gamma and Delta squads, to this location. We still need them to hold the power core, or all of this is for nothing. Once all of our reinforcements arrive, see what we have to work with, and I'll leave it to you to allocate them as you see fit."

"Roger that, sir," Quentarus replied. "They're dug in pretty well at the power core. They should be able to hold for a while, but we've got some work to do here, and they will need some reinforcements there as well. Anything you can do to buy us more time would help."

"Understood. I have a few ideas. Chief, you and your team continue your work. At the four-hour mark, I want you to transmit everything you have to Admiral Vincenze's ship, then, Jackson, I want you to activate the QE device."

"Aye, sir," Johansen replied, Jackson nodding in agreement. "I'll instruct my team in the power core to send us what they have now, just in case we lose comms. I'm sure they've got some solid data by now as well. We'll then keep the data feed going through the Quantum Entanglement matrix to ensure that it makes it back to Command if we don't make it."

"Very good. Jackson, Winters, secure this room. We have four automated phalanx turrets that I want set up on the entry to the Shroud chamber. Let's make sure we have every trick we've got up our sleeves ready if they make it this far; understood?"

Jackson and Winters looked at one another for a split second, then back to the admiral. "Understood, sir," they said in unison.

"Jackson, hang back a second. The rest of you, dismissed," the admiral said, the rest of the team moving off as he lowered his voice, Jackson moving in close as the two of them spoke. "I want you to get out of here and retreat with the Fleet when the next wave of dropships comes to reinforce us."

"But, sir—"

"Will, we can't afford to lose you. I let you take on the Mantis mission and come here because I believed in you and your skills. You've done a fantastic job, but we're past that now. If we fail here, there is no plan B without you. You may be the only hope the Confederation has. Only you can wield the Light weapons, and you're simply too valuable to risk here, for what very well may be a last stand."

Jackson pushed back the urge to respond, trying to keep his emotions in check and considering the admiral's words, thinking about the big picture and knowing he was right.

He took a deep breath, nodding slightly, then met the admiral's eyes once more. "I can't argue with your logic, sir. And you're right. Tactically, I shouldn't be here…but I *am here*, sir. And if the Ancient Quantum Entanglement device stops working, I'm the only one who can reset or troubleshoot it. Getting that data out could be the difference between success and failure. If this mission does fail, and that data doesn't get out, then all of this will be for nothing."

The admiral was silent for a moment as he considered Jackson's argument. "It's too great a risk, Will."

"Sir, please. I couldn't live with myself if…if you all didn't make it and I left you all here to die, when I could have made a *difference*. Please, sir, you know I can."

A moment passed as silence hung in the air, Jackson dreading the admiral's next words, unsure if he'd be able to obey the order if it came. To leave his friends and abandon the mission. To leave behind the mysterious woman who looked exactly like his dead wife, and to run away to safety while they all stayed and risked their lives.

A wave of agony rippled through him, the feeling telling him that he was meant to be there. The sense of clarity hit him like a bolt of lightning. The certainty that if he died on this mission, that at least it would be with all of them, and it would count for something.

Finally, the admiral spoke. "All right, Will," he said softly. "But you're not to take any unnecessary risks, and we'll only use you if we absolutely need to. Otherwise, your job will be to hang back and protect the Shroud chamber at all costs until we complete our mission. Is that clear?"

"Yes, sir. Thank you, sir," Jackson said, the feeling as though a cinder block had been lifted off his chest washing over him, despite knowing he may have just signed his own death certificate.

"Go and help Commander Winters with the preparations. I'm going to contact the Fleet," the admiral said, Jackson moving off before he opened a channel to Admiral Vincenze. "Admiral, do you copy?"

"I'm here."

"We're going to hold, Jim."

Silence filled the comm for a moment before Admiral Vincenze replied, "Are you sure?"

"I am. We have a chance to win this war, and the bugs know it. We need to get this done."

"Very well. We'll do everything we can to get back as soon as possible. You have my word. In the meantime, what can we do to help?"

"Can you send me any remaining mechs, armor, weapons, anything you can scrape together, along with anyone who wants to volunteer? The fortress is cleared out, but we took heavy losses, and we're spread pretty thin down here, so every last person and piece of hardware will help."

"I'll check with the rest of the Fleet now and see what we can come up with. I'll have the dropships send you everything we can in the time we have left."

"Thank you, Admiral. There's one more thing I need you to do before you jump out. I want you to fire on the main entrance to the base and collapse it. It will buy us more time if the Insectoids have to dig their way in."

"We'll make a hell of a mess for them, and we're leaving a few surprises in orbit as well. We've co-opted their remaining weapons platform network and are redeploying them now. There were close to three hundred and fifty that were out of range when we attacked, so they're undamaged and still in standby mode. It should be an unpleasant surprise when their own weapons platforms turn on them."

"It will indeed."

"Just hold on. We'll be back to kick their sorry asses."

"I know you will, Jim."

"May your gods protect and watch over you, Ren."

"And you," Admiral Valentyen replied. "We'll be transmitting our final data uplink in approximately four hours with everything we've gathered up to that point. It should be of some help if we don't complete our mission. Our last resort will be to destroy the Shroud systems here so they can't get it back online. We're also initiating the Quantum Entanglement matrix, so we can keep feeding Command data as long as possible. The other QE device is already set up at GCH Intelligence and will send anything we find directly there for the androids to analyze."

"Copy that. Good hunting, Admiral. Vincenze out."

Over the next several hours, the dropships dropped off more than eight hundred officers, sixty suits of various armor, and hundreds of crates of weapons, just outside the main entrance to the complex. The officers, all volunteers from the ships holding the system, quickly moved the gear inside, making their way to the cargo bay with the power core and command center to reinforce the troops there.

Right on time, Admiral Vincenze watched as the Insectoid fleet jumped into the system several million kilometers out, their ships breaking off into attack groups as they swarmed towards them.

"Order all remaining ships to jump out immediately," he commanded, watching as the rest of the Fleet, just three hundred and ten ships of the over five hundred that had conducted the initial assault, departed. "Confirm that all of our people and equipment are clear of the entrances to the complex."

"Confirmed, sir," his tactical officer replied.

"Ops, let them know we're initiating the plan. Tell them to take cover," he said, waiting a full minute before he continued. "Tactical, target the main entrance, set for maximum structural damage. Fire!"

Three torpedoes launched a moment later, impacting the main entrance to the mountain fortress and the surrounding area, followed by several blasts of plasma fire. The tactical officer then adjusted the target location, firing again and collapsing the peak of the adjacent mountain, creating a massive rockslide, which buried the area outside of the main entrance under tens of thousands of tons of rock.

The admiral nodded. "Switch viewscreen to the incoming fleet."

In the distance, over twelve hundred ships appeared, many of them moving rapidly towards the lone GCH vessel while the admiral stood his ground.

Suddenly, the viewscreen lit up as hundreds of small explosions filled the image. "Looks like they found our first surprise." The admiral smiled as dozens of Insectoid ships collided with the cloaked mines and were torn to pieces.

The rest of the Imperium fleet came to a full stop, their

overconfidence suddenly turning to caution. A moment later, they sent a handful of ships ahead to scout the path for further defenses. The admiral watched as two of the scouts were destroyed, further robbing their enemy of their resolve to test the web of invisible defenses, knowing they'd bought the team on the ground more time.

"Let's just hope they don't realize we only had a few hundred mines and that they're spread pretty thin," he said. "Tactical, send the signal to the co-opted weapons platforms in orbit to hold off on targeting the Imperium ships until they move into orbit and start landing their ground forces. Instruct them to focus their fire on the dropships as soon as the first wave launches, then turn on the rest of the fleet. Let's give our people on the ground every second we can possibly buy them."

"Aye, sir."

"Helm, prepare to jump out and rendezvous with our fleet."

"Standing by, sir," the helm officer replied.

The admiral paused, saying a silent prayer for the brave souls on the surface below. "Just hold on down there," he whispered, turning and giving the order to jump out, knowing he'd be back soon and that the fight for Stornoway was far from over.

CHAPTER 16
THE SIEGE OF STORNOWAY

Thirty-six hours later, Admiral Valentyen's comm beeped, shattering the silence. Jackson awoke with a start, the sound the only thing echoing in the cavernous space.

He moved to roll over, a flash of pain washing over him, his body screaming out in agony as he fell back to the ground. The sound continued, and Jackson forced himself to move, pushing through the pain, nearly passing out from the lightning bolts shooting through his body as he twisted onto his stomach, his cracked ribs crying out from the torment of his weight upon them. He tried to take a deep breath to steady himself, and another jolt of pain rewarded him for his efforts as the taste of blood filled his mouth, causing him to cough while he struggled to breathe.

He pulled himself forward with his arms, every movement a new level of suffering as he struggled to reach the blinking light on Admiral Valentyen's wrist. The soft glow became brighter as he pressed on through the darkness surrounding him. Finally, he hovered over it, trying to focus his eyes through what he knew was a severe concussion as he reached down, wiping away a layer of dirt, debris, and what appeared to be dried blood.

He pressed the button to activate the comm.

"Hello?" he said, his voice weak and hoarse.

Admiral Vincenze replied, his voice urgent, "Admiral Valentyen, do you read?"

"This is Captain Jackson. The-the admiral's here, but it's dark. I think he's unconscious."

"Acknowledged," Admiral Vincenze said, the concern clear in his voice. "Are you okay, Captain?"

"I-I don't know. I'm badly injured, sir. It's pitch-black in here. I don't know if we're alone or if the enemy's still lurking."

"Hold tight, Jackson; we'll be there soon. Just hang on."

"I'll be here, sir. And, Admiral… The Shroud… We did it," he said, slipping out of consciousness, his eyes closing involuntarily from sheer exhaustion.

The next several days passed in a blur as Jackson was taken by a medical team and put into a portable medpod. He awoke in what appeared to be a hospital room with half a dozen sensors attached to his body, his eyes aching against the dim morning light.

A nurse arrived a few minutes later, alerted to his having regained consciousness. She checked his pupils and bio-signs before helping him lift his head and giving him some water.

"Where?" he asked weakly, struggling to speak.

"You're safe, Captain. You're back on Archon in a GCH medical facility. You're going to be okay," she said, giving him a nod as she helped him take another sip.

"What happened?"

"There'll be time for that later, but for now, you need to rest. Get your strength back."

"Okay, you're the boss." He smiled, attempting to adjust his position slightly, his legs feeling sluggish. "My legs?" he asked weakly, suddenly terrified as he realized he had no feeling in them at all.

"You were very badly injured. Your spinal cord was severely damaged, but the doctors believe you'll make a full recovery, in time."

He nodded, feeling weak and helpless, trying to think of the last thing he could remember.

"Get some rest," she said, pulling up his blanket to tuck him in, then adjusting the IV patch he hadn't realized had been attached to his left arm. "You're still groggy from post-op. Your head will clear after a few more hours of rest, and you'll start to feel better."

The word *post-op* rang in his mind as he suddenly recalled awakening in the blackness, disoriented and in terrible pain. "Okay," he said, closing his eyes, the IV adjustment the nurse made willing him back to sleep.

He awoke the next morning, his head much clearer, and another nurse entered the room to check on him shortly after. "How are we feeling today, Captain?" she asked cheerily.

"I've been better," he replied, his voice still raw. "But at least my head seems to be clearer than it was yesterday, and my vision's not blurry anymore."

"That's a good sign," she said, making a note on the holo-chart beside his bed. "I know that Command has been eager for you to wake up and are looking forward to debriefing you."

"Debriefing?" he muttered as, suddenly, all of it came

crashing back, his mind reeling as he tried to steady himself. "What day is it?"

"Well, that's a loaded question, considering you just came from another world and don't even know what planet you're on."

"I'm on Archon."

"Very good." She nodded. "Well, it's Trivsday here on Archon, but for you, it's been six days since the rescue teams found you and were able to stabilize you on Stornoway before evacuating you here."

"Six days." The number didn't seem real as he tried to account for the lost time, his mind falling short.

"Don't worry, you'll get caught up. It happens. I'll get you something to eat; that will help," she said, walking over to a food synthesizer in the wall and bringing him back some eggs with bacon, toast, and juice. "These came up on your profile as favorites. They should help you regain some of your strength. I'll come check on you in a bit."

Bit… *Bits*, he thought as the nurse left the room. "Bits?" he said softly. "You there, buddy?"

"I'm here, William," Bits replied somberly.

"What happened?"

"I'm afraid I've been ordered not to discuss it with you until after your debriefing."

"Right. I get it. No worries, buddy. I'm just glad you're here."

"I'm just glad you're going to be okay."

"My legs?" he asked, afraid to know the answer.

"A serrated leg from an Insectoid pierced your spine just above your L5 vertebrae after you went down and lost consciousness. I was forced to reroute all available medical nanites to keep you alive, and the doctors only began to repair the damage once you arrived here. They've installed a new medical implant that will continue the work, and the tissue regeneration appears to be going well."

"That's good to know. How are the others?"

Bits hesitated a moment before responding. "I'm afraid that I'm not permitted to comment or speculate on their conditions at this time either, William."

Jackson's heart fell at the thought of not knowing if his friends were dead or alive, and fearing the worst, that Command was keeping this information from him to keep him focused for his debriefing.

"I'm sorry," Bits added, pulling him from the darkness filling his thoughts.

"It's okay. Orders are orders. I know how it goes. Let's just hope we can get some answers soon. It's all still hazy, but more and more of it is coming back, and I..." he said, trailing off, struggling to piece together all of the images flooding his mind.

"Why don't you get some more rest? Your body still needs considerable time to heal."

"Okay," he said numbly, the jumbled images haunting him as he drifted back to sleep.

The next morning, a GCH officer in a white uniform followed the nurse into the room, holding a similar uniform out for him as he approached. "It's time, sir."

Less than an hour later, the officer pushed his hover-chair into an elevator, then out again on the top level of the Admiralty building in the heart of the GCH Command complex. The officer guided him into a large conference room where a group of senior officers awaited him.

Fleet Admiral Lighton led the proceedings, flanked at a crescent-shaped table by a dozen other members of the top brass, including Admirals Vincenze, Easton, Scott, Janus, and, much to his surprise, Admiral Thompson.

The official debriefing came to order as Admiral Lighton stated the purpose for the record, then turned to him. "Captain Jackson, will you please detail the events that took place, as best as you can recall, after Admiral Vincenze and the rest of the Fleet jumped out of the Stornoway System."

"Yes, ma'am," Jackson said, taking a moment to organize his thoughts before beginning. "The Fleet began pulling out at 11:49 hours, local time, just under fourteen hours after the initial assault on the Stornoway System began. Before they left, Admiral Vincenze's ship fired, destroying the primary entrance to the complex, sealing us inside and buying us time."

Jackson looked at Admiral Vincenze, giving him a small nod, then continued.

"We continued to fortify our positions and clear the corridors approaching the command center and the cargo bay, where the Shroud power core was, disposing of the bodies of the Insectoid troops as we went. Teams of mechs worked carefully, moving the bodies of our fallen soldiers into other parts of the complex while the heavy armor cleared out the remaining debris to open up our lines of sight as we prepped for the impending Imperium counterattack. They piled the wrecked armor and debris farther down the tunnels, blocking the Imperium advance and using the choke points to set up automated defenses. During that time, I focused on securing the chamber to the Shroud control center with Commander Winters, while Chief Johansen and his team worked on cracking the encryption to the Shroud's command systems, hoping to take control.

"I'm not sure exactly how many of us there were defending the command center, but I think it was around five hundred and fifty officers on the barricades, plus a mix of mechs and armor. We also had another hundred or so people packed into the command center, ready to rotate onto the barricades as needed, and around forty of us in the room where the Shroud controls were located. We'd set up multiple defensive zones, and I was with Admiral Valentyen as part of the last line of defense, dedicated to protecting the engineering teams and giving them as much time as possible to complete their work. Lieutenant Quentarus rotated around, spending several hours with the squad leaders optimizing their defenses and using everything the Fleet had sent down to us to shore up our positions. The admiral then ordered everyone to get some sleep so that we were ready for when the Insectoids arrived.

"A little over four hours after, the Imperium fleet finally managed to land their ground forces – well, some of them anyway. The surprises the Fleet left for them certainly took a toll, from what we could tell by accessing the sensor drones left in the system. Even deep inside the mountain, we could still hear the impacts from what we could only assume were dozens, if not a hundred, enemy dropships crashing to the surface after their own weapons platforms turned on them." He smiled slightly, picturing the image in his mind, imagining the Imperium's surprise as their ground forces were wiped out while still in orbit.

"We then hunkered down, and most of us managed to get some rest, with help from our AIs. I'm not sure exactly when, but approximately three hours later, Chief Johansen and his team broke the Imperium's encryption algorithm and gained access to the secure network that controlled Shroud of Darkness. Another hour and a half later, he gained admin access, all without alerting them to our presence in the system. He had to be extremely careful, though, not to tip his hand, or they could still lock us out with their own admin access if they discovered him in the system. The team of engineers spent the next few hours carefully learning everything they could about the system, looking for other weaknesses and transmitting the data back using the advanced Quantum Entanglement matrix that we set up at GCH Intelligence before we left.

"Finally, after learning all he could about the Shroud's systems, the admiral conferred with the chief, Lieutenant Quentarus, Commander Winters, and me, and we discussed our options. After some debate, it was decided that we would leave the rest of the Shroud active until we were certain that we could get a message back to Command."

"Why didn't you just deactivate the Shroud as planned?" Fleet Admiral Lighton asked.

"We discussed it at length, ma'am. We figured we could do it for a time using a weakness one of the techs found in the system, but the chief felt that the network had too many redundancies in place with each of the sites able to function independently. Unless we could find a way to lock out the Imperium from all of the sites at once, he knew they'd find a way to regain control eventually. Admiral Valentyen didn't want to risk it if the Fleet wasn't ready to take full advantage of the Shroud going down. Even with the preparations that were being made, he said that it would take time for the Fleet to attack in force once we could start identifying targets of opportunity. And with a large group of our ships on their way to rescue us, we knew that the impact any attack would have would be limited before the Imperium could regain control. We figured we would only have one shot at this, so we didn't want to waste it." Jackson paused, looking around the room, and noticed several of the admirals nodding.

"Instead, we came up with a new plan. We created a virus. One that would silently infect the entire Shroud network, allowing us to inject a series of new command subroutines into the core programming. It was risky, though, as the virus had to be perfect and remain undetected. It also had to replicate to all the Shroud control sites to be successful. If it worked, however, we could kill their admin access at all sites simultaneously, bypassing the redundancies they had in place and locking them out permanently.

"Since we'd taken one section of the Shroud down, we knew that the Imperium was aware that we had access to the controls here and were likely already working on a way to disconnect Stornoway from the rest of the network. So, we had to make a choice. Take the entire Shroud down now for – we didn't know how long – hours, days, maybe a week if we were really lucky. Or keep our presence in their system hidden and try to find a way to cripple the system or take control of it for good," Jackson said pointedly, looking at each of the admirals in turn. "Admiral Valentyen had the chief split his team into two groups, one to work on crippling it and the other on taking control. But we had to act quickly.

"The chief linked the AIs of nearly three hundred and fifty of us, increasing the processing power available to develop the virus while he and a group of techs got to work on the design. He knew it had to be perfect, so he used our AIs to run tens of millions of scenarios, while layering additional subroutines and various other contingencies throughout the virus's programming. After he and his team were satisfied that they'd thought of everything they could, he uploaded the virus into the Shroud's network while running a hacked diagnostic log collection routine to cover its tracks. During that time, we continued to shore up our defenses, laying mines and setting up auto-turrets, grav-field generators, and other traps while the Insectoids continued to dig out the main entrance, and we waited to see if our gamble with the virus paid off.

"The virus entered the network as planned, the chief breaking it into hundreds of small fragments, each disguised as simple diagnostic log files to remain undetected. These were automatically uploaded as part of a larger automated diagnostic system that ran every six hours on the network. The virus would spread once it reached the core control system, co-opting the entire diagnostic log system and injecting the new code using our admin access. Once the core was infected, the diagnostic program would copy the virus out to each of the other Shroud control sites over time, sending reports back to confirm once it was everywhere. But we knew that this could take days until we received confirmations from all of the sites and could trigger the virus. Our hope was that it would allow us to take control of the entire system, but if it failed to replicate everywhere, then at least we could use it to cripple the infected sites."

"Why didn't the Imperium cut off the control system at Stornoway when you shut down the Shroud there?" Admiral Janus asked.

"Good question, ma'am. This was one of our initial fears after we took down the Shroud at our site and why we decided to create the virus in the first place. As the team learned more about the network and how it all worked, Chief Johansen believed that they couldn't cut it off. At least, not easily. The sites were simply too interconnected, coordinating traffic across thousands of light-years and allowing ships to navigate through the blackout field cast by the Shroud between each region. The system, as he explained it, was more of a mesh, with each control site linked to one another. It's quite complicated, but he believed that cutting off one site from the rest of the network would take a lot of time. At least, that's what we bet on. We figured that they'd try to retake control of Stornoway, rather than cutting it off and having to go to the trouble of reconnecting it to the entire mesh network. We were betting on their arrogance, essentially, that they would take back control of Stornoway and not need to go to the trouble of cutting the site off." Jackson paused, waiting for a moment to see if there were any additional questions, then continued. "So, that's why you didn't see the Shroud fall as planned, ma'am. Our hope was that some of us would survive and be able to convey the information about the virus when the Fleet arrived, or that the QE device would work to let you know. As a fail-safe, the engineers rigged up a system to upload all the critical data to every officer's AI in an attempt to ensure that at least one copy would survive, even if we were all dead.

"Thirteen hours later, the Imperium forces finally cleared the main entrance and began flowing troops into the complex. We were able to monitor and significantly slow the Insectoid forces as they made their way inside with the defenses we'd set up, but their numbers were still *staggering*.

"The first waves were comprised of heavily armed Ants, with squads of Hornets providing air support. The engineers in the cargo bay were also able to reactivate some of the base's original automated defenses, which, along with the other ones we set up, hit the first waves hard as they fanned out throughout the complex. Unfortunately, this also caused the enemy to change their primary objective, we think. Instead of attacking our position right away, they routed a large force towards the power core to eliminate this new threat."

"Why didn't Admiral Valentyen move all of his forces back to the command center?" Admiral Easton asked.

"Sorry, sir, the timeline's a bit confusing, and I'm jumping around a little. As I mentioned earlier, he kept them there initially to ensure that the power remained active while we studied the Shroud and uploaded the virus. By the time these objectives were complete, the Imperium troops had already landed and had been slowly working their way into and throughout the base. Our defenses slowed them down considerably, but he didn't want to risk their lives trying to outrun a horde to get to the command center, or risk them setting off any of the traps we'd left for the enemy. In the end, he decided that their best bet was to stay put where they had the greatest chance to defend themselves, behind the barricades at the cargo bay."

Admiral Easton nodded, seemingly satisfied with the answer.

"The squad leader from Delta had his troops fire heavy weapons at the corridor two junctions away, collapsing it to buy themselves precious hours, but they knew that it was only a matter of time," he said, thinking of the soldiers and engineers in Gamma and Delta they'd left back at the power core. He hadn't gotten to know any of them aside from their commanders, but he knew that they were all elite troops, dedicated to ensuring the success of the mission above all else.

He swallowed, closing his eyes for a moment before he continued, trying to picture in his mind how the events which followed unfolded. "It was approximately 04:42 local time when the enemy engaged the barricade protecting the power core," he said. "The fighting was intense, with thousands of enemy troops charging their position. They held valiantly for nearly fifty-five minutes, repelling wave after wave before the Insectoids finally gave up the attack, deciding to switch tactics. We could see from a few of the drones that were left outside the base to monitor the main entrance that their engineers had further excavated the opening, and now larger, deadlier creatures, such as armored beetles and Arachnids, began pouring into the complex.

"I'm not sure exactly what happened next…it all happened so fast," he said, his voice cracking somewhat as he recalled hearing the events over the open comm. "But we believe that a small squad of Insectoids made their way around to one of the rear entrances of the cargo bay just as the heavy reinforcements began a new offensive at the barricades. We think that they broke through one of the rear entrances, hitting our forces there from behind."

Jackson lowered his head, staring down at his hands folded in his lap, recalling how helpless he'd felt listening as the Insectoids broke through the cargo bay's defenses. He looked back up and met Fleet Admiral Lighton's eyes. "It was a slaughter, ma'am. We lost contact with the squad leaders shortly after that. One of the engineers, De'Silva, I think, kept an open comm and blew the charges to disable the core. We lost contact seconds later and never heard from anyone in the cargo bay again."

Jackson paused for a moment as he tried to picture the engineers and the soldiers from Gamma and Delta squads, unable to recall any of their faces as a wave of guilt washed over him.

"We double-checked and triple-checked our defenses, but the power was completely out in that part of the complex after the core went offline, so we waited in the darkness for the Imperium forces to come for us. We were fortunate that the bombardment Admiral Vincenze provided had also collapsed or partially blocked several other corridors between the main entrance and the command center, buying us additional time as the enemy was forced to dig through.

"At approximately 07:44 hours, the first waves of enemy soldiers assaulted our position at the command center barricade. Lieutenant Quentarus coordinated the main defensive effort from within the command center, and we rerouted all available drones to provide us with as much intel on enemy positions and strength as we could. As the first waves approached, the soldiers on the lines and our armored units laid down heavy fire. Multiple portable shield emitters were set up along the barricades, which limited our troops' exposure to return fire, and we had nine additional T21 phalanx cannons that came down from the Fleet set up to take out any enemy projectiles or fast-moving airborne units.

"The bugs sent wave after wave at us, but we held our position, the bodies piling up as we gave them no quarter, making them pay for every millimeter of corridor they took," he said, his voice hard. "After nearly twenty minutes, the enemy pulled back, finally realizing they were outgunned and forced to withdraw while they waited for more heavy reinforcements. At approximately 10:21 hours, the next wave of the assault began. The bugs sent in a variety of troops, from large Arachnids to small centipedes, moving along the floors, walls, and ceiling. We were able to take out all the

Arachnids before they reached our lines, but the centipedes were less than half a meter in size, and at least twenty-five to thirty of them made it through. They were fast and highly venomous, with razor-sharp mandibles, powerful enough to pierce our suits' armor. We lost forty soldiers before we were able to take them out.

"Wave after wave of enemy troops followed, forcing us to split our attention between those that breached our lines and keeping the rest at bay. We needed some time to regroup and shore up our lines, so the admiral ordered our last two bunker-buster rockets to the line. They struck the ceiling about ninety meters from the barricade, collapsing the corridor," he said, recalling the deafening sound of the explosion and subsequent collapse. "It took them over four hours before they could mount their next major assault, and our snipers and remote drones picked off their workers while they attempted to clear the debris, slowing their progress.

"By 14:40 hours, however, they'd cleared enough of the wreckage to begin sending multiple attack waves through. While the wreckage was being cleared, we'd mined the hell out of the majority of the space between there and our position, turning a stretch about fifty meters long into a death trap. It didn't stop them all, but it solved the issue of the centipedes getting through and took out some of their heavy hitters before they could get close enough to do any damage."

He looked down at his hands once more, recalling the sense of inevitability he'd felt as the Insectoids just kept coming, wave after wave of them, no matter how many they took out.

"We held fast for the next hour and ten minutes as, one by one, they whittled down our numbers. The shield generators were fully drained by then, and most of our heavy weapons were spent, forcing our troops to use rifles and small arms to hold the enemy back. Admiral Valentyen then made the call to send out a large wave of mechs down the corridor to buy us time while our forces redeployed, putting the majority of our armor on the front lines. The mech assault held the enemy at bay for a time, buying several minutes for the engineers to connect portable zero-point generators to the armored units to recharge them and for us to get the wounded out. Not long after, though, the waves of enemy forces started coming again, faster and with more varieties of Insectoids to repel. The armor held the line through nearly twenty minutes of intense combat, but we knew it would only be a matter of time before the bugs broke through and the ZPGs drained entirely from the relentless combat.

"As we watched the feed from the drones, I looked to the admiral, asking if it was time to activate the…*classified* weapons we brought with us," he said cagily, his eyes flashing to Fleet Admiral Lighton and Admiral Thompson for guidance. "I tried to convince him that we needed to act, but he was determined to wait for as long as possible, wanting to keep them as a last line of defense to buy time for the Fleet to return," he said, looking to Fleet Admiral Lighton once more.

"Everyone here has been briefed, Captain; you can speak freely," she said, sensing his hesitation.

He nodded. "Our forces continued to hold as best we could, falling back behind the barricades one row at a time before, finally, the officers in the armor switched to sentry mode, abandoning their units and making a run for cover. But the bugs swarmed, overtaking some of them, pulling them to the ground and tearing them apart," he said, his voice cracking once more as he thought of the terror they must have felt in those last moments. "The squad leader activated the remote detonation sequence on the armored units, taking out hundreds of their troops and putting our fallen out of their misery, and the explosions momentarily halted their advance.

"The admiral then gave the order for our remaining forces to fall back, and once everyone was clear, Lieutenant Quentarus triggered the heavy gravity emitters the engineers had affixed to the ceiling, setting them to proximity mode. We watched as the Imperium forces moved into range and the crushing gravity field activated, annihilating their forward ranks, leaving a deadly trap for them to overcome while the lieutenant triggered a set of charges to collapse the hallway to the command center by the barricades.

"There were just over a hundred and eighty soldiers out of the five hundred and fifty or so we had manning the barricades at the start of the battle that made it into the command center," he said, their losses hitting him hard once more. "Exhausted and sealed off, we took a moment to catch our collective breath, many of us having taken shifts at the barricades or helping to pull back the wounded. Meanwhile, the sounds on the other side of the entrance echoed through the walls. Thousands of Insectoids scraping and clawing, intent on breaking through… We knew it was only a matter of time.

"The admiral was…*amazing*. He walked through our ranks, stopping to check in on each and every soldier, many of them wounded or bloodied. He put his hand on people's shoulders, talked to them, thanked them for their courageous actions. The boost in morale was noticeable as men and women, some nearly broken moments before, found their will to fight once more," he said, still impressed with Admiral Valentyen's ability to inspire. "After a few minutes to rest, Lieutenant Quentarus and the admiral organized us into teams, staging the wounded near the rear of the command center to rest and provide support as a last resort. They then set up the rest of us throughout the command center, creating kill boxes and cross fires, as well as fallback locations with fresh weapons caches.

"At just after 16:11 local time, they finally took out the grav-generators and broke through the entrance, spilling into the command center. The collapsed entryway was too small for the larger Insectoids, but smaller creatures like Ants and Skifters, along with several other species I didn't recognize and dozens of smaller creatures, poured in. Despite our preparations and several phalanx units, the surge and sheer numbers, most with no regard for their own lives as they rushed through, quickly pushed us back. Our front lines were forced to pull back, and we knew it was just a matter of time until we would be overwhelmed.

"They continued to flow into the room, more targets than we could possibly hit. Dozens of frag grenades launched into the horde, but it barely thinned them out. We created a concentrated wall of fire with our flamethrowers, killing them by the hundreds, but they just kept coming. Twenty soldiers moved forward with sonic rifles, ripping them to shreds and stemming the tide momentarily. For an instant, it seemed like it was over… Then the next wave came. Then the next. Lieutenant Quentarus threw two amber grenades at the hallway opening, sealing it momentarily, while the rest of us, now less that a hundred of us still uninjured and combat ready, cleared out the remaining enemy targets. The lieutenant threw two more grenades, creating a barrier ten meters thick, buying us precious time to regroup. The admiral quickly had us pull back the wounded and reestablish proper firing lines and kill boxes. But we could hear them on the other side of the amber, pounding on it. Chipping it away.

"I looked around the room, taking stock of our numbers and dwindling defenses, knowing that we could only hold out for a short time longer. The admiral pulled up the last two active drones we had, and we could see the corridor outside, every square inch teeming with Insectoids. He looked to me, then Lieutenant Quentarus, each of us knowing that we were about to be overrun. Before any of us could say anything, a call came over the comm. A group of eighteen soldiers were still alive out by the barricades. Part of the last barricade had collapsed, trapping them in a corner. They'd hidden in the bodies and debris, knowing they were surrounded. Then one of them was discovered, and we could hear them firing, listening over the comm as they screamed for help."

Jackson shook his head, recalling the sounds of their voices, barely audible over the staccato of weapons fire.

"That's when the admiral finally gave me the nod, and I activated the Ancient device on my belt – the tactical forcefield generator – and went on the offensive," he said, trying his best to recall the events that followed through the haze of adrenaline-fueled memories.

"I ran for the amber barricade, flipping the field to the intangibility mode, running right through it and dropping half a dozen frag grenades in my wake once inside the hallway to clear it out. I then darted out of the hallway, turning right and flipping the field to attack mode. The forcefield around me glowed red and grew to twice my height, claws forming where the field represented my hands and feet. I rushed forward, cutting my way through the ranks of Insectoids in my path, slashing and tearing them to shreds. The grenades detonated behind me, killing most of the Insectoids in the hallway. The ones attacking the surviving soldiers suddenly turned, coming at me.

"Everything became a blur as I hacked and slashed at anything that moved as I cleared out the enemy troops, appearing before the last eleven survivors standing atop a sea of corpses. 'Be ready!' I called, turning back as a wave of enemies poured into the open space I'd cleared behind me.

"My AI flipped between combat modes several times, changing from the red attack mode to the green impact mode, and I took on several huge Arachnids, the power of the forcefield throwing them back with each strike like they weighed nothing, smashing them into the walls and crushing scores of their troops. I went back to attack mode after that, cutting through their lines as their forward assault ceased, and their focus turned entirely on me as I charged into their ranks, taking down everything they threw at me."

Jackson took a breath, focusing his mind, remembering the sense of righteous vengeance that had filled him as he took the fight to the enemy. "I was out there for"—he shook his head—"I don't even know, maybe eight or ten minutes, just fighting with everything I had. My AI kept my stamina up, hitting me with battle stims and watching my back. I took out more of their heavy hitters, the forcefield devastating anything that came my way. I was like an unstoppable juggernaut, slicing and smashing through the Imperium ranks with impunity," he said, his voice quavering as he recalled the rage he had felt at seeing the bodies of the soldiers who'd died defending the barricades, driving him further into his bloodlust. "I honestly have no idea how many Insectoids I took out, hundreds for sure, maybe thousands. I honestly don't know…

"Lieutenant Quentarus rallied around twenty-five officers, and they took down the amber barricade and moved back into the hallway, laying down heavy fire and taking out hundreds more targets while they were preoccupied with me, pushing the Insectoids back, farther and farther from the barricades. Another team, led by Commander Winters, followed Quentarus and rescued the soldiers trapped at the barricades, finding nearly a dozen more hidden under debris or Insectoid bodies, many barely alive. They got them back to the command center.

"I was halfway down the corridor, over two hundred meters from the barricades by this point, when another massive wave of enemy reinforcements came at me. I switched the forcefield generator to full-shield mode, an orange hue surrounding me, then tossed six shockwave grenades into the massive sea of Insectoids. The grenades went off seconds later, throwing me back but keeping me safe in my protective bubble as the shockwaves ripped through the enemy, wiping out huge numbers and creating a gap in their assault. I then pulled the two Ancient pistols from my hips and opened fire. The deadly beams lanced forward, ripping through the enemies' shields as though they weren't there, dropping hundreds more.

"I kept up the attack for a few more minutes, firing wildly before the pistols finally ran out of power. The forcefield generator's power was starting to get low as well, down to just a quarter left. I switched it to the purple intangibility mode as another wave of Insectoids approached from the darkness, and I ran straight into their ranks! I passed through them as though they were mist, turning the corner to the next corridor, then pulled the portal ring from my back. I activated it and targeted an area a few thousand kilometers above the planet, then opened the portal aperture to its maximum size, just a little over four meters in diameter.

"The sound of rushing air and screeching was deafening, as thousands of Insectoids were sucked through the portal into the vacuum of space while I stood where I was, untouchable and unaffected by the chaos around me. I watched for several seconds, everything around me a blur as it whipped by, the force of the decompression devastating. Finally, my AI alerted me that the forcefield generator was down to just five percent power, and I closed the portal. I stood there, suddenly completely alone in the blackness of the nearly empty corridor. How many Insectoids, I couldn't even guess, maybe thousands, were simply gone. Sucked out into space. It was the strangest feeling. Being surrounded by all that surging life, all that chaos one second, then suddenly alone in the darkness the next…

"I snapped out of it and ran back towards the main corridor and the barricades, just as the forcefield generator fluctuated. Lieutenant Quentarus and the officers with her watched my back as I made it to their position. We stood there in silence, the feeling still surreal, like the quiet calm before a storm. Not a single enemy contact emerged for over five minutes while we stood and watched. Finally, one of the drones deeper in the fortress alerted us to another wave heading our way. We tossed dozens of frag grenades set to proximity mode, then headed back through the entrance into the command center. The lieutenant and two others launched three rocket-propelled grenades into the ceiling just outside the hallway, bringing a large part of it down, along with rock from the mountain. They then filled the hallway with the remaining amber grenades they had, filling half the tunnel. Finally, she collapsed the rest, sealing us in the command center once more and buying us time," Jackson said, recalling the feeling of hundreds of eyes on him as he entered the command center, the soldiers there awestruck by what had just happened.

"Just over an hour and a half later, the Insectoids broke through the entrance to the command center once more. The fighting that followed was intense. We tried to contain them from getting through, but it wasn't enough, and the gap they created was steadily widening. Just when it looked like we were about to be overrun, Lieutenant Quentarus and the admiral rallied our forces, holding the line and repelling wave after wave after wave, pushing them back, then plugging the hole once more with several foam grenades, creating a temporary reprieve. The barrier bought us precious seconds to regroup, but it didn't last long.

"A few of the engineers had been hard at work, rigging up a portable forcefield generator, and they came forward and quickly set it up in front of the entrance while we stood ready to provide cover. They activated it, creating a makeshift barrier at the entryway. It actually worked far better than any of us could have hoped, and the force field it created kept them at bay for nearly half an hour before the power ran out." He paused, shaking his head slowly. "After the field came down though…they broke through. And everything descended into utter chaos.

"We'd set up our final phalanx, which was only partially operational, and deployed the last of our tactical drones, but it wasn't nearly enough. They came at us fast and hard. The first in were a large group of armored beetle-like creatures that scuttled forward and had powerful shield generators, clearing a path for a group of Wasps, which quickly took flight, swarming the room. We lost nineteen people in a matter of seconds. Several of us, including me, had cryo-weapons and micro-missiles embedded in our suits, and we used them to bring the Wasps down, then took them out quickly, before they could recover. Somehow, despite their increasing numbers, we continued to hold them back for several more minutes, giving ground but keeping them contained for the most part.

"We threw everything we had at them as we fell back, step-by-step, our only advantage the limited space in the room and the increasing piles of Insectoid bodies, which limited their attack vectors. Despite that, they pressed forward, pushing through everything we could throw at them, the piles of corpses coming almost like a wave moving towards us, the horde behind using their fallen as cover. Our forces continued to weaken as they overwhelmed pockets of us or forced groups back into alcoves where they made their last stand. I fell back to the Shroud chamber with a small group as their numbers became overwhelming, narrowly escaping the command center before it was completely overrun.

"I…" Jackson paused, closing his eyes and swallowing hard. "I didn't see what happened to Lieutenant Quentarus or the rest of our people who were trapped in the command center," he said, forcing the words out through the pain in his chest. "We lost contact with them after multiple grenades went off. Seconds later, the first of the Insectoids made it through the breach we'd created from the command center into the Shroud chamber. We took up defensive positions with clean lines of sight, attacking anything that came through the hole from multiple vectors, stemming the flow by choking it off with Insectoid bodies. I can't say for certain how much time passed, but we held our position for at least five minutes before the first of their centipedes slipped through. They unleashed at least thirty of them at us, forcing most our group to focus their fire on picking them off and creating an opening for a swarm of Wasps and a group of heavily armed and armored Ants to enter the room.

"It's mostly a blur after that. We continued to fight, but they took us out one by one as more and more poured through the breach. I saw..." Jackson looked down, trying to breathe as the image replayed itself in his mind suddenly. "I saw a blast of plasma fire hit the overhang above Chief Johansen and one of the engineers. I..." He clenched his fists, holding back his emotions, trying to get through the final parts of his report, the memory of what had happened and the losses of his friends finally hitting him. "I don't think that he could have survived."

Jackson took a moment to center himself, then pressed on, knowing he owed it to all of them to tell their stories. "I can't say exactly what happened next. I was up on a catwalk with Commander Winters. Another wave of Wasps had made it through, swarming the room. We were attempting to take down as many as we could, but they were coming at us from all sides. That was the last time I saw her..." he said, shaking his head, recalling how they'd been standing back-to-back just seconds before, firing in both directions.

"The next thing I remember, something, an explosion of some kind, rocked the entire complex. I remember falling. It must have been ten meters, maybe more. My thrusters fired at the last second, but I hit the ground hard, and two huge Ants came at me. I scrambled to my feet and leapt forward without thinking, launching into them with my thrusters and using my suit to form blades to stab and slash at them, my rifle lost in the fall. I finished the last one off when an

Arachnid got the jump on me, one of its legs impaling me. I… I remember getting off a quick shot from the plasma cannon in my suit, then falling back and hitting the ground. I thought I was done for…"

Jackson closed his eyes and bit the inside of his lower lip as he attempted to find the words to continue. He took a deep breath, pushing the emotions down deep inside, forcing himself to finish his report. "The last thing that I remember is Admiral Valentyen running over to me, laying down heavy fire. I… I couldn't move my legs, and I was lying on my back out in the open. My left arm had been badly slashed and was nearly useless as I fumbled for a nearby pistol. The admiral, he…he stood above me with a rifle in one hand, and I remember him reaching down. He must have grabbed the sidearm as well.

"It was chaos all around us. Wasps still buzzing, Ants and Arachnids closing. But he held his ground. He stood over me, firing in both directions, taking on…I don't know how many enemies. Staying out in the open to protect me, even though he knew it was hopeless. He was…" Tears streaked down Jackson's face. He looked up, meeting the admirals' eyes. "*He was amazing*," he said proudly, nodding his head slowly. "Against impossible odds, he protected me, protected the mission. To his dying breath, he fought for all of us. Never giving up. He… He was a true hero."

Jackson sat in silence for a moment, thinking of his friends and his mentor, knowing that he wouldn't be alive if it weren't for all of them.

"The next thing that I remember is waking up to the sound of the admiral's comm beeping. I crawled over, tapping the controls on his wrist, and that's when I heard Admiral Vincenze's voice. He said that the Fleet had taken the system and that ground troops were on their way."

Jackson shook his head. "I honestly have no idea how I'm still alive. I'm sorry, but that's all that I can tell you. Perhaps my AI can fill in some more of the gaps."

"I want to thank you, Captain Jackson, for your report and for your service to the Confederation," Fleet Admiral Lighton said kindly. "I'm very sorry for what you and everyone on Stornoway went through and the sacrifices you all made. You should know that our rescue teams found Lieutenant Quentarus in the command center. She was in a collapsed alcove, barely alive. She's in critical condition at a hospital on Delconia, receiving the best care possible, I assure you. Chief Johansen was also found. His legs were crushed, and he was very badly injured, but he's still alive and in intensive care here at a medical facility on Archon."

Jackson couldn't believe what he was hearing, that somehow, they had miraculously survived. He wanted nothing more than to go and see them, but he hung on, praying for news that the admiral had somehow made it as well.

"There were four other survivors in the command center," Admiral Lighton continued. "Captain Lauzon, Lieutenant Ferish, Ensign Coleman, and Commander Winters. Ferish, incredibly, was found at the barricade. A damaged support beam had fallen, trapping him in a corner and knocking him unconscious. The Insectoids must have thought he was dead. Ensign Coleman was in the command center, and, like Lieutenant Quentarus, when the ceiling collapsed, it sealed him in. Lauzon and Winters were the last two standing in the Shroud chamber, and they, along with the admiral, are the reason that you're still alive.

"Captain Lauzon used his last cluster of missiles to bring down part of the ceiling, which apparently had been weakened during the explosion you mentioned that rocked the complex. The ceiling took out a large contingent of the Insectoid troops as they were entering through the breach and closed it. With the room sealed, he and Commander Winters managed to pick off the rest of the remaining enemy troops, and she was able to stabilize you with a med-kit. Admiral Valentyen had been gravely wounded, but both reported that he fought right until the end, only collapsing after the last enemy soldier was down."

Jackson nodded numbly, completely speechless, picturing the admiral as he'd last seen him, the image burned into his mind. A swell of pride filled him at the man he knew. The man who'd saved him. The man who never gave up until the job was done.

"Thank you once again for your exemplary service, Captain. You'll be taken back to the hospital for further treatment, but I'm told that you'll make a full recovery in time," Fleet Admiral Lighton said, giving him the slightest of nods. "Dismissed."

"Thank you, ma'am," Jackson said, saluting, the memories of everything that had happened weighing heavily on him.

Fleet Admiral Lighton signaled to the medical officer who'd brought Jackson in, and he was taken back to the hospital.

As the next week unfolded, the events of Stornoway changed everything.

CHAPTER 17
CELEBRATION AND SADNESS

Shortly after Jackson returned to the hospital, Daria came to visit. She'd been to see him several times in the previous days, but he'd still been unconscious, forcing her to delay their reunion. This time she arrived just as he was waking up, having fallen into an exhausted sleep after the physical and emotional toll his debriefing had taken on him.

He looked up, smiling as she entered the room. "Hey," he said, her presence like a warm blanket wrapping around him.

After a quick reunion, she took him in a hover-chair down to the cafeteria, where they sat in a quiet corner, basking in the sunlight from one of the huge windows and talking quietly.

"How are you doing, Will?" she asked delicately.

"Still sore, but I'm told that I'll be okay. The feeling has finally started to return to both of my legs, so I'm excited to try walking again. I start *traction* in a few days. So that should be fun," he said, allowing himself a half-hearted smile. "They've said not to set my expectations too high to start, but I'm optimistic I'll be back on my feet soon."

"That's wonderful; I'm glad to hear it," she said, her face brightening. "How are you coping with everything?"

"It's a lot…but I'm okay. The news about the admiral, I… It's… It's hard to believe he's gone." He shook his head, still trying to come to terms with everything that had happened.

"I know. It seems like it's impossible, doesn't it? Like there's been a mistake somehow. That there's no way someone like Admiral Valentyen could be gone. But…he is, Will," she said, placing her hand on his, the two of them sitting in silence for a moment before she changed the subject. "I checked in on Hen last night. He was only conscious for a few minutes, but he said to say hello and to tell you he's so relieved that you made it out as well."

"How's he doing?"

"He's in pretty rough shape. His legs were crushed just above the knees, and he would have been too if it wasn't for a metal beam that came down next to him and kept a bigger piece from crushing him altogether. He's got lots of other injuries, including some damage to a few organs and a few broken ribs, but all of that is easily fixable. They're starting the procedure today, actually, to regrow his legs. He'll be unconscious for a few days while the biosynthesizers and genetic sequencers operate, and even though he'll have his legs fully back in a day or two, it'll be at least a couple of weeks before he'll be ready to start walking again. It's going to be a long hard road to recovery for him, unfortunately," she said, her expression darkening slightly. "Bio-regeneration of entire limbs, especially legs, takes a heavy toll on the body, but he should recover in time."

"I'm glad that he's going to be okay. I'd like to see him soon, but the doctors have been telling me to focus on my own recovery first and to consider being well enough to go and see him one of my goals," he said, his thoughts shifting and his face turning grave. "Have you heard anything about Kelara?"

"Not much. She's still on Delconia. I went to see her before making the trip here, but she was back in surgery again. The doctors are quite frankly amazed that she survived. I took a quick look at her file, and to be honest, I am too. Collapsed lung, broken clavicle, severe concussion, her right arm severed above the elbow, dozens of shrapnel wounds, multiple stab wounds, internal bleeding, and the list goes on. How she held on, I have no idea."

"Must be that Quentarus stubbornness. She was never one to give up at anything."

Daria nodded and smiled. "I'm going to go and see her once she's been downgraded, but for now, she's still in the ICU in critical condition. The doctors are hopeful, however, that she'll pull through."

"That's good to hear. She did an incredible job. She and the admiral held things together. We wouldn't have lasted half as long as we did without them."

"There's one more thing," Daria said delicately. "The funeral for the admiral is tomorrow morning, and there's a ceremony planned later that afternoon to honor those who fell at Stornoway. If you're able to, the brass would really like you to attend."

Jackson nodded slowly. "Okay," he said softly, an ache in his chest at the thought of burying the admiral.

"I'll come and pick you up in the morning. Don't worry. I've taken care of everything."

"Thanks, Daria," Jackson said, placing his hand on top of hers. "You're a good friend."

The next morning, she returned, picking him up from the hospital a few hours before the funeral. As promised, she'd taken care of everything, sending over a fresh dress uniform for him and having the hospital staff assist him in getting ready. For the first time in several days, he felt a sense of focus, of purpose.

Today, that purpose was to honor the admiral and those who had fought with them, and he was determined to do his best to see it through.

The ceremony for the admiral was perfect.

Exactly what he would have wanted, Jackson thought. A formal professional tribute to all of his years of service, with a smaller personal touch focusing on his family and friends.

Admiral Thompson gave a heartfelt eulogy, speaking about their years of friendship and recounting several humorous adventures from their earlier days serving together. A few other officers spoke, offering similar tributes to the late admiral and sharing how he'd influenced their lives and careers, Jackson only then realizing the number of lives his mentor had touched and the impact one person could have.

As one of the officers spoke, Jackson recalled the admiral moving through the ranks before the final battle of Stornoway, taking a moment to check in with each and every soldier in the command center, and the effect his presence had on them.

That's what leadership looks like, he thought, hoping that one day, he could be even half the leader Admiral Valentyen had been.

Several smaller personal tributes, including eulogies from family members, concluded the ceremony, and afterwards, dozens of people gathered in a large room with food and drinks, sharing memories and smiling as they remembered the incredible man whose service, dedication, kindness, and honor had touched so many.

As was common in the GCH, Admiral Valentyen had been married several times, and after the funeral, Jackson had a chance to briefly speak with two of his former wives. The admiral's first wife—he learned during one of the eulogies—had passed away after forty-one years of marriage. They'd had one child together, a daughter, who had gone on to serve in the Fleet. She'd been killed in the line of duty many years later, crushing them both. After that, both he and his wife, Shaelyn, had poured themselves into their work. She died a few years later from an outbreak of the Nuvarian plague while working at an Outlier colony, providing aid after a large, devastating hurricane had struck.

He'd met his second wife, Miranda, just under a decade later, and they had been together for fifty-three years, having had three children before they finally, amicably, decided to part ways, their paths diverging as he went back to the Fleet and she returned to academia. Just over twenty years later, he married his last wife, Julene, whom he was with for thirty-eight years.

He had kept in touch with both of his ex-wives, and they'd still shared dinner on their former anniversaries each year. They also saw one another at family gatherings and kept in touch over subspace. Each described him in their speeches as an honorable and caring man, dedicated to the protection of the Confederation, and as a wonderful father and husband.

Miranda worked as an administrator now at the largest university on Galathon, Jackson learned while they chatted. She was tall, with long black hair, thin cheeks, and a soft voice. Julene worked as an instructor at the tactical academy on Balath. She was shorter, with shoulder-length grayish-blonde hair and a kind but serious face. Both had heard about him from the admiral and were delighted to meet him in person. He expressed his sincerest condolences for their losses, a terrible secret guilt hanging over him that the admiral had given his life to protect his own.

Finally, he met the admiral's sons, Tristan and Nate, and his daughter, Emilie. Nate bore a striking resemblance to the admiral, while Emilie had the same sharp gray eyes. As they briefly chatted, he found it difficult to look at either of them for more than a few seconds, a sorrow filling him at seeing his former mentor reflected in their faces.

Daria came to get him a few minutes later, taking him out for lunch before they headed to the ceremony at the Fields of Remembrance. She told him that they had planned to build a monument to the Siege of Stornoway, as it was now being called, and brought him to a large circular field surrounded by beautiful gardens where the future site would be and the ceremony was being held.

Jackson was given a place of honor in the front row, along with Captain Lauzon, Lieutenant Ferish, Ensign Coleman, and Commander Winters. Daria parked his chair near the center of the row, between them and several other senior officers, including Admirals Easton, Carter, Scott, Thompson, and Janus, along with Captain Delgado. Jackson looked down the row, meeting each of the survivors' eyes and giving them a silent nod.

As his eyes met Winters's, the sight of her caused his heart to race in his chest. She was stunning. Her blonde hair was just barely visible near the top of her forehead, while the rest remained neatly tucked under her dress hat. Her piercing blue eyes met his own, and they shared a silent exchange while she stood at the end of the row, tall and proud.

The ceremony began a few moments later with the usual formalities, and after several minutes, Jackson found he began to grow numb to everything around him. The speaker, Jackson couldn't remember his name, listed off the numbers of ships and soldiers lost during the initial assault. He then went on to recount the statistics during the thirty-six hours that passed while the GCH forces held the base after the Fleet departed.

As he spoke, Jackson's mind drifted back to the present, the realization that tears had unconsciously begun to stream down his cheeks hitting him, along with a wave of raw emotion washing over him at the staggering price the GCH had paid to retake and hold the Stornoway System.

He turned his head slightly, looking over at the other surviving officers—Lauzon, Ferish, Coleman, and Winters—each of them brushing away fresh tears of their own. Jackson didn't attempt to hide or wipe his away. He simply listened as the speaker listed the numbers of lives lost, recounting several of the valiant defenses mounted and courageous sacrifices made, telling stories on behalf of each of the survivors and their fallen comrades.

The speaker shared how Gamma and Delta squads, along with the engineers, had fought to their deaths to hold the power core, allowing the team in the command center time to complete their mission.

He recounted stories of the assault on the main entrance and the battle above the planet when the Fleet returned to retake the system. "The two armadas were locked in a bloody battle, the Imperium forces holding the line with greater numbers as another six hundred ships jumped in just before our ships arrived, tipping the odds in the enemy's favor. Despite being outnumbered, our Fleet pressed on, taking the attack to the Imperium, desperate to get to the brave souls who stayed behind on the planet below. The battle raged on for nearly fifteen minutes, each side taking heavy losses, until a daring maneuver by Admiral Thompson broke through the enemy blockade, attacking the Arachnid command ship at the rear of the formation and taking it down!

"It was this same Arachnid ship that crashed into the surface near the complex, nearly taking it out entirely. The shockwave and ensuing devastation wiped out all of the remaining Imperium ground forces outside and collapsed huge sections of the base, stemming the flow and undoubtedly saving the lives of the last few soldiers still standing.

"With the command ship gone, the Imperium lines crumbled, forcing them to pull back in an attempt to regroup. Admiral Easton charged forward with the *Vengeance,* along with seven other ships, creating a wedge in their lines and unleashing the power of both the dreadnought's broadsides at once, devastating the stricken enemy ships. Seeing an opportunity, Admiral Carter's attack group barreled into the enemy's left flank, the *Alexia* pounding them and swinging around to box them in. Admiral Vincenze pressed the forward attack, hammering the Insectoids with all they had, breaking their lines entirely. Moments later, Admiral Thompson's ships returned to the fray, swinging around the right flank, our forces now surrounding the enemy and pummeling them relentlessly, routing them in the ensuing chaos."

The orator stopped, allowing a silence to hang in the air for a moment, his voice lowering, his cadence slowing. "Within minutes, the last of the Imperium fleet was wiped out, and the skies above Stornoway were ours once more," he concluded triumphantly, his voice rising at the end.

The speaker went on to detail how the Fleet then launched hundreds of shuttles filled with ground troops and medics, rushing to reach the GCH forces inside the base as quickly as possible, in a desperate hope of finding survivors.

As the stories played out in Jackson's mind, a sudden awareness of where he was, of what they'd accomplished, and of his shared place in history began to take hold.

This was his D-Day. His defining moment.

The defining moment of the entire war.

As the speaker continued, Jackson closed his eyes, envisioning each of the events in his mind while he listened, the orator recounting in riveting detail the final stand at the command center, holding his audience breathless.

His tone was high and full of life as he described how they held out against incredible odds, then his voice lowered, his speech slowing to a somber tone as he described how they fell.

Jackson felt an overwhelming sense of pride in himself and his fellow officers while he listened to the mosaic of stories.

The finale of the speech concluded with Admiral Valentyen's last stand, selflessly giving his life to defend the wounded Captain Jackson, who, it was noted, uncovered the location of the Shroud in the first place and helped to plan the attack. He explained how Captain Lauzon sealed the chamber and, together with Commander Winters and the mortally wounded Admiral Valentyen, cleared the room in a last-ditch effort to survive.

The orator ended his vivid narrative with Jackson answering the admiral's comm to let the Fleet know that they were still alive—and the revelation for all assembled that they had discovered the secrets of the Shroud of Darkness.

"And that is why the Siege of Stornoway will be remembered throughout the ages as *the* turning point of this war. It is a tragic loss of life. A tale of ultimate bravery and sacrifice. And a triumph that will echo throughout the ages as one of the noblest defenses of the Confederation of all time!" he said dramatically, finishing the tale.

After a moment of silence, the speaker shared that ninety-seven other survivors had also been found since the Fleet arrived and were recovering from their injuries on other worlds and, thus, could not be there that day. He then thanked each of them for their sacrifices before turning the proceedings over to Fleet Admiral Mendez.

The Fleet admiral, one of the five who held that title, the highest-ranking position in the GCH military, presented each of the officers in the first row with the Order of Dalath—the highest honor in the service—recognizing their sacrifice for the greater good of all of humanity.

She then addressed the assembled crowd. "Today is a day to look back. To reflect on the sacrifices of those who made this pivotal victory possible." She paused, gesturing to the survivors in the front row. "And today is also a day to look forward," she said, her powerful voice resonating in the open air.

"Over the past week," she continued, "our engineers have used the information gathered from the Siege of Stornoway to turn the enemy's Shroud of Darkness against them! The trojan virus, designed and inserted into the Imperium network by Chief Technologist Henrik Johansen, was activated by GCH Command just days ago, and all of Shroud's command systems came under our control. Our engineers then *reversed* the Shroud, leaving the Imperium forces blinded in their own space, while we gained the ability to see their entire fleet across tens of thousands of light-years, along with all of their military assets."

She paused, allowing the revelation to hang in the air for a moment as the assembled crowd quickly realized the devastating consequences of the Shroud of Darkness turning on its masters. "Over the past several days, GCH Command has conducted Operation Onslaught, consisting of wave after wave of our armadas entering Imperium space and eliminating enemy targets and installations. Since that time, our Fleet has destroyed thirty-nine enemy supply outposts, fourteen bases, seventy-eight mining operations, sixteen supply convoys, two military research facilities, and nearly sixty-three hundred enemy vessels in just over a span of seventy-two hours," she said proudly.

"At 05:00 hours this morning, Archonian Galactic Standard Time, the Imperium Council officially contacted GCH Command with an offer of a ceasefire," she said, pausing as all in attendance took in this new development. "Fleet Admiral Lighton led the response, consulting with me and the other fleet admirals, along with the GCH Council, sending them our terms shortly thereafter. These included the immediate withdrawal of all Imperium ships, soldiers, and occupying forces from *all* systems seized by the Imperium during the war. Furthermore, we dictated that a region of space twenty light-years wide will be created as a demilitarized zone of neutral territory between our empires, following the existing Holt Line and occupying the territory currently on their side. This effectively pushes the Imperium back, stripping them of hundreds of systems along the Line, while significantly weakening their ability to threaten our borders again.

"The GCH will also maintain control over the Shroud of Darkness *indefinitely*. All facilities that maintain the Shroud are to be abandoned by Imperium personnel, and any attempts to regain control of them will be viewed as an act of war. Finally, all Imperium fleets will be allowed a limited window of navigation to pull back and may not reside within a twenty-five-light-year distance from the demilitarized zone after that point. Only unarmed transport ships will be allowed to enter the DMZ in order to evacuate their troops and occupying forces on the worlds they conquered or must cede as part of the terms.

"These terms were *nonnegotiable*," she added sternly. "And we concluded our message with a warning that further military actions were pending following a brief ceasefire period of no more than two hours. Our response was clear that if they did not respond within this time, indicating their immediate acceptance of these terms, we would continue our campaign against them."

The Fleet admiral paused for a moment, allowing all of what she'd just told them to sink in, as the audience of nearly a hundred and fifty people sat in complete silence.

"The two-hour window passed with no response, and a massive GCH armada attacked two of their major systems, annihilating over four thousand of their ships, along with dozens of stations, shipyards, and other military assets seventy-eight light-years from the border, deep inside their space. A show of force to display our resolve and demonstrate that none of their systems were safe from our reach while we controlled the Shroud.

"At 13:27 hours this afternoon, just over an hour ago, we received a communication from the Imperium Council that they have unconditionally accepted all our terms." She paused, her voice rising as she continued. "Ladies and gentlemen, it is my great honor to inform you all that the war is now officially *over*!"

The assembly cheered, tears of sorrow changing to tears of joy, as one of the longest and bloodiest conflicts in GCH history had finally come to an end.

Jackson, and the other survivors in the front row, took in the news that their sacrifices, and those of the brave officers they fought with, had not been in vain and that their mission had been a success.

They'd made a difference.

They'd turned the tide of the war.

They'd changed the course of history.

CHAPTER 18

RESURRECTIONS

Several weeks passed while Jackson's recovery moved at a frustratingly slow pace. Though he continued to get stronger every day, the toll on his body had been severe, and he found his overall lack of energy and soreness kept him from making progress quickly.

Winters had come to see him the day after the ceremony, much to his surprise, and they sat, talking easily and of simple things, the immediate connection they shared evident to both of them as the hours slipped by effortlessly.

She returned again several days later, then again, the day after that. Soon, her visits became the best part of his day.

He was finally released from the hospital nearly three weeks after first arriving, and she took him out for dinner to celebrate. She'd bragged that she knew an amazing Cicarrian restaurant in the old town of Panthos City on Archon, and the meal, especially after weeks of synthesized hospital food, didn't disappoint.

They ate and laughed, sharing easy conversation while they sipped wine, their eyes meeting across the candlelit table. By the end of the night, they ended up back at Winters's hotel, their clothes scattered around the room as they lay entwined in one another's arms in her bed, the soft moonlight flooding the room while they talked late into the night.

The next morning, Jackson awoke with a pit of guilt in his stomach at the thought of betraying Verris. Despite everything she'd said to him, he still loved her and harbored a hidden hope that, one day, she would come back to him.

Most of all, though, he felt the weight of guilt for allowing himself to believe that Winters might somehow be Amy.

That she'd somehow come back to him. And that being with her was somehow a betrayal of the memory of his lost wife.

He knew all of the so-called facts and science on reincarnation, but he'd still never really believed it.

Meeting Sierra Winters had changed all of that.

She, in turn, was amazed at how quickly and completely she'd fallen for Jackson. She wasn't certain if it was the way he looked at her, or his kind, confident demeanor, or if it was something else, but she felt as though she was floating, the experience sweeping her off her feet like nothing ever had before.

Two days later, Jackson paced anxiously around the hotel room while she showered, clenching and unclenching his hands.

Today is the day, he told himself, determined that he had to be honest with her.

He ordered room service, and they sat at a small table near the floor-to-ceiling windows, sipping their coffee, stealing secretive glances at one another, the soft orange light of the early-morning sun bathing them in its glow. His heart pounded in his chest as he stared at the woman before him, like something out of a dream, and in that moment, he realized that he couldn't go through with it.

He couldn't tell her.

What if she somehow really is Amy or another version of her? he argued with himself, unable to bear the thought of pushing her away, of losing the woman he loved once again.

And if she wasn't, then it was just a happy coincidence, he tried to convince himself; and it doesn't matter, he reasoned, desperately clinging to the need to be with her.

And so, he said nothing, unable to deny himself a second chance at happiness with the woman he was falling in love with all over again.

The days turned to weeks, and soon they were living together in an apartment on Archon, both taking time off from the Fleet, having more than earned the break. They avoided talking about their past and their time in the service, focusing instead on living in the present and enjoying one another's company.

Henrik slowly recovered and was finally released from the hospital a few weeks after Jackson. Daria walked him out to find Jackson, along with Winters, waiting for him. Jackson embraced his friend in a hug, so grateful that he was still alive after thinking he'd lost him.

Kelara, meanwhile, was still progressing slowly. She was downgraded to stable condition, and Jackson went with Daria and Henrik to visit her on Delconia as soon as she was cleared for guests. Most of her wounds had healed, but her head trauma had left her with lingering balance issues and headaches, along with a few injuries that needed more time to fully heal. Her right arm had been replaced with a cybernetic limb, which she had opted for instead of having her arm regrown. Her new arm looked completely natural but was made from a highly durable military-grade alloy. It enhanced her strength significantly, which she gleefully demonstrated, holding a metal cup and crushing it before their eyes, a wicked smile crossing her lips.

Their visit, although brief, helped her immensely, and her recovery began to pick up speed shortly thereafter.

The next few weeks passed as Jackson and Winters spent most of their time together, sharing dinners with friends and touring various sites across Archon and Delconia, the Fleet and their past far from their minds.

After the second month of leave, both Jackson and Winters began slowly talking of returning to duty, each wanting to do their part to help rebuild after the war.

Henrik and Daria had both returned to work a few weeks before. The chief was keen to study everything that the GCH had learned about the Shroud and its underlying technology since Stornoway, and the doctor returned to her lab, resuming her work from before the war.

Lieutenant Quentarus finally recovered from her injuries, the crew taking her out to celebrate. While happy to be free from the boredom and confinement of the hospital, she learned that it would be months before she would be cleared to resume active black-ops duty. Without a purpose, she struggled to find a path forward, uncertain of her place in the Fleet after years spent fighting endless battles.

Kelara went to visit her mother for several days, the two seeing each other for the first time in nearly a year since the ceremony to honor the *Viceroy*. She returned to Archon a short time later, meeting up with Jackson and the doctor for coffee shortly after she got back.

Quentarus had seen Jackson and Winters together now a few times, and it left her feeling numb after her short romantic liaison with the commander, uncertain as to how she felt about seeing them together. Jackson picked up on the awkwardness, and Winters later explained what had happened after a tense battle against the Canids and the night at the bar that brought them together. Both of them decided it was best for Winters to hang back as Jackson and the doctor went to meet with Quentarus, not wanting to make things any more awkward than they already were.

"I'm just not sure what I'm supposed to do now," Quentarus said, the frustration clear in her voice as the conversation turned to how she was reacclimating to things.

"Maybe you just need some time," the doctor offered, knowing Kelara had seen some of the most intense action of anyone during the war.

The lieutenant shook her head slowly. "I know, it's just... The Fleet's been my life, you know? I was born into it. It's all I've ever known. And now, without it, I don't know who I am anymore."

"This could be a good thing," the doctor pressed. "You should take some time. Find yourself. Get out there and see the Confederation. See what it is you've been defending all these years."

Jackson nodded. "I've been doing the same thing. Sierra and I..." He paused, catching himself, instantly regretting mentioning Winters's name. "It's been good to remember what life outside the Fleet is like. To see normal people going about their lives. Different cultures, art, and the beauty all around us that we've sacrificed so much for." He paused, reading Kelara's expression, sensing that she was drowning across from him, desperately searching for something to cling to. He turned, giving the doctor a quick look.

Daria let out a small breath, giving him the slightest of nods, already knowing what he was thinking.

"We've been talking..." he said slowly, the lieutenant meeting his eyes, noticing the shift in his demeanor. "About picking back up where we left off before the war…" He trailed off for a second, recalling the destruction of the *Viceroy* once more. The moment the war began. The one that sent Kelara down the dark path she'd been on. "I reached out to Fleet Admiral Lighton a few days ago, and she's agreed to see me…us, a few days from now. We're going to ask if we could resume the search for Ancient sites now that the war's over."

Quentarus noticeably perked up as Jackson spoke, her expression turning dower a moment later. "You… You were going to leave me behind," she said, the revelation hitting her. "Why?"

The doctor gave Jackson a worried look, then turned to face Quentarus. "We honestly thought you needed a break. You've been through so much, and it was on that mission where all of this started. We didn't want you to feel that you had to come."

"You would have left without me?" she said, the hurt clear in her voice.

"We were still figuring it out. We don't even have permission to go, or a ship or anything. Daria, Hen, and I have just been talking, is all," Jackson interjected. "Of course we want you with us, Kelara, but we didn't know if it was what was best for you. We've all been worried about you." He paused, meeting both of their eyes. "We're not just a crew – at least not to me. We're more than that. You're all like a family to me. You're the only people I have. After I thought you and Henrik had died on Stornoway, I..." He trailed off, unable to hide the pain he'd felt, looking away for a moment. "I can't bear to lose any of you again. We've already lost Verris, your father, and the admiral. And I keep thinking that maybe we'd be better off giving up on this mission, but at the same time, I want to finish it, if not for us, then for them."

"I understand, Will. I do," Quentarus said slowly. "I *really* do. And I agree; we owe it to all of them to continue this. And I want... I *need* to be a part of this."

Jackson nodded slowly, realizing that in his efforts to protect her, he'd nearly taken something away from her. Something precious. The ability to honor her father and the admiral and their legacies by completing the mission they'd both laid down their lives to protect.

"Okay then," he said, a smile crossing his lips as he looked at his friends. "Let's go find some Ancient sites."

Several days later, Jackson, Johansen, Quentarus, and Dr. Duratis met with Fleet Admiral Lighton, along with Admirals Janus and Thompson, and Jackson petitioned them to be allowed to continue their original mission to search for Ancient sites and recover more technology.

"There're a few other loose ends that I'd like to track down as well, Admiral," Jackson said, addressing Fleet Admiral Lighton specifically. "There's the bioweapon that attacked the Insectoid colony and whoever deployed it. We believe that there's something larger going on that we still can't see. There's also the former GCH officer you met with, sir. The one who added the program to track me," he said, turning to Admiral Thompson. "We still don't know what happened to him and whether he's the one that saved us at Praxian Prime, but that's our current theory. We also believe that there's potentially another player out there who's not yet revealed themselves. The person who hired the Reptilians to go after me on Brestin III. And then there's the Shroud of Darkness itself. Alura, the Ancient I spoke with, said it was Phague technology. We don't know how the Insectoids got it or why they used a Ularan power core at Stornoway, but the Ularans were the ones that brought me to this time, and Alura called them the protectors of their legacy, so there could be a link there as well. From what I understand, they invested significant resources and fought to the death to try to keep me but still have nothing to show for it a decade later. They seem to be involved in this somehow and already tried to grab me once."

"Admirals," Johansen chimed in. "I've read all of the data and analysis available on the Shroud, and I've seen it with my own eyes. It's a marvel of engineering. The ability to shadow thousands of light-years of interstellar space is astonishing, to say the least. Fully reverse engineering it will take us years, perhaps even decades. It seems a stretch that the bugs simply acquired some Ularan tech and suddenly created the Shroud from the ground up. It's hundreds of years, if not more, beyond their capabilities, and, quite frankly, I don't think they're that creative."

"And there's still the Ancient site on Praxian Prime," Jackson added. "We only barely got to explore it before we were ambushed, but our scans indicated that it might contain a hangar bay. We may be able to recover an actual

Ancient ship. That alone should be reason enough to continue. And there's—"

"All right, Captain, you've made your case," Admiral Lighton gently interrupted. "And I concur that continuing your mission would both be of great service to the Confederation and would serve to honor the memory of our dearly departed comrade, Admiral Valentyen, and the sacrifice the *Viceroy* made to protect you all," she said, her eyes moving to Lieutenant Quentarus as she gave her a nod.

"Thank you, Admiral," Jackson said sincerely.

"There's still the matter of *how* you're going to continue with your mission," Admiral Janus said, speaking for the first time. "Your ship was lost, and we're not exactly brimming with extras after nearly a quarter of the Fleet was destroyed and another third is still in need of major repairs."

"However," Admiral Thompson quickly interjected, smiling ever so slightly, "a new state-of-the-art stealth ship just came off the line at the shipyards in Cicarrus two weeks ago, and I believe it's nearly completed its shakedown cruise. It hasn't been assigned a post yet or given a name. Perhaps this could meet your needs?"

Admiral Janus bristled slightly but said nothing while Jackson smiled brightly. "I think we could make that work, sir."

"Well then, I suppose that we should add the name *Phoenix* back into the registry then?" he suggested, raising an eyebrow.

Jackson turned and looked at the faces of his crew, then looked back to the admirals. "Yes, sir, I think that would be perfect."

Jackson thanked the admirals for their continued support, assuring them that the investment of time and resources would be worth it.

Before they left, he requested that Commander Winters be assigned to their team to replace Lieutenant Verris, and, after a brief conversation, the admirals agreed.

Jackson stayed behind after they were dismissed, chatting with Admiral Thompson for several minutes. The admiral explained how Admiral Valentyen had reached out to him while they were planning the mission to Stornoway and convinced him to come back to active duty.

He shared some of the details with Jackson regarding his now-famous maneuver, leading a small strike force through a weak spot in the Imperium lines and taking the fight directly to the Arachnid command ship, forgoing all other targets while their ships took a pounding in going after the lead enemy ship with everything they had.

He then recounted how the badly damaged command ship had tried to make a suicide run into the mountain fortress, and the admiral, commanding the *Waverly*, dove into the atmosphere after it in a desperate attempt to stop it.

"It was closer than most people realize," the admiral said, keeping his voice low. "It had a good lead on us, and we couldn't manage to knock it off course. I ordered the helmsman to dive straight for the planet at full speed, knowing that our only chance was to catch it. The two ships raced towards the surface, our broadside still hammering it from a distance as we went, trying everything we could to stop it. We finally hit with a dozen spatial-disruption torpedoes, the impacts knocking it off course. As soon as we were sure it was clear, we followed up with two precision strikes from our mass drivers, knocking it further off course for the base and punching enough holes through the ship that it finally lost power. The ship hit about a hundred and fifty klicks from the fortress. The kinetic energy, along with the ship's core detonating upon impact, created the massive shockwave that devastated an area nearly five hundred kilometers across!"

"That's incredible, sir. Thank God you were there," he said. His heart warmed at seeing the admiral back to his old self, recalling the kindness he'd shown him back when he first arrived in this time. "I know Admiral Valentyen would be proud."

Admiral Thompson nodded. "I hope so too. I sure as hell am damned proud of him. And you," he added, giving Jackson a pat on the shoulder. "You've come a long way, my boy, since that confused soul we rescued all those years ago."

"Thank you for everything you did for me, sir, and the patience you showed me. I truly get it now, and I see why you and the other admirals would do anything to defend the Confederation. It's something that's worth protecting."

"I'm glad to hear it. You've become a fine officer, Jackson. And if you ever need anything, please know that you can count on me."

"Thank you, sir," Jackson said, leaving a moment later to meet up with the rest of the crew, who were waiting for him in the lobby.

As they left the Admiralty building, Jackson explained that he wanted to surprise Winters, having the rest of them promise not to say anything until they'd returned to the Hideaway and he could show her everything.

Later that day, he took her out for lunch and told her that she'd been assigned to his unit on a top-secret op. "I'm going to work with the crew to prep. We've got a bunch of things that we need to do, and I want the mission to be a surprise. I'll send you a comm to meet us once we're ready."

Winters agreed, deciding to go and spend the week visiting with her parents while the rest of crew met that evening, putting together a list of everything they'd need. They used the next two days to prepare, gathering supplies and requisitioning tech and weapons, along with a new state-of-the-art Guardian Mark V armor. Dr. Duratis collected medical supplies, while Quentarus focused on provisions, weapons, and exo-suits, and Jackson made the trip to Cicarrus to pick up the new *Phoenix*. Johansen headed back to his lab on Delconia and focused on getting them the latest scanning and analysis equipment, along with some new toys.

The four of them met at the landing fields near GCH Command two days later, loading the *Phoenix* with their haul before preparing to depart.

"Wow, I have to say, I'm impressed," Quentarus said, sitting at the tactical console while the crew ran the ship through a final series of diagnostics. "They've added a second forward torpedo launcher, doubled our complement of missiles and countermeasures, and given us an arsenal of four different types of torpedoes, along with new state-of-the-art plasma cannons and particle emitters. I haven't seen this type of armaments on a ship this small before, aside from black-ops tactical strike ships."

"I think that's where this ship may have been destined for," Jackson commented. "The first *Phoenix* was an Infiltrator class covert-ops ship, but this one is something else altogether. It's called an Avenger class. I haven't heard of it before."

"That's a black-ops strike ship class," Quentarus replied. "This must be a redesigned version of it. I've been on a few of these, and they're tough little ships."

"It's got a bunch of upgrades over the original *Phoenix*, including state-of-the-art stealth and hypervelocity drives and a small IRC," Johansen said excitedly. "The hull is ten meters longer to fit it all in."

"Just don't get lost. The internal layout's different too," Jackson said. "I've gone for coffee twice now and ended up in the med bay."

"Sounds about right," Johansen teased. "You really don't function well until you've had a cup or two."

"What can I say? I'm a deep sleeper. Coffee and a combat alert are the only two things that seem to wake me up in the morning," Jackson replied as the crew continued to banter while preparing to depart.

The *Phoenix* exited hyperspace in the Jankara System eight hours later, setting a course for the fourth planet, the icy rock where they'd staged for the mission to the Reptilian battle station. The admiral had decided to stash some of their gear there after the events on Brestin III, fearing that the Hideaway may have been compromised by the mole in Command or the tracking signal, and the team hadn't returned since.

After several hours of loading the ship, they met in the mess for a meal, discussing next steps.

"We'll take a break and spend the night here," Jackson said, the long day having worn him out, suspecting that Quentarus and Johansen were equally exhausted as they all got back up to speed from their injuries. "I want to make one more stop before we head to the Hideaway."

"Where are we heading?" the doctor asked.

"Well, the ship's shakedown cruise only finished the day before we picked it up, and the commander at the Cicarrus shipyards said that they just had time for the basics."

"Makes sense," Johansen chimed in between bites, clearly famished from the travel and hard work. "It only came off the line a few weeks ago. The paint's barely dry, let alone the ship's systems having gone through their break-in period."

"My thoughts exactly. I'd like to run it through its paces for a few days to make sure everything is combat ready and properly field-tested before we head out there again. There's an uninhabited system about half a day from here with an icy asteroid belt and a few nasty gravitational anomalies. Verris and I ended up there on a rescue op a few years back. It was brutal to navigate and had lots of fast-moving rogue asteroids that should make for some challenging targets, especially near the gravity fields. It's the perfect place to run some battle sims and test out the weapons systems and should also give the sensors and propulsion systems a good run for their money."

"Good call, Captain," Quentarus said, flashing Jackson a quick smile. Despite his rank, he'd mostly worked alone since getting promoted and had never had a crew serve under him, aside from the few days when he was in command of the first *Phoenix*. "Never go into battle with an untested weapon."

"You read my mind, LT. And since I've been told that I seem to have a knack for finding trouble, I figured we might as well prep for the worst before we head out there for real and stir something up." He smiled mischievously.

"I can launch a few dozen probes in the system and set them to a patrol mode. We can use them to run intensive scans to test the stealth and cloaking systems," Quentarus suggested.

"That's a great idea. We can also use them to help us fine-tune things," Johansen added. "The ships systems were calibrated for ideal conditions back at the shipyard, but without ample field-testing, our cloak and stealth drive may still have flaws. Giving it a run in a war-games scenario is a great way to get them dialed in, along with the rest of the ship's systems."

"Sounds like a plan," Jackson said.

"What about Winters?" the doctor asked. "When's she meeting us?"

"I told her I'd send her a comm once we were ready and that we could be about a week or so. She'll grab a shuttle and meet us in the Kilgaren System after I message her. I wanted to get everything ready first, before she joined us. It's going to be a lot to take in, but I think she'll be excited. She's been eager to get back out there and help in some way."

"I've got to admit, I'm excited too," the doctor said. "I haven't been out of my lab since the last time with all of you, and with the war looming and everything that happened, it was a stressful time. Getting out there now, with the Imperium broken and the Reptilians still caught up in their own conflict, it just feels different. Like anything is possible and there's not this enormous shadow looming over us, you know?"

"Yeah, last time we were racing against time. This time, we can explore more, and we'll call in the Fleet if anything goes south," Jackson said, hoping to reassure his crew and keep things light. After all they'd been through, the last thing any of them wanted was another battle. "Anyway, once we get her up to speed, I figured we'd head back to Praxian Prime and see if we can finish exploring the base there. I'm still hoping we might find an Ancient ship."

"Are you sure you want to go back there first? We could try another site. There were lots of them on the Ancient map that we could check out," the doctor suggested.

"I know it's going to be hard to go back, but I think the longer I leave it, the harder it will be to face it. Besides, I really need to tell Sierra about Verris and what happened. It's going to come up sooner or later, and it's better that she knows up front. I don't want to keep anything from her," he said, a wave of guilt flashing in his mind as he thought about how he still believed that she was somehow Amy. He'd tried to separate her from Sierra in his head; they were different… yet so much the same that it was nearly impossible not to see his wife when he looked at her.

"It would be good to find out what happened to the ship that saved us," Quentarus said. "I've thought about it a lot over the past few years, and after you told us about the man who met with Admiral Thompson and the ship he had, I think it's worth checking out."

"Yeah, about that… Are we sure we want to find this guy?" Johansen said. "He seemed pretty intense and maybe not all quite there. If it was him in that ship, we wouldn't stand a chance if he suddenly decided he wanted us dead, even with the fancy new *Phoenix*."

"I think we look for clues about him while we're there, but I agree, he's probably not someone we should be seeking out," Jackson said. "Let's focus on the Ancient site and save chasing down trouble for another day."

"Wow, you really have changed, Will." Quentarus smiled. "Where's the brash idiot who stole a ship, sabotaged his friends, then went off half-cocked and out for revenge?"

"He finally had some sense beaten into him. Dying a couple of times does that to a person." He smiled in return. "Besides, brash idiots don't make great captains, so I've heard."

"Hey, what about Kirk!" Johansen blurted out. "You love Kirk!"

Jackson laughed. "Yeah, well, we can't all be Captain Kirk. Besides, I'd need some red shirts to hang out with me. Any takers?"

The doctor and Quentarus both stared at them, shaking their heads.

"What is it Verris used to call you two?" the doctor asked.

"Nerds!" the lieutenant called, relishing the word as they all shared a laugh, feeling as though they were back to a simpler time, before the war. Before Verris and the admiral were gone.

The shakedown and war-games exercises took four days to complete, each of them running various systems on the ship through their paces. Johansen spent several hours each day tweaking the ship's systems and adjusting the cloak while Jackson calibrated the sensors using the skills he'd learned from his time on the Algeron to optimize them. Quentarus focused on the weapons and defensive systems, finding a misalignment in the optical targeting sensors that the chief was able to correct. The doctor, meanwhile, prepped the med bay, set up the mess, and focused on tweaking some of the settings on the science station to increase the bio-scanners' sensitivity.

By the end of the fourth day, they each felt that the ship was as ready as it would ever be and were eager to put it to the test for real.

Jackson set a course for the Kilgaren System, sending a message to Winters with the coordinates to join them. They arrived nine hours later and were still getting settled in when Winters's shuttle arrived at the waypoint.

Jackson activated the command for the corridor in the asteroid field, and Winters docked at the station a few minutes later, exiting the shuttle and embracing him, the two having barely spent more than a day apart, much less over a week, since they'd started spending time together after the war ended.

"Okay, so I'll admit, I'm intrigued," she said after giving him a kiss and looking around, the excitement written across her face. "A clandestine meeting at a secret, off-the-books black-ops site. You sure know how to show a girl a good time."

"If you like that, then you'll love this," Jackson said, gesturing to the empty space at the other side of the hangar bay, waving his hand as the *Phoenix* decloaked.

"Oh, wow!" she said, taking in the sleek, deadly strike ship. "If you're trying to turn me on, you're on the right track." She cracked a mischievous smile. "That's one hell of a ship, Captain. Care to give me the tour?"

"I think that could be arranged, Commander."

"Where are the others?" she asked, looking around.

"They're all working on projects. We won't be missed for a few hours."

"A few hours?" she said, raising an eyebrow. "Someone's feeling ambitious today."

"What can I say? I missed you. A week's a long time to be away. I feel like I just got back from a Deep-X mission!"

"Well then, lead the way, sailor."

"Copy that, Commander. Follow me."

The crew ate together later that evening, sharing a few drinks, then calling it an early night, each of them eager to get started with the mission the next morning.

Jackson and Winters lay in his bed on the station, cradled in each other's arms, catching up on the past week.

"So, are you finally going to tell me what this mysterious mission is we're going on?" she asked after he finished telling her about the shakedown cruise.

"All will be revealed in the morning, I promise. I don't want to spoil the surprise."

"I can't wait."

"I'm pretty sure you won't be disappointed. Remember how we were talking a few weeks ago about coming back to the Fleet and making a difference?"

"Yeah," she said, turning to look at him.

"Well, this is a chance to make a real impact for a lot of people. If we're successful, our mission could have far-reaching results."

"Not overly dramatic or mysterious at all," she teased.

"Yeah, well, what can I say, I'm just full of drama and intrigue."

The crew assembled in the briefing room the next morning, each wearing fresh uniforms with the insignia Admiral Valentyen had created on their shoulders, in honor of their fallen leader. Jackson stood at the front of the room, a holographic map hovering in the air.

"So," he said, turning to Winters, "there's a lot to catch you up on. But first, let me show you this. This is a map of the galaxy from over four hundred thousand years ago." He paused, letting the map hover above the table for a moment. "Before the war, our team was tasked with finding specific sites and exploring them. Bits, can you overlay the current galactic map and adjust for galactic drift?"

"Of course, William," Bits replied over the conference room speakers.

"As you can see, there are a lot of potential locations to explore, with several promising new sites now possible in systems that were, until recently, part of the Imperium. As part of the terms to end the war, they've had to pull back by twenty light-years to form the new DMZ, which opens up some options for us to explore. But first, we have a site that we want to revisit where we think there might be something special," he said, pausing dramatically for a moment. "An *Ancient* ship!"

"Wait, did you say...Ancient?" Winters asked.

Before he could answer, the station's proximity alarms went off.

"Report," Jackson called, while Quentarus pulled up the station's main sensor array and ran a scan.

"A ship just jumped in near the waypoint. It's pretty small. Getting a lock on its transponder now. It's just a shuttle, and it's...hailing us."

"On screen," Jackson said.

Verris's image appeared a moment later, causing Jackson's heart to skip a beat.

"Hey, Jax, long time no see," she said casually, as a mix of guilt, dread, and joy washed over him all at once.

Johansen, Quentarus, and the doctor looked at one

another, then at Jackson, each of them frozen in their seats. "Hey, Ver, it's good to see you too. Uh, how are you?" he asked.

"Better, sort of. Mostly. Some memories started to come back a few months ago. I'm still missing a bit, but I'm starting to feel like my old self again."

"That's... That's, uh, wonderful to hear," he said, unsure what else to say, quickly realizing the ramifications of what she was telling him.

After a brief moment of awkward silence, she spoke again. "So, are you going to leave me out here all day, or are you going to invite me in?"

"Uh, yeah. Of course. Hang on. Opening up the passageway now. Proceed to the main, uh, h-hangar," he stuttered.

"Yeah, I know the way. See you in a few."

Winters looked at the rest of the crew's stunned faces. "What is it? Who was that?"

Jackson stood frozen, unable to speak as his mind reeled, his head shaking slowly as he tried to process what had just happened. He turned to Winters, a blank look across her face as he tried to find the words. "I..." He trailed off.

"We'd better head down to the hangar bay," the doctor said, hoping to buy Jackson a minute to collect his thoughts, noticing the stunned look on his face.

The crew fell in and started making their way to the hangar bay, Jackson knowing he needed to tell Winters something, and quickly. He grabbed her hand, and they fell further behind the rest of the group, the two stopping for a moment while the others went ahead.

"This was going to be part of the briefing... Well, sort of. So, Verris and I were...together," he said, his eyes darting to meet hers, then looking away as he continued. "She was critically injured on a mission just before the war, and when she finally woke up, she didn't remember any of us anymore."

"Were you…married?"

"No," he said quickly, putting his hands up, instantly regretting downplaying his relationship with Verris while his heart and mind raced, still trying to process what was happening, feeling as though his heart was tearing in two. "But we were together for almost three years."

The sound of the hangar bay door opening a moment later pulled them both back to the moment, and he tipped his head towards the hangar bay, the two falling into step as a feeling of panic took hold while he tried to figure out what to do.

He was finally happy again after years of feeling lost and alone. He'd found a place with Winters and a sense of peace after the long, bloody war that had been missing from his life for too long.

But Verris coming back changed all of that.

Verris exited the shuttle, the doctor and Johansen both going to her and giving her a hug, while Quentarus gave her a firm nod, as high a greeting as she ever gave.

Finally, Jackson approached, giving her a hug, but careful not to get too close lest she try to kiss him…or he her, his mind still racing and his heart pounding in his chest.

As they pulled back from their embrace, he turned to Winters and introduced her. "And this is Commander Sierra Winters. She's part of our team now."

Jackson felt an enormous rush of guilt in everything that he had omitted from his introduction, such as *And I think that she's my former reincarnated wife, who I've fallen back in love with, but I haven't told her anything about my past, including you.*

The two women shook hands, both sensing the awkwardness that hung in the air.

"So, what happened with your memory after all of this time?" the doctor asked, attempting to break the tension and change the subject.

"I don't know for sure," Verris said. "I was out on a mission when the war ended, and when I got back, there was a huge party happening at the station, so I went down to check it out. I can't say for sure what it was, but I watched the news vids about what happened at the Siege of Stornoway, and there was an image of Will that appeared on the screen for just a few seconds of him receiving an award and sitting in a hover-chair. I don't know what it was, but something just kinda…I don't know, flipped a switch in my brain, and suddenly, I felt a bit dizzy. The next day, I took a shuttle to see a specialist on Kishara Prime, the neuro-something-doctor who I saw every couple of months for checkups. She said that my brain scans were different. A bunch of stuff about neural pathways healing or regenerating. Anyway, over the next few days, I started to get some memories back. Rescue ops I've flown, the rookie that I lost, and stuff like that. Then it all stopped for a while," she said, shrugging.

"I went back to work, waiting to see if more would come back and checking in with the doctor again, who said that this sometimes happens, that I might get more back or that might be all that I ever get. I was frustrated, but I returned to work since there was nothing else I could do about it. A month or so passed, and then, one day, I was sitting in the bar when Meratta was telling some story about Will, and I was in it. As he told it, I just, I don't know, I just started to picture it in my head, and then suddenly I actually remembered it. Before I knew it, I was telling Meratta to fuck off because he wasn't telling it right. When I finished telling the story, it was like a fragment of a picture that had been there before had started to slowly reveal itself. I quickly went back to my quarters and watched the vid message that Will sent when he died."

Winters shot Jackson a look, and he shrugged, giving her an apologetic *I'll explain later* look, while Verris continued. "And when I watched it, it suddenly all came flooding back. That was three days ago."

"Wow, that's incredible," Johansen said. "Then what happened?"

"After that, I asked Vees if I could take a shuttle out for a few days to go and see Will. I contacted Command, but they were cagey with me, so I reached out to Fleet Admiral Lighton, who knew me from before. And she told me you were coming back to the Hideaway, so here I am."

Silence filled the room as the crew stood awkwardly, no one seeming to know what to say.

Jackson was about to speak when Bits interjected over the hangar's speakers. "I'm sorry to interrupt, William, but there is something urgent that you must see *immediately*. I'm afraid it cannot wait."

Jackson turned to the crew. "Let's go," he said, leading the way as they headed back towards the briefing room, welcoming whatever terrible new crisis was getting him out of this one while he tried to think as the two women he loved both followed him.

CHAPTER 19

POINT OF NO RETURN

Bits activated the holo-display as soon as they arrived in the briefing room. "This recording was taken by the GCH cruiser *Everest* in the LN-391 System three hours ago. The system is just nine light-years from the border on the Imperium side and was one of the systems that, as part of the terms to end the war, the Imperium was forced to abandon and cede to become part of the new demilitarized zone," Bits explained, showing the position of the system relative to the GCH. "Since the end of the war, GCH Command has sent small task forces to monitor as the Imperium pulled out of dozens of systems just like this. The effort has been happening along the Holt Line for the past several months and, as per the terms of the treaty, the Insectoids were only allowed to send unarmed transports in order to retrieve all of their soldiers and occupying forces from each system."

The holo-display updated, the bow of the *Everest* coming into view along with a group of GCH ships in the distance, overseeing the Imperium transport operations while streams of small vessels rose up from the surface, filling their holds. Suddenly, a small vessel about the size of a corvette appeared out of hyperspace in close proximity, opening fire without warning on the Insectoid transports.

The *Everest*, along with the two other GCH ships, returned fire, moving to put themselves in the way to protect the unarmed transports. Seconds passed as the unknown ship shrugged off the assault, firing a wave of ion energy and causing the power to fluctuate on the GCH ships, the view from the camera flickering before stabilizing once more.

The unknown ship then surged forward, destroying the rest of the Imperium transports in a matter of seconds. Not satisfied with the devastation, it turned towards the planet, launching several volleys of high-yield torpedoes at sites where hundreds of thousands of Insectoids had congregated, grouped together, awaiting evacuation.

The torpedoes detonated, thermonuclear explosions rippling out across the planet, killing millions of Insectoids in a matter of seconds.

The *Everest* recovered from the ion wave a moment later, closing the distance and opening fire once more. The unknown vessel ceased fire and broke off, its shields absorbing several more hits from the powerful battleship. Seconds later, it jumped out of the system less than two minutes after it arrived.

Scans appeared beside the visual display of the planet, showing that all Insectoid life on the surface had been annihilated, the shockwaves from the nuclear detonations still radiating outward as the plumes of smoke and fire continued to rise higher and higher.

The crew stood in stunned silence, watching as the holo-display faded to black.

Bits quickly rewound the vid-feed, leaving an image of the attacking ship on the display while bringing up a three-dimensional representation next to it.

"When did this happen?" Jackson asked, still trying to process everything.

"Four hours, sixteen minutes ago," Bits replied.

"How far was that system from here?"

"Just over three hours away."

"Who sent this to you?"

"Fleet Admiral Lighton."

"Could that really be an Ancient ship?" Johansen asked in disbelief.

"The *Everest* is an Allegiant class battlecruiser," Quentarus replied, "and it didn't even scratch it! What was that ship, maybe a sixth of its size? The *Everest* alone should have decimated it, but it not only took out those transports in less than a minute but bested three of our ships without even trying! Whatever the hell it was, it's unlike anything I've ever seen before. An Ancient ship may be the best guess."

"But where would an Ancient ship even come from? How could it even function? Don't they only work for the Ancients?" Winters asked, clearly confused.

"That's right. How is this even possible?" Dr. Duratis chimed in. "It can't be. Will was right here the entire time, and only he can use Ancient tech."

Winters looked at Jackson, puzzled. "What does she mean?"

"It's complicated. I was going to tell you at the briefing today. It was going to be a surprise, actually. It's just that..." Jackson didn't even know where to start, every word he said feeling like he was just digging himself into an even deeper hole while everything in his life seemed to fall apart right then and there. "I'm different, you see. I have this *ability* that no one else has. I can activate Ancient technology. That's what our mission was all about. Our job is to search for it. I was literally about to tell you about five minutes ago!"

"But if only you can activate it, then who did that?" Winters said, looking at the screen.

"I don't know. It shouldn't be possible," he said, shaking his head while he considered for a moment. Then, when no one else spoke, he continued. "There's more," he said, looking Winters in the eyes, knowing that it was time to come clean about the rest. "I've been wanting to tell you, but the timing just hasn't been right… It's complicated…but you see, I'm not actually from this time."

"Wait, what?" Winters snapped. "Wait… You're *William Jackson. The* William Jackson? The one that the Ularans brought through time from nine hundred years in the past?"

"How… How did you know that?" he asked.

"I was assigned to the temporal response team that assaulted the Ularan base on Yanara that rescued you!" Winters said. "Fuck!" she yelled, shaking her head in disbelief. "How could I have been so stupid?! I knew I knew you from somewhere when we first met! How the hell could I not see it? It was right there in front of me all this time!"

She stormed across the room for a moment before turning back. "You all knew about this?" she asked, turning to the crew.

Johansen and the doctor looked away awkwardly, not wanting to meet Winters's eyes, while Quentarus folded her arms across her chest, her stone face as enigmatic as ever. None of them dared to speak and risk drawing her wrath.

She turned and walked back towards Jackson, pressing her finger into his chest accusingly. "When I first met you all those years ago, you were a mess. You looked so different. Longer hair, unshaven, radiation burns. But you awoke for the briefest of moments while we were interrogating the Ularan scientists, and you looked at me and said a name. Annie or Amy or something. You clearly recognized me! What the fuck was that?"

The rest of the crew winced as she said the name, all of them knowing who Amy was.

"That… That really happened?" Jackson asked, genuinely surprised, looking away for a moment, having convinced himself that somehow it was all a dream.

"Oh, Will," Verris said breathlessly, bringing her hand to her mouth, recalling a picture of Amy that Jackson had showed her once.

Winters looked at her. "What? What!"

Verris looked at Jackson, tears welling in her eyes, suddenly realizing what was happening. The awkwardness of their reunion. This woman. All of it came crashing together.

He was with her. He was with this woman who looked exactly like his dead ex-wife.

Jackson hung his head for a moment, gathering his courage. He let out a breath, lifting his head and looking directly at Winters while he spoke. "You look exactly like… And… Oh God… I can't even believe it myself, but I think you might be the reincarnation of my wife, Amy, who died more than nine hundred years ago."

Winters froze, taken aback for a moment, her anger wavering as she processed Jackson's words, the strange connection they'd shared since meeting on Stornoway suddenly becoming clear.

Just as she was about to reply, Bits interjected, "William, Fleet Admiral Lighton is hailing us, priority Alpha."

"Shit! They must think I did this. That I'm seeking revenge against the Insectoids. That maybe we all are," he said, turning back to the holo-display. "On screen," he said numbly.

Fleet Admiral Lighton's face appeared, her anger barely contained. "Have you seen the recording I just forwarded to your AI from the *Everest*?"

"I have, ma'am," Jackson responded. "Just now."

"Can you explain to me what an Ancient warship is doing attacking an Imperium colony that was in the process of evacuating?"

"I can't, ma'am. We've been here the entire time."

"I'd like to believe you, Captain. But the Imperium is furious and wants answers, and we have precious few to give. If it wasn't for our ships attempting to defend their colony, we might be at war again already!"

Jackson nodded, understanding the gravity of the situation.

Fleet Admiral Lighton continued, "The *Everest* was able to scan the ship before it jumped out. The alloys in the hull match those from other Ancient sites, and the readings confirm that a humanoid male was on board. They were able to get a partial reading from his AI's transponder. *Your* transponder, Captain! So, I will ask you again to explain yourself!" she said, anger and betrayal filling her voice.

Jackson looked around at the faces of his crewmates. "I'm afraid that I can't, Admiral. We were on a shakedown cruise, then here the entire time. I swear. We didn't do this!"

"I'm sure that our AIs and the station's logs can confirm that we were here, Admiral," the doctor interjected.

"I wish that I could believe you, Doctor; however, I had GCH Intelligence pull the full logs from your AIs, and we've detected a significant unexplained anomaly in each of them. We cross-referenced this with the diagnostic logs from the original *Phoenix*, and it appears that you shut its systems down, along with your AIs, and altered the ship's logs after the events on Brestin III. You hid your tracks well, a credit no doubt to Chief Johansen's technical expertise, but I'm afraid this casts a significant shadow of doubt upon your credibility."

"Admiral, I—"

She cut Jackson off, glaring at him. "You came to me a week ago, asking to be allowed to continue your mission. I sensed that there were still things that you weren't telling me from before, but I never imagined this. You went through an extremely traumatic experience on Stornoway. You all did. And I wanted to honor the memory of my dear friend, Admiral Valentyen, and allow you to continue his work. I thought it would help you all to come together and heal." She paused, her anger rising once more. "And this—this is how you repay me?! You take revenge on the Imperium, nearly plunging us back into a Gods damned war!" She slammed her fist down on her desk, rattling a nearby cup.

"If we did this, Admiral, then where is the ship?" Quentarus asked defiantly.

Fleet Admiral Lighton gave Quentarus a look that quickly took her down a peg. "That's one of the many things that I plan to get to the bottom of, *Lieutenant*," she said, turning her attention back to Jackson. "As soon as the report from the *Everest* arrived, I recalled you mentioning a possible hangar on Praxian Prime which might contain a ship," she said, letting the assertion hang in the air for a moment. "I rerouted the *Ulysses*, which was on patrol only fifteen light-years from the Praxian System, and had them run a detailed scan of the planet. Imagine my surprise when the scans showed that a tunnel was recently cut from over thirty meters down, up to the surface."

"It wasn't us, ma'am," Jackson said, trying to remain calm. "Despite what the evidence suggests, it—"

"Don't lie to me, Captain!" Fleet Admiral Lighton snapped, pausing for a moment, reining in her emotions before continuing. "I'm afraid that all of this evidence simply cannot be ignored. Until we can hold a formal hearing to figure this out, I'm ordering you and your crew to stand down and stay where you are. I've dispatched the cruiser *Oberon* to come and escort you all back to Command. It will be there within the hour."

"But, Admiral—" Jackson began.

"You have your orders, Captain. Stay there and cooperate. I will do what I can for you, in light of all that you've done for the Confederation, but this act of blatant revenge cannot go *unpunished*," she said. "We'll get to the bottom of this, I assure you, but as of this moment, you are all formally under arrest. Lighton out."

The admiral's face disappeared from the viewscreen while the crew stood in silence, trying to process what had just happened.

"Bits," Jackson finally said, "is there any way to prove that this wasn't us?"

Bits responded over the conference room speakers. "I'm afraid not, William. We can submit the logs from the Hideaway, the *Phoenix*, and each of your AIs to prove where you've been for the past week; however, they may not believe them. The discovery that the logs from the first *Phoenix* were altered, along with shutting down your AIs in order to cover up your actions, is a court-martialable offense. Even if you explain the dangerous nature of the Ancient technology you recovered from Brestin III, the revelation of this deception, along with the presence of your transponder ID in the LN-391 System, will cast significant doubt on your innocence."

"How did they get your AI transponder ID?" Verris asked.

"That's a good question," the doctor replied. "Can that be faked?" she asked, turning to Johansen.

"Yeah. It's not easy, but if you have the unique transponder ID, then it's possible."

"The officer… Arkamus," Jackson said. "The one who got to Admiral Thompson and had him under his control for a short time. He's the one who tampered with Bits's code and sent the signal to track us."

"Wait, what?" Verris asked.

"It's a long story," Jackson said. "But that's how they kept finding us."

"That may be the answer," Bits interjected. "When my code was compromised with the tracking signal, the transponder ID was part of the data packet sent to whoever was receiving the messages. It's possible that they cloned the ID to implicate you, William."

Jackson thought for a moment, then looked back to his crew. "What are our options?"

"They have you at the scene of the attack…at least, your digital signature," Johansen said. "Along with an Ancient ship that only you can use. At least, that we know of."

"And they have a powerful motive," Quentarus interjected. "We all have more than enough reasons to hate the Imperium."

"And now, they have proof that we've altered logs before to mask our trail…" the doctor said. "Shit," she added, swearing for the first time that Jackson had ever heard.

"If we let them take us, we may never be able to prove our innocence," Quentarus said. "God knows we each have enough reasons to want revenge on the Insectoids and that our feelings are still raw. If Command has to give them something, then they may have no choice but to indict us to placate the Imperium. Even without the Ancient ship as evidence."

"The admiral was smart too," Johansen added. "She retraced our steps and checked on Praxian Prime before we could. If what she said was true, then there *was* an Ancient ship there, and we need to find it and whoever was piloting it. It's our only chance to prove our innocence."

They each looked at one another—the revelations between Jackson, Verris, and Winters forgotten for the time being.

Jackson looked at Quentarus, who stood defiantly with her arms crossed, her mind clearly made up.

He turned to the doctor and Johansen, each of them slowly nodding.

He looked at Verris, who gave a small sad smile, then nodded.

"Ver, you just got here. You could still walk away from all of this," he offered.

She shook her head. "We started this together; we finish it together."

He smiled, meeting her eyes for a moment, the woman he loved looking back at him.

Finally, he turned to Winters, who stood slightly apart from the rest of the crew, her arms still folded across her chest. She looked back at them, then to the empty viewscreen for a moment before closing her eyes and giving the slightest of nods.

"I know you all didn't do this. Despite everything else that just happened, I'm at least certain of that," she said, taking a breath, then continuing. "I was there the day you arrived in this time. I helped to set all of this into motion. I want to see it through."

Jackson paused, meeting each of their eyes, resolving himself, then addressing his crew.

"It's settled then," he said decisively. "We run."

EPILOGUE

A lone figure stood resting on a cane atop a small rise, overlooking the village below, the sun setting in the distance. It had been too long since he'd seen a sunset. Of all the thousands of years he'd lived, the countless days, the endless nights, he couldn't recall the last time he'd allowed himself the simple pleasure of taking a moment to bask in one of nature's most basic and awe-inspiring sights.

As he watched the giant ball of gas and fire slip below the horizon, he knew that this would be among his last.

His eyes wandered to the village below, thinking of his people: cold, hungry, a shadow of what they once were. Of all the things stolen from them. Of the fight they'd so nobly fought and the price they'd paid in doing so.

Was any of it even worth it? Was there any future left for the next generation to inherit?

He'd lived more lifetimes than any man had any right to, and yet, despite all of that, despite all he'd sacrificed, all he'd lost…there was still a sliver of hope deep within him.

Darkness stretched out across the land, the gentle breeze growing colder, his bones aching to his core.

Death was coming for him and for his people. The last of their legacy lost to the ashes of time, forgotten.

Betrayed.

He hardened his will, knowing that just as the sun sets, it must inevitably rise once more.

His people's time may be at an end. An end that would come soon…but… A small smile crossed his lips, the sliver of hope there once more, tenuous as his frail breath hanging in the cool evening air.

…But not yet. Not yet.

To be continued in Legacy: *The Fates of Time*

BRADLEY ELLIOTT

is a writer based near Toronto, Canada, where he lives with his wife and two children. He's an avid hockey fan, board game fanatic, and lover of the great outdoors. An unabashed geek at heart, he's always up for discussing sci-fi, fantasy, movies, or why Han shot first and Greedo had it coming.

You can find out more by visiting:

WWW.BRADLEYELLIOTT.CA

Printed in Dunstable, United Kingdom

80990310R00190